For all the dreamers who aren't afraid to turn imagination into reality

1

I'D NEVER FELT SO VULNERABLE. THE OCEAN CLOSED ABOVE ME, swallowing the shuttle into a suffocating vastness that made me itch to claw at the 360-degree windows. Obviously, that would have been useless, but it was hard to turn away from the unending view. So I hugged myself in an attempt to stifle my panicked urges and found a seat in the circular back-to-back rows of the luxury pod.

Not only were there thousands upon thousands of tons of water pressing in on us, but now that it was too late to change my mind, a million reasons not to go raced through my brain. The faster we accelerated toward the bottom, the less convincing my reasons for coming felt. The engineer in me studied every rivet, weld, and seal and found them flawless—beautifully designed actually—but that did little to sooth my near-panicked emotional state.

The other fifty people onboard crowded close to the impossibly thin AC glass, gawking and chattering like they were viewing the Grand Canyon for the first time and not an endless darkness illuminated by the blue glow that caught the occasional school of silver herring. The new technology that allowed such a thin barrier had been thoroughly tested over the years, but that didn't mean I had to like it. Proven or not, I couldn't help but long for the days when glass for underwater vessels had been four to six inches thick. My father and Jackson stood front and center with the other sheeple, smiling like they hadn't a care in the world, like we didn't just leave Mom, weak and battered by chemo, all alone on the surface.

Her unnaturally thin face was all I saw behind her smile, the smooth skin of her scalp visible through the woven texture of her large brimmed hat.

"I need you to go," she'd said for the fourteenth time, framed by the sun like an angel with a halo.

She'd finally convinced me with her crazy, characteristically unselfish wish that I play nice with Dad and the woman he'd cheated on her with.

"Excuse me, Miss Meadows, but you look a bit peaked."

I stared up into the plastic face of Dr. Candice Lawry, chief operating officer and artificial intelligence guru of Bennet Systems. *Wonderful.*

Candice always looked like she swallowed something horrible but was trying to smile through it and not let on. I suspected it had something to do with being as high ranking as one can get inside Bennet Systems, yet not being a complete insider, aka literal part of the disfunction that was the Bennet family.

"Thanks," I said, taking the hydropod she held out to me in the hopes it would be enough to send her on her way.

"Your profile shows you are at an increased risk for DSI," she said, sitting on the edge of the seat beside me and crossing her long legs.

"Depth sensitivity illness is a made-up term to excuse the psychological effects of being crushed beneath a million tons of ocean water," I said, taking a sip from the malleable pod she'd handed me. A genius invention, the bubble-shaped object held the perfect amount of electrolyte-enhanced water, and when it was finished the thin skin remaining could be swallowed as well.

She smirked. "I'll let that comment go, considering the symptoms include lowered inhibitions and heightened anger."

I took another swig, not wanting to feed into it. She leaned in, elbows perched on knees, glassy green eyes unnervingly close as she tapped her thumb and finger together like she had an invisible castanet.

"Let's not have any issues that might spoil this demo trip for anyone. If you feel like you can't control yourself, there's always the option of stasis until it's time to leave."

Did she just threaten to put me to sleep for a month in a box if I didn't behave?

She rose while I remained speechless and cleared her throat to get the attention of the fourteen other families. Bennet Systems, or BS as I lovingly referred to them, was all about family. Frankly, to me, it was more like a cult that kept everyone close enough to monitor. As Candice warned, those who misbehaved were dealt with.

"Welcome!" she chirped in a fake voice that sounded like an animatronic gone wild. "And congratulations on reaching this milestone. You will be the first people to enjoy the new luxury resort, Paradise Atlantis."

She paused for applause.

"We at Bennet Systems are thrilled to be able to offer our very own employees and their families this opportunity before opening our doors to the public. You've worked hard to make this happen, and we extend all the finest luxury to each of you in thanks. You will experience AI like never before as all of your needs are met, and hopefully exceeded, by our artificial staff members. If there's anything you need, just press one of the silver call buttons located throughout the grounds and buildings, and you will be showered with assistance. Enjoy the ride, we should be docking in less than an hour."

Everyone erupted into more applause and chatter as Candice waited, clearly not finished.

"One last surprise. We are not the only ones spending a month on Paradise Atlantis."

A hush fell over the shuttle as people began to pay attention.

"The Bennets have decided to join us. Mrs. Bennet wants you to know that you are all part of her extended family."

With this information, Miss COO disappeared into the crowd, which seemed to swallow her whole.

The entire Bennet clan? For a month? Trapped down beneath the waves with us? My mind immediately went to the only Bennet I'd ever been interested in meeting, Mason. My mouth dried up despite my hydropod. I'd never been able to string two words together around him. One look at his sparkling eyes or glorious physique, and I was destined to become a tongue-tied adolescent all over again.

Pull it together, Sam, I told myself, tightening my ponytail. I needed to focus, for shit's sake. I was twenty-six years old and had a master's of engineering in Artificial Intelligence from MIT. I'd be starting work on my doctorate once Mom was healthy again. Not only did I not have time for a man, Adonis-like or not, but I did not have time for frivolities while Mom suffered.

I would simply tour the gallery as often as possible, inspect what I could about the engineering while avoiding certain people, and stay in my room the rest of the time. I closed my eyes and leaned my head back, seeing no reason to keep them open and stare at the dark beyond. Planning would keep me focused on the right things.

"At least somebody here isn't ogling a window with a view of nothing," said a deep voice to my right.

My eyes popped open and took in the face of the dark, handsome stranger. His deep brown eyes reminded me of the woods above land. Thick hair framed his face and carefully trimmed beard.

"Travis Gould." He held out a large hand to shake.

It was warm, but calloused, and he didn't hold back on the strength of the welcome.

"Samantha Meadows," I said. "What department are you in?"

He scoffed. "None. I refused the work study. My parents, unfortunately, did not. My dad is head of Interior Design, and my mom is the main vital-systems engineer."

I nodded. Bennet Systems notoriously hired females for lead science roles. With the exclusion of my father of course, since he and my mother met Mrs. Bennet back in college. He'd been a fixture since the start, which meant the rest of us were as well.

"Why'd you refuse the work study?" I asked, curiosity getting the better of me.

"I will never work for those assholes."

I smiled despite myself. Maybe we had something in common.

"I don't work for them either," I said. "Dragged here with family, same as you."

The shuttle lurched like it'd been hit by a torpedo, and I froze, clutching the armrests of the seat. My head pounded as my blood pressure skyrocketed.

"You okay?" Travis asked, his thick eyebrows furrowing into one as he stared at my white knuckles.

"What was that?" I breathed.

He grinned and pointed toward a giggling group of girls by the glass. They waved and made silly faces at a dolphin that hovered on the other side. The creature appeared to be smiling ear to ear. I was confused for another moment until one girl put her hand on the glass and the dolphin headbutted it, making the whole vessel seesaw.

"What if it breaks the AC glass? Or it knocks us off course?" I asked, staring at the horrible sight. The engineer in me knew it was a ridiculous fear, but the terrified woman in me disagreed.

Travis laughed, bringing my attention back to him. The rest of my blood rushed to my face and down between my legs when he set his hand on mine. I guess not getting laid in over a year had unfortunate effects on my body.

"It's a dolphin, not an enemy submarine. I'm pretty sure even the assholes could've predicted that. In all seriousness though, are you sure you're okay? If you're afraid of the ocean, this is not going to be a pleasant trip."

"Thanks, Captain Obvious. I'm good." I stood up on shaky legs and strode as confidently as possible over to join my father and Jackson. Alyssa was off chatting with Candice, so it was as good a time as any to make a half-assed effort.

"Sammie." Dad held out a hand for me and I took it, forcing a smile. I promised I'd try after all. "Enjoying the view?"

"Jackson sure is," I said, noting my brother's wandering eyes, which were locked onto his newest target, a young woman with the body of a super model, too much of which showed beneath her tangerine romper.

My six-foot-two brother bumped me with his hip, making me stagger.

"Are you eight or twenty-eight?" I asked, downing the remainder of my water and popping the rest in my mouth.

My father's smile was worth it though. The way his eyes crinkled when it was genuine always warmed my heart. If only he'd reserved it for our family and not shared it, first with BS and then Alyssa.

"Stand over here, Little Dragon," Dad said, repositioning me with a clear view of the glass. My heartrate sped up, but he held me tightly from behind, grasping my arms for security.

"Dad, I'm not twelve anymore," I said, making light of his pet name, given because of the way my nostrils flared when I was super angry, like I was about to spit fire.

"You'll always be my baby. Now if you look a bit down and to the left, you'll be able to get a first glimpse. It should come into view any minute, and this is the prime spot. That's why I've been staking it out."

I bit my lip so as not to make a snarky comment. I promised Mom I'd try. I should at least do so for the first day, I supposed.

Within the next thirty seconds or so, a glowing light appeared in the dark waters. As we swooped toward it, the shining bubble seemed to rise from the depths of the Atlantic, revealing a ten-mile-wide snow globe of something out of a 50's futuristic B movie. Emerald green pastures dotted with bright red and yellow blooms punctuated the circular space. In the center of the maze-like perimeter stood a speckled white statue of some sort. Around it, gleaming silver buildings of rounded glass and metal shone beneath what appeared to be...sunlight.

"How?" I asked, unable to take my eyes off the scene. The cheesy brochure I threw in the recycling can upon receipt didn't do it justice.

"They're called nanosuns," Dad said, reading my thoughts. "I developed them myself. They even dim and wane into a moonlight effect at night that follows the actual cycle of the moon."

It was amazing. But I was not admitting that to him. If that's what started his years of absence from our home—from Mom, then I refused to compliment it.

"Please prepare for docking," Candice chirped.

"Prepare?" I said, unable to control the high-pitched way it came out. "Is it dangerous?"

Jackson laughed, no doubt enjoying torturing his sister. It was like we'd gone back in time to elementary school. I shouldn't have been surprised. We hadn't spoken much since he took the job at BS in our father's department, working under him. Better that than in AI with Alyssa. Truthfully speaking, she was closer in age to him than our father. Youngest woman to ever earn a PhD in Artificial Intelligence from Bennet University, she was the logical choice to take over the position from Candice when she was promoted to the equivalent of second in command four years earlier. That's when the affair started and when Mom's first bout of cancer was diagnosed, which made it that much worse. Before that, we'd all gotten quite good at pretending it was normal for Dad to never be around —always working.

I wondered where Alyssa was. It was entirely possible she was avoiding me. That thought brought a big smile to my face.

"You have nothing to worry about, Little Dragon. Just a formality to announce the docking procedure."

I nodded and leaned back into Dad's chest, allowing myself to feel safe for once. It was almost perfect until I heard Alyssa's voice.

"Oh, I'm so glad you two are getting along!"

I pulled away from my dad and hugged myself, stepping far enough away to make a point without saying it. She didn't seem to notice, though, as she cozied up to him, taking my place in his arms. Her perfect face with her perfect, smooth, dark skin and perfect long lashes, and perfect straight smile lit up as though from within as he rocked her slowly side to side, wrapping his arms around her.

My stomach swam as if the angelfish outside the closest window had crawled inside it.

"Have you enjoyed the ride, Samantha?" she asked, continuing to beam like a bunch of nanosuns.

"Not really," I said. Dad's crinkle smile faded behind her, and I almost regretted speaking the truth.

Before anyone could say anything else, the shuttle lurched slightly. To calm down, I tried to convince myself it was another dolphin. But I soon realized it was the ship slowing for the docking procedure Candice mentioned.

It looked like we were about to smash straight into the giant glass bubble when we came to a full stop and dropped downward like an elevator until the view was replaced by a bright green door that slid open to admit us. Smooth as silk, the shuttle slipped inside and the door closed. The water around us drained through the grated floor and a second door opened, offering an upward slope festooned with marble mermaid and merman statues lining the glowing path.

"Impressed yet, sis?" Jackson asked as the oohing and ahhing crowd around us pushed their way outside.

"Too gaudy for me," I said, feet stuck to the ground.

Jackson narrowed his hazel eyes at me and drew a hand back through his tawny hair as understanding lit his face.

"Come on. I'll help you."

Heat rushed to my pale cheeks. I'd never been able to hide a blush, so instead of arguing I accepted his offered hand. It was better than being stuck in the shuttle for a month. I scanned ahead and caught sight of Travis at the top of the incline. His sharp gaze bored into me, causing a tingle of anticipation to spread throughout my body. And together with my somewhat estranged brother, I moved forward, focused on possibilities I hadn't originally considered, as opposed to the oppressive view.

2

MY NEWFOUND OPTIMISM CRASHED AS I TOOK IN THE SURROUNDINGS at the top of the ramp. The bubble was enormous—maybe a half-mile high—but crystal clear. No matter what direction I looked, no matter how amazing the architecture or design, the impending enormity of the dark water beyond cemented my view. It was a million times worse than the pod, and I didn't know if that was because of the size ratio, the depth, or what. It hardly mattered when every time I looked out beyond the AC glass shield, my heart threatened to escape through my throat.

I was still squeezing Jackson's hand with my sweaty one. Thankfully, he hadn't complained yet, but he would eventually. Maybe if I did it in baby steps I'd get used to it.

I turned so my gaze fell more toward the middle of the crowd and lifted my eye level enough to spot the familiar leather jacket I'd used to force myself out of the shuttle. Travis chatted with tangerine-romper girl, who was all but bouncing on her heels with excitement. He once again focused on me, which caused a flood of excitement to rush all the way to my pants. It was probably from the fight or flight response I was stuck in and my hormones being in overdrive because of it. I didn't usually go around getting physically excited by random guys staring at me.

"Damn," Jackson whispered from my side. "He does move fast."

I followed his stare and ended up at the same couple. Travis was competition for my brother for sure.

"You know him?" I asked.

"Just by reputation," he said, doing a double take as he realized Travis was staring at me. "So stay away from him. Trust me, he's not your type."

"Player?" I asked. "Do you just recognize each other by scent?"

"Very funny," he said, prying his hand from mine.

"Maybe if I distracted him you'd have a chance with tangerine romper."

Jackson huffed. "Her name is Tasha Graves, and she works in the botany department. For somebody so into treating women right, you sure have a funny way of showing it."

He was right. Damn that pissed me off. Luckily, I didn't have to respond because the squelching sound of good old-fashioned feedback demanded everyone's attention. Wincing, I turned toward the noise to find a platform with a polished lectern on top. The woman responsible for everything perched behind it. Not just Paradise Atlantis Resort, but my father's workaholism and ultimately him cheating on my mother. Stacy Bennet stood regally behind the mic, though even with six-inch heels, she was barely tall enough to reach it. It didn't matter. I'd seen her intimidate men over six-feet tall with her steely eyed glare, power suits, and short cropped, two-tone hair.

"Welcome!" Her voice carried throughout the open pavilion. Her red lipstick was visible from all the way back here. "My family and I are delighted to join you for a much needed and well-deserved vacation."

I followed her gesture outward to find her tall, tan trophy husband and two adult children, Nicole and Mason. The former was a young version of her mother but with long blond hair that must have included extensions, and a designer dress that, while professional, didn't leave a lot to the imagination. Not that she had an ounce of body fat on her, but who knew how much of her was real with all her mother's money and company innovations.

Mason was more a mirror of his father but with a young surfer vibe. He was dressed far less formally than the rest of his family, with a Hawaiian shirt, muscled arms folded across it, and white Bermuda shorts that made his smooth, tanned legs stand out even more. I didn't have to see them to know his cerulean eyes could've melted me at a glance.

Oh man, maybe I needed to get laid so I didn't keep falling to pieces when I saw a hot guy. Next thing I knew I'd be carrying around binoculars. I did notice another difference from his family, as far as Mason went. He wasn't happy, or at least wasn't politely smiling for the crowd like the rest of the Bennets. That piqued my curiosity.

"I want to get to know you all better while we're here. After all, we're family," the she-devil continued. "So let's start with personal introductions, shall we? And Friday night we have a get-to-know-you gala in the Oyster Ballroom at Mermaid's Cove. Attendance is mandatory because I have a few more surprises to present. Let's get this party started!"

Stacy backed away from the microphone to applause as Candice took her place.

"Please form one line and limit your hellos so we don't keep everyone from finding their hotel rooms. The staff will escort you to your rooms after your greeting with the Bennets."

I gawked open mouthed at Jackson, who grinned ear to ear and slowly clapped in response with everyone else. What the fuck? So now we had to form a line like these people were actual royalty? Screw that. Also...what staff? I thought we were the only ones down there. I was tempted to go find the hotel on my own as a protest, when Dad and Alyssa appeared out of nowhere.

"Let's get in line," Dad said, leading the way to the rapidly forming string of people snaking its way toward the spot we all came in.

When I looked, I realized the ramp entrance was gone. The grass-covered ground was perfectly manicured, uniform, and level all the way to the edge of the shell, with no sign that anything but dirt existed below us. I was distracted enough to be ushered along by the group, but I couldn't help feeling trapped. I hugged myself to quell the shivers.

"What do you think?" Dad asked, beaming with expectation and pride.

My stomach cramped. It was a look I used to crave so badly that I would have done almost anything to receive it. Until I realized it only appeared when I demonstrated my aptitude for science and engineering.

"Impressive," I said, measuring my response. I wanted to scream for him to take me home because this was a big mistake, but I had to control myself. "How does it work? I mean the ground cover. Clearly there are parts below, since the docking ramp seems to have vanished."

"Absolutely. The action is all down below. The offices, machinery, everything you can imagine, but the idea is for the guests not to notice any of it. It should feel like magic when you're here." He smiled at Alyssa.

"Effortless," she agreed. "Wait until you see the sliding tubes."

"Sliding tubes?" I repeated.

"Yes. They're exterior arms made of clear polycarbonate that extend out from the resort and provide tours to the guests. You can follow whale pods or sea turtles as they move in their natural environments."

"That's amazing," I choke out, vowing not to take a ride in one for fear of being sick all over the tube.

"You have to explore the *Calhoun*," Alyssa said, practically dancing.

I glanced at my father for explanation.

"Sunken ship," he said as we inched forward another few steps.

"So, Alyssa," I asked, steering the subject matter to something more interesting to me. "What's the difference between the AI at Paradise Atlantis versus the original Bennet Systems AI that made the company so famous?"

She turned to me, eyes lit like I just made her day. "It's far more nuanced. It can alter its decisions in milliseconds depending on the emotional reaction of the guests. I can't wait for you to see it yourself. You'll have to let me know what you think. From what I hear, you're almost as much a prodigy as I was."

We continued forward in line as the awkward comment hung in the air. It reminded me of the real reason I hadn't gone for my PhD yet. I wanted to separate myself from the dysfunctional Bennet "family." Why couldn't I have inherited my mother's propensity for art instead?

"Well..." Apparently, Alyssa felt the need to fill the silence. "This is going to be a very healing trip for all of us."

"How so?" I asked through gritted teeth I tried to pass off as a smile.

"I mean the timing is perfect. Not that there's ever good timing for cancer of course. But it worked out perfectly for your mother, and it'll be good for us to get along."

What the fuck was she trying to say? My neck heated up, and I felt my nostrils flare. Little Dragon was in the house, and I seemed to have little self-control. Before I exploded, I felt my brother's hand on my shoulder, squeezing.

"Excuse me?" he said, his voice strong, and when I heard he was on my side for once, I relaxed slightly.

Even my father turned to Alyssa, the lines on his face hard for once and not doting.

"I haven't given them the letters yet," he said in place of a reprimand.

"I thought that's what you were doing when I left you alone on the pod," Alyssa said, horror written on her face.

"What letters?" Jackson asked for us. At this point I was speechless.

My father sighed and pulled two envelopes out of his pocket to hand to us. My mother's curling script sprawled across the back, spelling out our names. I took mine and stared at it. It was sealed to the edges. My hands trembled out of fear of what lay inside.

We were almost at the front. One more family ahead. I couldn't look now. I couldn't risk breaking down in front of everyone, least of all the Bennets, so I stuffed the letter in my own pocket for safe keeping. I would be alone when I opened it to give it the time and attention it deserved.

Jackson followed suit, a dark shadow covering his face.

"If it isn't the Meadows clan!" Mrs. Bennet exclaimed, reaching her hands out to our father in greeting.

"Pleasure as always," he said.

"And Dr. Forbes," she said, moving along to Alyssa for a quick hug.

"Pleasure to meet you all," Nicole said, offering a hand to my brother.

I hung back, but Mrs. Bennet reached for me and clasped my hand in hers. "I've heard so much about you, Samantha. But I haven't seen you in person for years."

"I've been busy with college," I said coolly.

"I understand you're on hiatus now," she said, and I was flabbergasted that she somehow knew so much about me. "Not that I blame you with your mother's health. I'm so very sorry. Family always comes first."

I felt the color drain from my face, and I swayed slightly. What was it she knew exactly? What was in that letter? I couldn't stop myself from nearly hyperventilating right there on the stage. What was wrong with me? I wasn't usually this emotionally out of control.

"I'm so sorry for my mother's callous comments."

I looked up into the face that had hung on my bedroom wall as a teenager. Mason's fame was the kind that came from *being* famous. Of course, it didn't hurt that he was also filthy rich and stunningly handsome. Mason's eyes were the blue the sea ought to be, and right then they were filled with concern for me, only inches away. The tropical scent of salt and hibiscus enveloped me. The urge to see what he tasted like overwhelmed me on top of the rest of my emotional loss of control. I stayed still for fear of doing something I'd regret.

"She meant well," my father quipped from somewhere to my right.

Mason didn't take his eyes off me. Instead, he took my hand in his and lingered after he shook it. His skin was smooth and soft, and I wondered what it would feel like on my body.

Holy shit, I needed to stop this. He was a Bennet for fuck's sake.

"I'm Mason," he said. Even his voice was dreamy.

"Sam," I managed to respond.

The moment was interrupted by Tangerine—Tasha Graves— who nearly shoved me out of the way for her turn at Mason. But every time I glanced back over my shoulder, his eyes were locked on me, and a shiver of excitement lit in my belly.

"Excuse me, ma'am, are you in need of assistance?"

I turned my attention to the male voice and was startled to find an android had slipped silently up beside me. It was human height with a metal body, like a person but more of a sci-fi movie manservant robot kind of look rather than realistic. It was made of matte black metal and white plastic shielding with glowing red light emanating from beneath its chest. The bottom of its feet appeared to have wheels built in, as it glided forward a foot or so as though on roller skates. Onyx orbs for eyes both reflected the light and felt like they hid something important. I shivered at the sight, attributing it to the Uncanny Valley reaction of seeing something that closely resembled a human, but wasn't quite...right.

"You are Samantha Meadows, Mermaid's Cove room six thirty-four."

"Uh, thanks," I said, still creeped out by the totality of the black in its eyes. "I prefer Sam."

"Understood, Miss Meadows."

Did it...do that on purpose? Were these capable of sarcasm? No way. I'd worked with the most up-to-date systems elsewhere, and nothing came close to that. It had to be a fluke. It was programed to use last names for the sake of politeness.

"Please accompany me to your room. We will retrieve your father and brother."

"I'm okay. Thanks. I'll find it on my own." I really could have used some alone time to deal with everything. I definitely didn't need a mechanical babysitter.

It rolled so close I felt the need to take a step backward.

"I have been instructed to accompany the Meadows family to their respective rooms."

"Back off, the lady said no." Travis stepped between us and shoved the robot in the shoulder.

The black eyes turned to this new variable as the machine spoke into a tiny microphone built into its shoulder. "Bartholomew to Finn. I have located Mr. Travis Gould. Please retrieve from this location."

"I'm sorry, did you just say your name is Bartholomew?" I asked.

"Correct. There are twenty-six model A's. We are named for each letter of the alphabet. If you will kindly accompany me as requested, I will enlighten you with further information about the unique offerings here at the resort."

Travis's fists clenched at his sides, and I was afraid he might dismantle the thing. Candice's warning about the stasis chamber flashed before me. I grabbed his arm.

"It's ok. I should go with my family. There are some things we need to discuss."

I watched as his jaw ground back and forth for a moment, then it stopped and he fixed his intense gaze on me. My insides once again leaped to attention. I was so shocked by this that I let go of our connection.

"Guess it's going to be hard to go anywhere without surveillance," he said. "I was looking forward to sneaking around with you later."

I was getting used to the blush at this point. A bit presumptuous on his part. Then again, we only had a month and we both felt stuck. Maybe hanging out with a kindred spirit would be better than spending the whole time holed up in my room.

"Excuse me, Mr. Gould. If you are ready, please follow me." Travis inhaled sharply through his nose before deciding to listen to the newly arrived "staff" member. I couldn't help but find it intriguing that its voice was different than Bartholomew's.

Dad, Jackson, and Alyssa strolled up to join us.

"Catch you later," Travis said, dark eyes raking me in a way that both sent ripples of excitement through my body and sent up warning signals in my head.

"If everyone is ready, please follow me," Bartholomew said. When I looked over, his head was turned toward us as his body remained facing forward and rolling along the manicured path.

I shuddered at the unnatural feeling of it but reminded myself it was a robot for all intents and purposes and could "see" the way ahead with its glowing red sensors.

Trying to focus on the scenery as opposed to the clasped hands of my father and Alyssa swinging between them was a challenge. Still, the architecture was admittedly well done, the layout of the entire resort being a spiral of sorts. According to our escort, the numerous buildings included everything: various hotels, restaurants, a full-on gym, spa, hospital, water park, and more.

"Wait until you see the aquarium," Jackson said, latching on to the intrigue in my eyes.

I laughed. "Aquarium? At the bottom of the ocean? Isn't that a bit redundant?"

"I'm afraid the aquarium is closed to the public at the moment,"

Bartholomew stated with what sounded like actual regret. "The dolphin trainers were not included on this first run. But allow me to draw your attention to the park grounds. We call it Poseidon Park, after the centerpiece."

We glanced over at the statue that was barely visible during my first glimpse. Now its impressive size and detail took my breath away. The gleaming, muscular sea god stood tall and held aloft a giant trident made of solid bronze, the tips glinting wickedly beneath the sinking nanosuns. I probably came up to the top of his toes on the etched platform he stood on. A twisting sea serpent surrounded him, frozen forever in battle, mouth open, fangs as long as the spears on the trident the god held aloft.

"It's breathtaking," I said. "It reminds me of Mom's work."

"That's because she designed it for us," Dad said, laying a tentative hand on my shoulder. "She wanted it to be a surprise."

I choked back the lump in my throat, and tears brimmed behind my eyes. Apparently, there was quite a bit she wanted to surprise me with. I knew the buildings down here in the resort included a gallery housing a collection of her life's work. It was part of the reason I was there. But seeing this was so shocking and overwhelming, I wondered if viewing the gallery would be more difficult than I anticipated. The letter in my pocket felt like a ten-ton truck.

"Ah, and here are your temporary living quarters," Bartholomew said, indicating what looked more like a cartoon palace than a hotel. "Mermaid's Cove."

We followed it through the enormous double doors carved with gaudy, topless mermaids as handles, and I nudged Jackson, who'd fallen into step beside me.

"Bet you can't wait to open those doors."

He rolled his eyes but granted me a smile that gave me some unexpected comfort. It was nice having my big brother around. I'd missed his company.

We stepped inside a ten-story domed structure, glass windows curving upward framed the view of each floor, ringed by a banister overlooking the center. In that center sprouted a color-changing fountain surrounded by elevators. It was dizzying.

"I feel like they had a hard time deciding between futuristic and gothic mermaid when it came to décor," I said.

"Each building has a theme," replied good ole Bartholomew. "This one is mermaids. It is the top tier of the available accommodations of course."

I trailed along toward the elevator.

"Greetings. What floor would you like?" Candice's voice greeted us from all around as we stepped inside the lift. It seemed she was vain enough to use her own voice to remind everyone she was the one who created the Bennet AI in the first place. Not that I blamed her for wanting to make sure she wasn't overshadowed by Alyssa. The woman tended to do that.

"Floor six, please," Bartholomew answered.

With barely a purr, the elevator lifted from the ground and we sailed smoothly upward.

Movement caught my eye through all the glass layers as a large shadow undulated past in the dark waters outside. Despite the distance, I couldn't stop myself from shuddering in response.

"Floor seven, as requested," Candice's voice announced as the doors whooshed open.

"Six," I said as we all froze in place. "You asked for floor six."

Bartholomew slid forward, pressing the silver call button in the elevator. "Floor six, please." Then to us, "Do not be alarmed. This is a first run, and I've already notified the proper authorities."

The doors closed and reopened moments later. "Floor six."

I was the first one off the elevator, trying to control the panic I'd been fighting to keep down all day.

"If it can't even get the floor right, how do we know it's safe to be down here?" I asked. Screw their feelings; I needed reassurances.

"The vital systems were the most carefully checked, Sammie,"

Dad said. "This is so trivial that they probably didn't even think about it."

"She's right, Tom." Alyssa placed a hand on my father's arm, instantly calming him. "I'm going to have to go down and double-check everything once we're settled in. I need to make sure it's not an AI issue."

"Here are your wristbands," Bartholomew said. Speaking of AI picking up on guests' emotions, I couldn't tell if he was or wasn't reading the room.

"Wristbands?" I asked, arching an eyebrow in suspicion.

"They are communication devices as well as room entry keys. They have been coded to your DNA and will open only those rooms you have access to. Yours is six thirty-four, Miss Meadows."

"It's all good," Jackson said. "This is my pet project. Phones don't get service down here, obviously, so these are the next best thing. You can call anyone by using their name and a call command, or message them the same way."

With a grimace, I slid the thin silver band over my wrist.

"Room six thirty-two for you, Dr. Meadows, and six thirty-three for Drs. Forbes and Meadows."

Great, so my father and Alyssa would be boinking right across the hall. Were we having fun yet?

"Listen, this is great, but I'm in need of a nap," I lied. What I really needed was some alone time.

"Of course. Want to meet for dinner?" Dad asked with a hand on my shoulder.

"No thanks. I'll order room service or something. Maybe tomor-row. Or the next day." Maybe if I could stomach being around Alyssa.

"Friday is the get-to-know-you gala," Alyssa said. "Make sure you wear your formal attire. It's going to be so much fun. I never get to dress up."

"Formal attire?" I repeated, glancing at Jackson for help.

"Didn't you read the brochure I gave you?" Dad asked with a

laugh. He probably figured I threw it out immediately. He knew me well. "You should have packed a formal outfit along with several appropriate for tropical climates, swimsuits, and workout clothes."

"Of course. See you soon then." I feigned a yawn and waved my bracelet in front of the entrance to my room. The shiny metal door, inlaid with holographic mermaids, slid open, and I disappeared inside, wishing I could magically reappear on the surface where I belonged.

3

THE DOOR WHOOSHED CLOSED BEHIND ME, AND I JUMPED BECAUSE OF the sudden and absolute blackness in the room.

"Lights," I squeaked out.

Nothing happened.

"Lights!" I demanded, louder this time, and they sprang to life, making me blink.

The accommodations were thrown into sudden relief. The design was done all in shades of white and silver. A soft cream-colored sofa sat front and center facing a metal and glass coffee table. A full kitchen stretched out behind a breakfast bar with two overstuffed, eggshell bar stools. The carpet was so soft I could feel the padding right through my shoes, which I immediately kicked off to the side.

My hand sprang to my head. Only then did I realize the extent of the ache behind my eyes. I winced. I was probably so tense from the situation that I hadn't even noticed the pain. That was pretty damn tense. I strolled through an automatic door to the bedroom, where my luggage waited for me on a bench at the foot of the enormous ivory bed. It looked soft enough for me to sink into and get lost in the satiny sheets and cloud-like duvet.

A bathroom fit for a king included a giant, step down Jacuzzi-sized tub I could swim in, and a walk-in shower with four heads. Off that lay a walk-in closet, already filled with my things.

My panic made a reappearance as I rushed back to my luggage to find the suitcases empty. I pulled open the drawers on the dresser and found everything neatly folded and entirely familiar inside. They'd touched my things. I shivered as I pulled out the top drawer to find my underwear and bras also perfectly folded and secured. To me that spelled creepy, not luxurious.

I sat at the edge of the bed, sinking in slightly, and found an envelope leaning against an overstuffed pillow.

Fumbling, I opened the envelope. A sharp involuntary intake of breath inflated my chest as I once again recognized Mom's scrawl.

I added a few things to your suitcase I thought you might need. Hope you like my taste in formal wear. We both know you didn't read the brochure.

Alone at last, I allowed the tears to slip from my eyes. I had another letter to read, but I wasn't sure if I was ready yet.

"I need some water," I said to no one in particular, unable to settle myself.

When I stepped back inside the living area, I spotted the large open windows with a view overlooking Poseidon Park and the rippling waters beyond the glass, with schools of colorful fish flitting about. I averted my eyes immediately and hurried into the kitchen, where there were no windows.

The fridge had nothing inside. Annoyed, I pushed the silver button on the wall near the door.

"How may I assist you, Miss Meadows?" came Candice's voice.

"Please close the shades on my window and keep them closed." I glanced over and sighed with relief when the ocean view darkened to an opaque black. "I'd also like some hydropods and maybe some food while you're at it." My gut grumbled in agreement, since I hadn't been able to stomach much earlier.

"Right away," Candice's computer voice said.

I hesitated. "Do you have any other voice options?"

"I can imitate any voice on record. Simply ask, and I shall switch." The voice around me was now my own and more than slightly disturbing.

"No. No thank you. Please revert to the original option. I need some fresh air."

Hugging myself, I shoved my feet back into my shoes and headed out of the room. But one glance at the elevator and I wondered if I had it in me to go in there alone. Sighing, I pressed another silver button.

"How may I assist—"

"Where are the stairs?" I asked, cutting it off.

"The stairs are not as aesthetically pleasing, so they are kept out of sight at the end of the hall. May I recommend the elevator?"

"Nope."

I took off down the hall and found the door half obscured by the continuous mural of a long-haired mermaid and a giant clam. Shaking my head, I opened it and bounced down the steps until I was finally free of Mermaid's Cove.

Disappointment sank into my bones as I tried inhaling. Even with nanosun technology, they couldn't do much for the air. There was no difference between the inside and outside. It was mentally stifling, despite the sufficient oxygen being pumped in from below. I headed for the center, not only for the outdoor atmosphere of the park, but so I was at the farthest possible point from the oppressive ocean views all around.

What I hadn't expected was to find Mason Bennet seated with his long legs stretched out before him on the grass in front of my mother's statue. I nearly turned around when I took note of a group of women walking the path opposite. Mason scooted closer to the base of the statue, effectively disappearing from view.

"Hiding in the open?" I asked, unable to help myself.

He looked over his shoulder. His face colored at being discovered as his eyes widened.

"I'll let you have your privacy," I said, realizing I was exactly what he was probably avoiding.

"No, wait," he said, scrambling to his feet and gesturing to the ground. "You're just the kind of company I was hoping for."

I stared.

"Sorry, that's not what I meant." He drew a deep breath and tried again. "I want someone to talk to that isn't after my family's notoriety."

"How do you know I qualify?" I asked, approaching him.

"Truth?" he asked.

"Truth," I said.

"I don't. But I remember you from when you used to come into the office with your dad. The other girls were always all over me. You kept your distance. I appreciated that."

He sat, and I sat beside him, in awe that he remembered me, let alone at the impression my shyness gave.

"Why'd you stop coming around?" he asked, leaning in so his Caribbean-blue eyes penetrated my soul.

"I was trying to escape," I said, honestly. "When I went to college, I thought for some crazy reason I might be able to disconnect from Bennet Systems and forge my own path."

"I admire that," he said, lowering his ridiculously long lashes. "I tried to escape with college also. Stanford. It put a good two thousand miles between myself and the dysfunctional duo. But sadly, it didn't last."

"Dysfunctional duo?" I asked, trying to hide a snicker.

He looked at me again with that smile and those eyes, and I was sure I blushed. Damn my towhead. "My nickname for my parents. If I don't laugh at it, I might cry."

Nice, handsome, and in touch with his feelings. My heart fluttered a bit faster. He hugged his knees to his chest, and I admired the way his biceps bulged at the edges of his sleeves.

"What about your sister?" If I didn't keep talking, I might have found myself inching even closer to his intoxicating scent.

"Nicole?" His brow furrowed. "She's a bitch. I avoid her as much as possible."

The harshness of his answer startled me out of my reverie. "I can't imagine that. I mean, my brother gets on my nerves, but he's always there for me." I didn't add the part about how I refused to talk to him for years.

"I expect most people have families far more pleasant," he said.

"Why'd you come on the trip if you managed to get away once?" I asked, again unable to help myself.

"Let's just say my mother likes to control everything and everyone. It's almost a fetish with her."

"So neither of us want to be here, but we're doing it for our families." I shook my head, looking up at my mother's statue, so beautiful compared to the rest of the gaudy décor I'd witnessed so far at this resort.

"It's nothing against Paradise Atlantis. I'm sure it's a fine resort," Mason said. "Maybe we just need to stop sulking and make the most of it."

He leaned in and put a hand on mine. My pulse fluttered along with the million butterflies in my stomach. I froze in his gaze, a prisoner, afraid to move or even breathe for fear he'd break the connection between us. His full lips parted ever so slightly, and I imagined what it might be like to press mine against them.

"Well, look who I found." Travis's voice startled me out of my trance, and I blushed like I'd been caught with my hand in the cookie jar. But his gaze was locked on Mason. If his chocolate eyes could've fired lasers, Mason would have been dead.

That couldn't be about me. I'd just met him—both of them really.

Mason stood quickly and offered me a hand up. I took it and was unprepared for the strength with which he hoisted me to my feet. I nearly fell, but he caught me. My head spun from the sudden proximity to him.

Travis cleared his throat, and I backed away, adjusting my ponytail.

"I guess I will see you around," I said to Mason, since the moment was broken.

"How about Friday night at the get-to-know-you gala?" he responded, eyes locked on me, not the brooding man to his left. "It's going to be unbearable without someone normal to talk to. Would you consider sitting with me?" Mason moved closer, and I glanced to the side to where Travis had moved back just enough not to intrude. He leaned sideways against a young tree so wobbly, I feared he'd knock it over. But the sapling held, and he remained as still as Poseidon. His dark eyes bored into me. Heat flooded my body again, which made me angry. What was with me? I turned back to Mason, placing my back to Travis.

Mason waited for me, hands tucked inside his pockets. I smiled.

"Sure. That sounds great. It'll give me some distance from my own dysfunctional duo." That way, at least my father would think I was making an effort. It was a win-win situation.

"It's a date." Mason smiled, flashing perfect teeth that I wanted to run my tongue over, then nodded to Travis with what looked like a wistful expression and strode away.

Date? I just made a date with a Bennet. What was I thinking?

I turned to find Travis staring at me, the muscle in his jaw working as he ground his teeth.

"Can I help you with something?" I asked with a bit more bite to my tone than I intended.

He had the audacity to grin. "Just thought I'd said hi. Sorry if I interrupted your fairytale. Sounds like you'll get to go to the ball anyhow though."

"Jealous?" I asked, feeling my nostrils flare like Little Dragon was making a reappearance.

"Of what? I wouldn't trade places with Mason Bennet for all the money in the world," he said, standing so suddenly that the small tree snapped back to its full height.

Oh God, I just completely embarrassed myself for no reason. This couldn't be normal. I started walking back toward the hotel, unsure of what else to do.

"Wait," Travis called as he ran to catch up. "That came out wrong. Look, Sam, I'm just worried about you, okay? He has a reputation."

"Worried about me?" I repeated, stopping dead in my tracks. Didn't Jackson warn me of the same thing about him? "Because you know me so well?"

His hand settled on my shoulder. His voice came soft, his breath tickling my ear. "Maybe I don't. Maybe I'm wrong about you. But I'm usually a pretty good judge of character."

"Well you're wrong about Mason. I can tell you that much. And FYI, he's just a friend. I'm not the type to fall so quickly. Could you tell *that* about me?"

Before he could respond, I whipped around and walked straight toward the hotel. That was enough "fresh air" for one day.

4

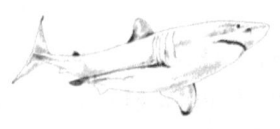

BACK IN MY ROOM, I NOTICED A HYDROPOD SITTING ON TOP OF THE breakfast bar, a notecard leaning against it. I snatched it up and read the typeface, drinking greedily.

> *Dear Ms. Meadows,*
>
> *We regret to have disappointed you with our lack of hospitality. Please accept our apology at this unacceptable oversight. You will find the refrigerator sufficiently stocked. Please let us know if there is anything else we can do to assist you during your stay.*
>
> *The Staff*

They'd been in my room again, and even though I suppose I'd requested it, I had pictured more of a room service situation where the bots came to the door and delivered something without trespassing on my space when I wasn't there. I downed the remainder of the pod and opened the fridge to find every possible space taken by hydropods. The freezer was similarly stacked with frozen entrees, ready to be thrown in the insta-oven. At the sight of it, my hunger won out over the creep factor. I selected a spaghetti and meatballs platter, which sat steaming on the table less than a minute later. I was still upset enough to be salty about how delicious the food was though. It wasn't like me to be this moody, and the fact that this situation brought out the worst in me stoked my anger even more.

Forcing myself to focus on more pleasant things meant I couldn't stop thinking about the two men at the park. When I thought of sitting with Mason at the gala Friday, my stomach fluttered again, and I could almost smell his salty, sweet scent. Then Travis's dark eyes made an appearance, and my libido went into overdrive. I wondered if they'd be into a threesome?

Holy shit, I did not just think that.

"Time for bed, Sam," I told myself, backing away from the table.

I tossed my ponytail holder onto the nightstand and unbuttoned my shirt. But as I pulled off my pants, I stopped, feeling the stiffness in the pocket. Mom's letter. I had actually forgotten, I'd been so distracted by hot men. That was unacceptable. Still, I wasn't ready yet. The thought of tearing open the fragile paper made my fingers tremble. So I tucked it away on my nightstand, promising to look later. After all, tomorrow was another day.

I thought I would be able to hide in my room, but the more I sat there, the more agitated and depressed I became. So off to wander the grounds it was. Fascinated by the tech, I made my way toward the Tube Exploration Center. While I had no plans to take an actual ride out into the ocean on one of the swinging arms, I did wonder about the mechanics.

The archway welcomed me with a sign stating THIS WAY TO DEEP SEA ADVENTURE! Naturally, the framed view was of the endless ocean, but I steeled myself, drew back my shoulders, and plunged beneath the sign. I had to work on getting over my fears if I was going to find anything positive during my month of isolation.

To my relief, only a few scattered groups seemed to be inside the visitor center, some browsing merchandise in a makeshift gift-shop, some reading holographic displays along the wall, learning about the ocean and sea life. One colorful picture popped to life in 3D. It was Candice in a yellow suit and matching heels as she gestured around her at what appeared to be a coral reef, teaming with life. Blue, yellow, and pink colors filled the air, surrounding the visitor with swimming fish of all shapes and sizes, and even sea turtles.

"Paradise Atlantis is more than a luxury destination, it's a symbiotic environment, working with the local ecosystem and supporting marine life. Here you see a coral reef brought back to life by our scientists by sharing our environmental systems technology with the reef after being ravaged by global warming. The subtle changes you and I feel are far harsher on oceanic life. Take a look at the difference we've already made."

The scene changed, and the reef all but disappeared, looking suddenly dull and dead, and far too small. Plastic trash floated down around it, and I wondered if it was an actual before picture or enhanced to make a point as it slowly transitioned back to the original thriving scene.

I tore my eyes away from the display, and my stomach knotted when I noticed Travis was among those in the shop section of the center. It took only a moment for him to sense me, his head shooting up from between a middle-aged couple consisting of a tall balding man and a curvy dark-haired woman. I smiled awkwardly as he made his excuses and joined me.

"Stalking me now?" he asked, hands in the pockets of his ever-present leather jacket.

"Happy coincidence," I said. "Your parents?"

"Yep. Promised family time." He made a fist and pumped it in fake excitement.

I laughed, relaxing slightly. "Don't let me interfere."

"Interfere? More like rescue." He grinned, and the familiar heat hit me low in my abdomen. "Join us."

"No thank you," I said, backing away. "I'm not here to ride. I'm here to observe."

His brow crinkled with understanding. "No problem."

Travis's cold stare above my shoulder alerted me to what I assumed was Mason's presence.

"Or maybe you were waiting for someone in particular?" Travis muttered under his breath.

I turned, verifying my suspicions with a sigh. Mason strode toward me from the entrance, face glowing and eyes locked on me. Was I a magnet for these two? Did I have a tracking chip on me or something?

"So nice to run into you here, Sam," Mason said, joining our little group.

I couldn't help but notice Travis's parents hurry out toward the entrance for the tubes upon seeing Mason. Did his whole family hate the Bennets? It didn't make sense when they worked for them.

"I was just saying the same thing," Travis said.

Mason moved so close to me that I felt the heat from his body. Confusion flushed through me along with desire, since I had no idea which man I was responding to.

I needed space. This wasn't why I'd come down here.

"Well, I hope you both enjoy the ride. I'm here to check out the tech." I gestured to the control panels in the glass booth behind the front counter.

"Not for the gift shop?" Travis said in mock horror, gesturing at a turnstile of stuffed jellyfish, sharks, and robostaff in the corner. I for one, had no desire to cuddle with any of them. Travis and Mason though...

I shook my head to clear it.

"You'll need access," Mason said, placing a hand on my shoulder. Was he marking his territory or being friendly? I stiffened.

"Oh, I didn't realize."

"No worries, I got you covered." He wiggled his hand, showing off his wristband. "All-access perks."

"Then by all means, let's take a look," Travis said through gritted teeth.

Fuck. This was definitely not what I had in mind. Still, the attention had me excited in more ways than one. I was beginning to get used to the high strangeness of two hot men fighting for my attention.

"We should go scuba diving to the sunken ship sometime," Mason said, turning so it was clear he spoke to me alone. My insides warmed, but my head started spinning with fear at the thought of it.

"She's afraid of water," Travis said with an infuriating smirk.

"What?" Mason's eyes widened. "How the hell are you down here then?"

"I'm not afraid of water," I corrected. "It's the ocean itself. Besides, it's not that bad. I can handle it. But maybe not scuba diving."

Embarrassment burned my face, but Mason's hand squeezed my shoulder reassuringly. "No worries. There's plenty to do aside from going in the ocean."

I nodded and started behind the counter for the control room, hoping they'd get the message to change the subject.

"Aren't your parents waiting for you?" Mason asked Travis as he waved his hand, opening the door to the control room.

"I'll catch the next ride," Travis said, shouldering his way inside.

"Wow," I said, pushing between them to look around at the semicircle of controls overlooking the tubes. Sure enough, the coral reef I'd seen in the hologram was out there, sunken shipwreck to the left of it. It was amazing enough that I forgot to be afraid for a full minute, staring at the clear arms swinging slowly through the waters above the scene, with people interspersed inside them.

"That's amazing," I said. "The movement is so smooth, it's hardly like I pictured it."

"You expected it to shake people around and toss them back inside?" Travis asked with a laugh.

I hit his arm. "I expected the motion to be jerkier. Like you."

Mason chuckled, but Travis and I shared a smile.

"Take a look," Mason said, coming around my other side and leaning over the controls. A whiff of his tropical scent passed over me. "There are settings so that we can send them in any direction. If someone asks to visit the other side of the reef for example—" He moved one of the empty arms with what looked like a joystick, and it glided over and around the reef, curving like a snake around the other side.

"Nice," I said. "There are your parents, Travis."

I pointed over at another arm, seeing them through the glass. Two other people I didn't recognize were inside as well.

"Dr. and Mr. Gould," Travis said into his wristband. "Hey Ma and Pops, want a ride to the shipwreck?"

"Sounds fun," said his mother.

Travis reached for the controls and smoothly guided them over to the other side of the shipwreck.

"See any buried treasure?" he asked.

"A shark," his mother said. "Glad we're in the tube."

"Releasing tube 3A." Candice's voice filled the room, and before it registered as the AI, the tube Travis's parents were in separated from the resort, floating out into the ocean before us.

Dr. Gould's scream burst through Travis's wristband as his hand jerked away from the controls. "What the fuck?"

"Computer, reattach arm!" I yelled.

"Unable to comply without correct clearance," said Candice's inflectionless voice.

"Bennet override, C12BQ11395," barked Mason, tapping buttons on the control panel.

"Clearance currently unavailable," the computer replied.

The loose tube swung out into the current, and the shark Dr. Bennet mentioned appeared, mouth opened to snap at the people trapped inside.

"We have to get them back," I said, unable to take my eyes from the free-floating tube.

Travis ran to the door, but Mason blocked his way.

"Move or I will kill you," Travis said.

"You can't go out there. Not only is there a shark, there's nothing you can do. We have to get clearance from someone the computer will accept."

"I'm not staying here doing nothing!" Travis screamed.

My hands flew over the control keyboard. The AI was off limits to me, but I managed to find a way into the mechanical overrides through a back door.

"Both of you shut up and stop fighting," I shouted, still focused on the keys and hoping they weren't tearing each other apart already. "I got this."

Travis and Mason appeared on both sides of me, faces strained forward like they could somehow will themselves through the window to the ocean outside. But why go out there into danger when the problem could be solved from right here, faster?

I stabbed one final key and clutched the edge of the control panel with my left hand, biting my lip in anticipation of my plan working. With my right hand, I reached for the joystick and prayed.

A second, empty tube glided out into the water toward its rogue sister. Carefully, I maneuvered the arm to scoop the loose one in, back toward the resort. When the clang caused a minor tremor beneath us, I knew I'd done it.

Mason leaped into action, running from the room, already barking orders into his wristcom for "all hands" to meet him at the tube ride docking station.

I sat, staring out at the reef and partially decayed ship, mouth agape, trying to make sense of what had just happened. When Travis's fist smashed down into the control panel, I jumped. His arm trembled, every muscle in his body taught with frustration and anger. His attractive face was twisted into something ugly and painful. A single tear slipped down his cheek.

My hand rose as I considered trying to comfort him, but something told me to let him be. I sat there, arm hovering in air, until the spell was broken by Mason's voice coming from my wristcom.

"Everyone is okay. The staff are using a blowtorch to create a new opening directly to the tube so everyone can climb through safely. Then it will be sealed off."

I sighed with immense relief and leaned back into the seat as Mason continued via the com.

"You saved them, Sam. You know that, don't you? If you hadn't reacted so fast and used the other arm to pull them in, they'd still be floating out there with the sharks, running low on oxygen."

Somehow, Mason's words did little to make me feel better. My throat was dry, and no response seemed enough with Travis standing next to me. I imagined he felt much like I did with my mother's situation. He had been just as helpless to save his parents. The difference was the Goulds' disaster had been averted, while mine was still ongoing.

"I'm going to go back to my room to rest," I said to no one in particular. "I've had enough excitement for one day."

"Thank you," Travis said as I reached the doorway.

"No problem," I said awkwardly as I stepped through the threshold without looking back.

Slipping out of the main archway was easy with all the attention on the emergency inside. People seemed to flow in from nowhere, apparently drawn by word of mouth. As I rounded the corner, cheers rang out, and my shoulders relaxed the rest of the way with the knowledge the Goulds and the others inside the tube had been properly rescued.

Still, the memory played through my head on repeat. Who had shut down Mason's override? And why? Clearly, the so-called glitch had become dangerous, whether Stacy Bennet wanted to admit it or not. Anger burned inside me, and I clenched my fists at my sides.

"Sam, wait up."

I swung around to find Mason hurrying to catch me.

Slightly out of breath, his smile glowed on his face as though the incident had brought him joy somehow. What if the spotlight was more important to him than the rescue?

"Those people could have died," I said, waiting for him to make up the distance.

"But they didn't, thanks to you." The huskiness of his voice drained some of my fury as he pulled me against his side.

"Something is very wrong with the AI here, and it needs to be fixed."

"Agreed," he said, looking me in the eye, face flushed, though what from I was unsure. "I for one feel safer with you around."

I didn't. What could happen if the AI broke down and compromised a vital system? I didn't want to think about it too hard. "Well thanks for the vote of confidence."

"You probably do need rest," he said.

I furrowed my brow, confused as to his train of thought.

"But it's early in the day. How about I pick you up at seven?"

"Pick me up?" I repeated.

"For some R&R. We have to be able to find some time here without a tragedy, right?" He leaned forward so a lock of his sunshine hair fell forward, making me want to tuck it away.

Was he asking me out? "We have the gala tomorrow, right?" I asked. We hadn't even had our first date yet, and he was already asking for a second. I knew I should be flattered, and I was, but the timing made me hesitate.

"I don't want to miss a moment," he whispered, and it curled my toes.

"I suppose it couldn't hurt." I looked down at the too-even, emerald grass so I wouldn't see his eyes. There'd have been no way to form any words had I fallen into those sapphire pools. "I'll meet you at the Poseidon statue at seven. And I'll pick the venue." That way there'd be no risk of scuba diving involved.

"Deal," he said. I peeked to find him grinning ear to ear.

5

I SPENT MOST OF THE AFTERNOON SOAKING IN THE GIANT TUB. I HAD no trouble with Jacuzzis, or swimming pools either. It was the unpredictability of the ocean that loomed in my nightmares and now my waking life. But with the relaxing tub and darkened shades, I almost forgot about its ever-present enormity. It also made it easier to avoid my mother's letter, whose presence I found harder and harder to ignore. Opening Pandora's box felt like too much after watching the arm of the tube float off into the ocean, those inside helplessly trapped.

Shutting down the images of what happened earlier proved harder than getting out of the tub when the time came and I could no longer avoid getting ready.

Shuddering at the memory for the hundredth time, I paused the application of my final coat of lipstick. I wondered how Travis was doing and if his parents had recovered from the shock of what had happened. I toyed with the idea of reaching out and contacting him, but something held me back. Maybe it was the rage that took over his whole body during the incident. I understood it, hell I even felt it for a moment, but something about it still gave me pause.

Seven came faster than I anticipated, and I headed out the door and down the stairs to the grounds. The walk to the Poseidon statue left me contemplating what I wanted to do with Mason. What I really wanted to do might be better done in the privacy of one of our own rooms, but we weren't quite there yet. So I needed to come up with a non-water-related activity.

I decided to give myself time to think over dinner. After all, everybody had to eat.

Mason waited near the base of the statue, pacing between the shrubs. He wore tight, faded jeans and a turquoise shirt that showed off his biceps nicely. He kept pulling a hand through his adorably mussed blonde hair. Clearly he was nervous, and that made my heart warm. Mason Bennet, nervous to go on a date with little ole me. Who would have guessed?

"Hey there," I said.

He stopped pacing and lit up at the sight of me, which I had to admit felt nice.

"So where are you taking me tonight?" he asked, falling into stride beside me.

"First we eat," I announced with what I hoped was an air of mystery.

"I can't argue with that. My stomach is always ready for a meal."

I led the way to a little place I remembered spotting on my walk that morning. On the path between a string of shops and hotels sat a fancy sit down restaurant and...

"Shipwreck Sam's," read Mason, nodding with approval at the small counter and smattering of picnic tables. "Sounds delicious."

"Come on, my treat," I teased, knowing nothing at the resort actually cost us a penny.

Grabbing Mason's hand, I tugged him up to the tiki-style counter in front of a life-sized model of the shipwreck outside the resort. I pushed the silver call button and scanned the menu.

"How may I help ye?" asked a disembodied voice in a bad imitation of either a pirate or an old sea captain.

"I'd like a bowl of clam chowder and a basket of fries," I said.

Mason smiled. "I'll take a bowl of chowder too, if the lady doesn't mind sharing a few fries."

I tapped my chin, pretending to debate. "I suppose."

"Yer order be right up," said the voice.

We chose a table beneath the most mature tree we could find, so we wouldn't be on the path and could maintain a private conversation.

Two minutes later, a compartment on the side of the ship popped open with trays of steaming food and silverware. Mason retrieved it, setting it between us with a laugh. "Gotta love the presentation."

"Oh, but I do," I said, grabbing a fry from the red composite basket and popping it in my mouth. "Not sure about the kraken though." I pointed at the eco-plastic sculpture attached to the side of my bowl, tentacles attempting to pull the treasure trove of soup beneath.

We laughed. We talked. We ate, feeding each other fries. My mind occupied itself with the pleasant conversation and excited tingle in my stomach, which grew with each brush of his hand on mine or stolen glance.

"So, you're a genius," he said after I'd told him about my degree.

"Please," I said, "You're surrounded by scientists and engineers. I'm nothing special."

"I think you're very special," he said, leaning forward and placing a hand on mine.

I wondered if he could hear my breath speed up or feel my pulse race beneath his touch.

"What's your degree in?" I asked, trying to get ahold of myself.

"Environmental studies," he said. "It was my idea to use the tech here to help the natural ecosystem."

I recalled the hologram I'd seen earlier at the visitor center and smiled in approval. "Nice."

"If I can't escape the family business, at least I can see to it that it's used for good and not evil."

"My mother would like you, Mason." The words slipped from my lips before I'd thought them through.

"I'd very much like to meet her sometime if she's anything like you."

He knew all the right things to say, that was for sure.

"I hope we have that chance," I said, staring down at my empty bowl, running a finger over the kraken's tentacles.

Mason's hands squeezed mine in the center of the table, and when I looked up into his kind, encouraging face, my heart cracked open.

"She has cancer," I said, letting the words fall heavy in the air between us. Once I'd uttered them, there was no taking them back.

His hands squeezed harder.

"It was hard leaving her there during chemo, but she insisted." My voice broke, and I stopped before the lump in my throat became tears spilling out of my eyes.

"I can't imagine how difficult that must have been," he said softly.

I nodded, still unable to speak.

"It's a gift that you're so close to her," he said. "I don't know her personally, but between her beautiful statue and amazing daughter, let's just say I'm a fan."

"Then you'll like the next part of our date," I said, the decision suddenly made. "I want to see the gallery filled with her life's work."

Mason smiled warmly. "I'd be honored."

I wanted to clean up our table, but Mason assured me a robostaff member would be by shortly to take care of everything. So hand-in-hand, we strolled the rest of the path to the museum as the nanosuns set, basking us in the soft blue light of a non-existent moon. The eerie absence of crickets and other nightly visitors wasn't as hard to swallow with Mason at my side.

"Here we are," he said, opening the door to the domed building.

It seemed none of the other visitors chose the museum as a nighttime haunt, so we had the place to ourselves.

We entered another enormous lobby, like that in our hotel, except there were no other floors to explore beyond the winding spiral of the sprawling structure. The glass floor lit beneath the touch of our feet, and glowing arrows guided us toward the right. Floating letters announced the entrance to the hall beyond as the Susan B. Meadows wing. A small gasp escaped me at the sight of my mother's name, and Mason pulled me close.

"You ready for this?" he asked, concern darkening his brow.

"Yes."

He waited until I drew a deep breath and led the way through the holographic words and into the dimly lit hall. Inside and along the walls hung my mother's paintings every six feet or so on the path, each individually illuminated by a spotlight so every piece stood out as a spark along the way, drawing the visitor's attention.

Spaced about ten paintings apart stood alcoves sporting the smaller sculptures I'd seen in my mother's studio growing up. Always in motion, usually featuring animals like horses or wolves, each one felt as though it were a snapshot of life.

When we reached the third group of paintings, I halted halfway down. Tears blurred my vision as Mason patiently held my hand. The fantasy world in the picture captured a wooded glen where a unicorn knelt beside a young princess, surrounded by a halo of fairy light. It had hung in my room growing up, where I spent hours staring at, wondering if I did so long enough, would I be able to slip inside and live in that world, like Narnia.

When I glanced Mason's way, I was stunned to find him contemplating the picture before us, head tilted and deep in thought.

"It's you, isn't it?" he asked, voice echoing in the silent hall.

"I suppose it looks like me," I said. "Though she painted it when she was pregnant with me."

"She knew your soul," Mason said, wiping the moisture from my face.

I smiled up at him, and he tugged me toward more works of art in the hall of memories.

When we'd finished following the spiral, we found ourselves facing a second opening at the back of the lobby. Before us a hologram of my mother smiled joyously, and words fell from the ceiling, forming a short bio of the artist.

Susan B. Meadows began painting at the age of two and never stopped. Her art evolved over the years to reflect the joy found in life's constant state of flux and motion. Susan's art is about finding beauty in the moments between. She strives to capture the happiness she feels when she is with her children.

"Your mother is an incredible artist," Mason said. It could have come off as placating except for the vehemence behind the words. "I love her philosophy of finding the joy in the moments between the motion. It helps me understand the Poseidon statue better. It's humanity facing nature, like a dance that should never be completely won, only kept in balance."

"Wow," I said, truly impressed. "You really do get it."

"Thank you for taking me here. I know this wasn't just a simple outing for you."

"Thank you for supporting me through it," I whispered back.

Mason didn't let go of my hand the entire way back to the front of Mermaid's Grove. When he finally paused to open the door, I stopped him from following me with a hand on his chest.

"I'd invite you up, but..." I let my voice trail off. My body wanted me to reconsider. But the emotional ache in my heart told me I'd regret it.

"I understand," he said, raising my hand, and letting his lips brush over the back of my knuckles.

Electric tingles ran from the point of contact all the way through me, igniting the yearning for more. But he stepped back, releasing me like a perfect gentleman.

"Tomorrow is another day. And I intend to show you a great time at the gala."

"I can't wait," I said, meaning every word. "Thank you again for tonight. It was exactly what I needed."

"I aim to please."

Like a magnet, I drew closer to him again. I didn't want him to leave without at least a kiss.

"Mason, you're needed." Stacy Bennet's voice blared between us from Mason's wristband, breaking the spell.

"It will have to wait, Mother," he said, eyes locked on me.

"It can't. Get down to Engineering. We've re-established your override authorization but have questions about the incident this morning. You have five minutes."

The reminder of the "incident" brought back the memory of the Goulds floating through the water and Travis trembling with rage. I hugged myself.

"I better get going," he said. "Duty calls."

I nodded and watched him reluctantly back out of the door to the lobby and away. I wanted a nicer end to the evening, but there was no doubt we'd sparked a connection. Now it was time to face Mom's letter. If I could handle the museum, I knew I could handle whatever waited inside the folded paper.

Still, I took my time, making my way upstairs and getting ready for bed. The day had been emotionally exhausting, and it was quickly catching up to me. I finally finished undressing and slipped under the covers with the envelope. It was actual paper, written in actual ink, by hand. Such a luxurious rarity must have cost her a lot. It made me even more scared of what lay inside. Ready for the worst, I slipped it open and bit my bottom lip.

Dearest Sammie,

Let me start by telling you how proud I am to be your mother. You have brought sunshine to my gloomiest days and smiles when I thought I couldn't anymore. This is the hardest thing I've ever had to write, but I knew that if I told you before you left, you never would have agreed to it. So here goes...

The cancer isn't responding to treatment and I have two choices. One is to give up, which isn't in my nature. The other is to pursue experimental treatment with nanotechnology that your father set up for me through Bennet Systems Medical Center in Spain. I'm choosing that option. Even with the best doctors and foremost tech, the odds are not exactly in my favor. That's why I couldn't tell you. That's why I needed you to go on this trip. I have to focus on me, not trying to pretend for anyone else, because that's what I do when you guys are around. The other plus side of you going is knowing that my family is whole if I don't make it. Sammie, there's a real chance I'll never see you again. If that happens, please, don't take it out on your father or Alyssa. I forgave them both. I need you to do that too.

My love for you will never die, even if my body gives out.

Love always,

Mom

I lay still, yet somehow, the paper trembled. Tears splashed down on the parchment, and I set it carefully to the side, not wanting what might be her last words to me to be destroyed. How was this possible? My mother, Susan Meadows, was the kindest, most loving human being there ever was. Surely if God existed, he wasn't going to take her from us.

"I have to get out of here," I said, sitting straight up. My breath came so rapidly, I started to hiccup, and I jumped out of bed despite my lightheadedness. I rushed for the closest silver button on the bedroom wall nearest the doorway and didn't wait for the fake Candice's greeting.

"How do I get home?" I asked, desperation coloring my words. What did it matter? This was a computer simulation I was speaking to.

"The pods will be available to relocate everyone to the surface at the end of your stay."

"No." I pounded a fist into the pristine wall. "I meant now."

A moment's hesitation was filled with only my heavy breathing, then, "The emergency pod cannot be activated without prior authorization from an appropriate party."

"Well get authorization," I said. "This is an emergency."

"I am sorry, Miss Meadows, but nothing qualifies as an emergency aside from a vital-systems crash. Unless, of course, Mrs. Bennet gives the override."

I pressed my eyes shut and beat my fist into the wall again in frustration. As if I didn't already hate that bitch enough. The narcissistic woman who had kept my father working odd hours during my entire childhood, basically programmed him to put work before his family, would never understand why I needed to go home early. I was stuck here.

6

I woke to see the nightstands at the foot of the bed. That is, until I realized I was actually lying backwards and upside down. I groaned at the heaviness of my body and hoisted myself into a sitting position. It felt like I had just run a marathon instead of sleeping, because my body was sore and my brain addled.

"What time is it?" I asked, pressing a hand to my head.

"It is 9:26 a.m.," reported Candice's disembodied voice.

I was about to crawl back under the covers the right way and go back to sleep when I heard a sharp knock at the door.

"Go away," I said, falling face-first back onto the bed.

The knocks came harder.

"Dr. Meadows is at the door," announced the computer. I decided that Candice's voice sounded even more annoying when it wasn't coming from her actual person.

I guessed if it was Dad I should probably get it. He was no doubt wondering how I was after reading the letter. Resentment cleared my mind as I wrapped myself in a silk bathrobe hanging on the bedroom wall.

"Come in," I said, "Just stop knocking."

The door opened to admit not my father, but Jackson. My

brother's six-pack showed beneath his open shirt. He wore trunks and flip flops.

"You going swimming?" I asked, wondering why he was so hell-bent on getting in my room if that was the case.

"Yes. A bunch of people are meeting at the pool, and you're coming. We have a whole day planned." He strode in and tugged at my arm.

"Hell no," I said, pulling free. "I never agreed to those terms. Besides this is my vacation, and I want to sleep in."

"Look." Jackson took my arms in his and waited until I looked him in the eye. "I promised Mom I wouldn't let you wallow here alone."

Low blow, bro. I bit my lip to keep my eyes from tearing up as I was reminded of the letter. He got one too. Is that what she asked in his? I deflated.

"I'm fine. I actually have plans already," I lied. "I'm going to explore the grounds with someone I met."

Jackson quirked an eyebrow at me, indicating his suspicion. "Oh yeah? Who?"

"Travis," I said. The only other non-family members I knew the names of were the Bennets and Tasha Graves, who I assumed would be at the pool. Mason would create more conversation than I wanted. But I was pretty sure Travis wasn't the social butterfly type, based on the enormous chip on his shoulder.

"Travis eh? Fine. Just be careful. I don't want some guy taking advantage of my sister when she's emotionally distracted."

"Thanks, but I'm a big girl. Now go swim with the piranhas." I pushed him playfully away and out the door.

I couldn't stay there. He was right. I'd only cry all day. A quick shower, jean shorts, my favorite teal shirt, and some makeup, and I was out the door. I doubted I'd ever stop sucking in that breath when stepping "outside," no matter how many times I realized the air was the same.

This time I chose a different path, one that headed away from the pool area, the tubes, and the museum. The grounds were beautiful, and the temperature was perfect, but it still just didn't feel right. I slid my fingers along the communicator on my wrist and toyed with the idea of calling Mason. Company would be a nice distraction, and I was already missing him. While the Travis excuse had worked, it had only been an out. I didn't really plan on hanging out with him, even if he was deliciously ripped.

When something brushed my elbow, I jumped and spun around to find Travis grinning at me as if my thoughts had conjured him.

"Planning on calling your new boyfriend?"

"What are you, my official stalker now?" I asked, stepping back.

"Sorry." He lifted both hands, which I noticed held steaming cups of coffee. "Will you accept a peace offering?" He held one out to me.

I hesitated. I didn't like how jealous he seemed when he found me with Mason, or the barely controlled anger he'd displayed yesterday. We'd only known each other two days. Then again, he also seemed to be a loner like me and felt the same about this whole scenario. I couldn't blame him for being so upset about his parents being in serious danger. He also had coffee that smelled very much like a caramel macchiato.

My stomach growled, winning out, and I snatched the proffered cup from his hand. "I'll consider it."

"What if I get a pastry to go with it?" he asked before taking a sip of his own and stepping closer.

I tapped my chin, pretending to consider it. "Something with chocolate would buy you brownie points. But I can't promise anything."

His smile made him look a whole lot less stalkerish.

"I'll be right back."

Within ten minutes we were walking toward the far end of the grounds, sipping coffee and taking bites of chocolate donuts.

"So where are you taking me?" Travis asked as we rounded the last building, which appeared to be another themed restaurant like Shipwreck Sam's. "My mother warned me about girls like you who lure men off to do horrible things."

I bumped him with my shoulder and jerked my head back toward where we came from. "I wanted to get as far from the others as possible. Actual destination though? No idea."

"Hmm." He stroked his neatly trimmed beard and tapped his chin. "I'm quite interested in the aquarium, which is as far off the map as possible."

My throat went dry, so I drained the last of my coffee and tossed it in a trashcan. "I thought that was closed."

"That's what our robot overlord said too," he agreed. "Which is why I'm interested. Come on. It'll be fun."

The idea of getting into some harmless mischief did have its appeal, so I followed along as he led the way to the sprawling building backed up to the oppressive depths outside. He leaned over the trackpad and fiddled with his wristband. Then he stood back as the door slid open, offering his arm with a bow.

"After you," he said.

The man had skills.

I strolled in, and the smirk fell from my face. The entire lobby was a micro-version of the resort, a small space enclosed in glass inside of an ocean teaming with life. My feet cemented to the spot as my breath came wild and far too fast, trying to keep up with my heart no doubt. I stared up, unable to blink as a hammerhead slithered above my head.

"Let's get a look at the—" Travis stopped when he saw my rigid stance. "Oh shit. I forgot you have thalassophobia. Sam, look at me."

I couldn't move. I'd lost control of my motor skills. The glass ceiling was going to break and drown us both, assuming a fish didn't eat us first. Travis appeared in front of me, and his hands took hold of my face, tilting it down so all I saw was him and his mahogany eyes.

"Focus on me, Sam. Just keep looking at me. I'm not so bad to look at, am I?" He grinned as he guided me carefully backward, step by step, hands firm and comforting as he fed me support.

I did like his eyes, and my body reacted to his touch. Confusion clouded my senses, and I nearly blacked out as I glanced to the side, trying to escape his gaze.

Travis scooped me into his arms and carried me the rest of the way out of the aquarium. He set me down on a bench and rigged the door closed before returning and sitting at my side.

"I am so sorry, Sam."

"No, I'm the one who's sorry, Travis. I should have realized what it might be like. Thanks for getting me out of there."

"No problem." He smiled again, and I had to stop myself from jumping him. The urge disturbed me.

"I should get back," I said, averting my eyes.

"So soon?" he asked, taking my hands in his and grazing his lips over them like Mason had last night.

Holy hell, he was sending sensations down my body that made me feel out of control.

"'Fraid so," I said, standing, and stepping away to give myself some space. The memory of his facial hair against my skin gave me goose bumps.

"Sam, wait," he called, grabbing my arm and pulling me back before I could bolt.

Anxiety at being restrained overrode my common sense, sending me spiraling right back into a panic attack. "Let go of me!" I yelled, yanking my arm away and rubbing the spot where he held on just a bit too tight.

We stood there, breathing hard, staring at each other with a mixture of want and confusion, until a staff member rolled around the side of a nearby building faster than I thought possible.

"Back away from this woman," the thing said, sliding between us and brandishing a short spear-like weapon of some sort. Blue electricity sizzled along the tip.

"Whoa, wait. I didn't do anything," Travis said, backing up.

"You will report to your quarters with me, where you will be sequestered until the matter is resolved." The robot held out the weapon a touch further.

"No need," I said, moving between the machine and a rather panicked-looking Travis. "There's been a misunderstanding."

"You yelled for him to let go of you," the robot said, tilting its mechanical head in a questioning gesture.

"He's my friend. It was a mistake," I said, holding my hands palms out. "He let go when I asked."

"What's going on over here?" Alyssa asked, jogging over from the path and tugging out an earbud. Sweat glistened on her skin, and her breath was ragged from exercise.

"This man has assaulted this woman," the robot said.

"No," we both said. "It was a misunderstanding. I already told you that. Can you help, Alyssa?"

She looked between the three of us and shook her head with disappointment. "You're dismissed, Terry. I have the situation under control."

The robot's arm, weapon and all, slid back inside it's body, and it rolled away. I released the breath I didn't realize I'd been holding.

"What are you doing out here all alone?" she asked, staring down Travis with a hand on her hip. "By the aquarium?"

"Just walking. We wanted some exercise, just like you," I said, gesturing to her dangling ear pods. "That thing is crazy. I mean, you gave it weapons?"

Alyssa pursed her lips. "That thing, as you call it, is programmed to save your life in a situation gone wrong. Listen, you should both go back to the hotel and relax before the gala tonight. It doesn't look good for you to be out here alone."

"I'm not a child, Alyssa," I said with a snort of indignation. This conversation was long overdue. She treated me like a stepchild when she was barely five years my senior.

"Your sex life is none of my business, Sam," she said, shutting me up. "But I'm trying to do you a favor."

She pulled me aside, and whispered, "Someone defaced the Poseidon statue last night."

"What?" I asked, stunned. "So, what? You think I'm angry enough to go throw paint on my own mother's art?"

Travis joined me at my side.

Alyssa's jaw dropped open. "How did you know it was paint?"

"Defaced property?" I said with a laugh. "Ever heard of tagging? What else would have happened to a marble statue the size of a house?"

"It just doesn't look good to find people out here so far from the main area," she said, glaring at Travis like the protective step-mother she wasn't.

"You were out here," I snapped.

Travis's eyes narrowed at her as he stroked his beard again. "She was sent out to look for anyone suspicious."

Alyssa shifted her weight to her other foot and glanced in the direction of the statue. But she didn't deny it.

"And I'm on the Bennet watch list. I'm honored," he said.

"You got a warning because you're with my fiancé's daughter. Don't make me regret it." Alyssa stuffed her earpiece back in and took off pounding the pavement.

"Did she just say fiancé?"

"'Fraid so," Travis said, reaching for my hand.

That little tidbit of bomb-dropping information was new to me. I backed away. "Look, I'll see you later. I have to go." Before he could respond, I ran back toward the hotel. I never should have left my room to begin with.

7

THE WALK BACK TO THE HOTEL HAPPENED IN A DAZE AS I TRIED TO sort through all the confusing and contradicting emotions I went through at the aquarium. By the time I stepped inside the elevator, I was ready to go upstairs and hide under the covers until the whole trip was over.

"Rough morning?"

Mason's voice startled me. I hadn't even realized someone else was in the lift with me.

"Let's just say this 'vacation' is off to a roaring start."

"I'm sorry to hear that. For me, it's starting out to be much better than I anticipated." Mason leaned forward, drowning me in those startling cobalt eyes and memories of our date at the museum. Still, I had to be careful not to let myself get carried away, at least until I untangled the crazy sensations that seemed to have taken over my body.

"That sounds like a line if I ever heard one," I snapped, surprising us both.

Mason straightened up. His mouth opened. "I thought we had a nice time together yesterday."

I winced. "We did. I did. Today has already been a tough one, that's all."

"If I said I'm really looking forward to tonight, will you bite my head off?"

"Not if you mean it." I recalled the easy time we had together the day before, not just easy, fun even. And he had been so sweet. Travis was the one who seemed hot and cold. Mason hadn't done anything but be nice and open up to me. Why was I blowing it?

"Let's hope you can tell that I do. I'd hate to be decapitated before getting the chance to dance with you."

A laugh bubbled up my chest and escaped as the elevator opened.

"I guess this is my stop," I said, hesitating at the threshold.

"Mine too." Mason joined me, letting the doors slide shut behind him.

"What are you doing on the sixth floor?" I was flattered if this was his way of trying to have some more time with me.

"I wish I was hanging out with you." He leaned close, seeming to read my mind. "Unfortunately, my dear mother has asked me to investigate a lead on the resident vandal."

"On my floor?" I asked, curious.

"It wasn't you, was it?" He grinned. "Personally, I think you taking a stand against my mother would be quite sexy."

"Hate to ruin your daydream, but I was locked safely in my room last night. What have you found out so far?" I had to admit, curiosity was starting to get to me.

"That's need-to-know." Mason raised a hand in a Boy Scout gesture.

"What if I need to know?" I asked, stepping in close. "I can be rather convincing."

"Do demonstrate." Mason quirked his mouth up in the corner, and I imagined tasting those lips. "I'm not beyond bribery."

I cleared my throat. "What exactly do you have in mind?"

"Well, you already promised me dinner this evening. What say we trade classified information for another date tomorrow? I'd say it's a fair arrangement." Mason's smile nearly blinded me as sparks flew to all the right parts of my body.

I pretended to think about his offer, tilting my head and tapping my chin. "I suppose it would be acceptable. Why don't you come in to my room, so we can talk?" Talking isn't all I wanted to do with him.

I led the way inside my quarters to the white sofa. I sat on one end, giving Mason his choice, and crossed my legs as casually as possible.

Without hesitation, he planted himself right beside me. He wrapped one arm over the back of the cushion and tilted his body so he could face me.

"Sometime last night around two in the morning, as far as we can tell, someone took a can of spray paint and left a message at the base of the Poseidon statue." Mason watched carefully for my reaction, I suppose knowing it was my mother's artwork. But I needed more information to truly process this on top of everything else that had happened. Was it possible to be so overrun with emotion that at some point there wasn't room for any more?

"What sort of message?" I asked.

Mason coughed, but it didn't cover his laugh. "Down with the bitch. Your reign is near an end."

"A threat against your mom?" I asked, unsure who else it could've meant. "Aren't you worried?"

"Nah. You don't get to where my mother is without making a few enemies. And let's face it, they pegged her just right." When he saw my face, he added, "Don't worry, I'm sure it's harmless. We did background checks on everyone before inviting them down here. She gets empty threats like this all the time."

That hardly made me feel better. Who would have done that while trapped down here with her? "So...why this floor?"

Mason furrowed his brow, seeming uncomfortable. "The security footage around the area blacked out for an hour, but so did the footage all the way back to Mermaid's Cove."

"Let me guess. The sixth floor went out too."

"Yep." Mason leaned forward.

"You can't seriously believe the person who did this is really on this floor." I snorted.

Mason straightened in his seat. "I think it's pretty obvious that's precisely where they are."

"It's too obvious. I mean, if someone had the ability to get through your security system, why would they be stupid enough to leave you a trail right to them?"

Mason's face blanked and then slowly broke into a smile. "Maybe we should put you in charge of the investigation."

"Leave me out of it," I said. "I mean yeah, I'm pissed that someone took it out on my mom's statue, but it's not like that's common knowledge, so curiosity is as far as I get with this investigation. Feel free to run things by me though."

"I'll take you up on that. You can be my secret weapon. Of course, if you demand payment, I'm not sure what more I have to offer." His voice lowered, sending tingles of anticipation down to my toes as he leaned in.

My heart thumped as those luscious lips finally met mine. I'd dreamed of this moment since I was twelve, and it didn't disappoint. His tongue slipped inside my parted mouth, gently probing my own, and my entire body responded. A moan escaped from somewhere deep in my throat as his hands slid beneath my shirt, running up the sides of my ribcage, prodding at the material of my bra.

When his thumbs found my nipples, I knocked him back onto the couch and straddled him, whipping off my shirt. I froze half naked on the man of my dreams, staring in disbelief at the small yet unmistakable smear of red near the entryway to my room.

"What's wrong?" he asked, voice throaty with want. "Sam? Are you okay?"

"I, uh." I stood up and grabbed my shirt, holding it to my chest. "This is moving so fast. I need some time. I'm sorry, but I need you to go."

Mason didn't hesitate. He stood and nodded, pulling a hand back through his mussed sunshine hair.

"I'm sorry, Sam. I really am. I shouldn't have moved so fast. Please tell me you'll still join me for dinner?"

I practically shoved him out the door with a strained smile plastered on my face as I reassured him that nothing could stop me.

Nothing could, except someone seeing that red mark.

Mason threw a hand on the doorframe, inches from what had to be an innocent mistake, *or a plant of evidence from someone trying to frame me for the statue incident.* I couldn't help but think it. Would Mason feel the same? Or would he condemn me based on what had to be faulty evidence?

"I promise to take it slow from now on, Sam. But please don't give up on me. The truth is, I've been infatuated with you since we were young, when I used to see you hiding in your father's office. I couldn't stand it if I ruined everything now that you're actually speaking to me."

"You didn't ruin anything," I said, hands still splayed across his chest. "The truth is, I had a crush on you too. But I want to know the real you, not just the posterchild for BS." I bit my bottom lip, realizing that I just used my pet name for Bennet Systems.

To my surprise, he chuckled and leaned in to gently brush his lips across mine. I momentarily forgot about the red spot on the door and contemplated throwing him back on the couch. But I stayed still, reveling in the scent of him as he nuzzled his nose against mine before stepping backward, away from my doorway.

"See you in a few hours," he said with a dazzling smile.

I nodded. I didn't trust my voice. The door slid shut between us, and I collapsed against it, letting the cold metal soothe my overheated head.

Knowing I had to face it eventually, I pulled away from the door with a deep breath and examined the smear of red. It was definitely paint, but how did it get there? I mentally flipped through the day. The only other people to come in were Jackson and Mason, neither of whom made sense. Could someone else have found a way to get in my room? The robotic staff certainly had access, based on the fridge and my unpacked bags. But it was an AI, and despite all the science fiction out there, it didn't make sense for it to turn on its boss and frame me.

Deciding a hot bath in the huge tub would settle my nerves, I yanked the ponytail out of my hair and headed for the bathroom. One glance in the trashcan by the door and my heart nearly stopped. With trembling hands, I scooped out the empty canister of "Scarlet Fever" spray paint from the bottom. I held it away from my body like it might infect me as I planted myself on the edge of my bed. Trying not to hyperventilate, I thought back to last night. Surely I'd have an alibi. But the last thing I remembered was slamming my fist into the wall because the AI informed me that only Mrs. Bennet could authorize an emergency departure.

I blinked, noting the red dots that suddenly stood out clear as day against the white sheets on the bed near the pillow. I called her a bitch. So did the vandal. Try as I might, everything after that moment was blank until Jackson pounded on the door this morning.

I would never...would I? Absolutely not. I'm neither a child nor that sloppy. Candice's words on the descent rang in my ears. *Your profile shows you are at an increased risk for DSI.* What were the symptoms she'd mentioned? *I'll let that go, considering the symptoms include lowered inhibitions and heightened anger.*

Lowered inhibitions would explain why I couldn't seem to get my mind out of the gutter when it came to certain men down here. Anger would certainly have described my feelings when I found out I couldn't leave last night.

I pressed the big silver button and leaned into the wall for support.

"What are the symptoms of DSI?"

"Symptoms of DSI can be similar to those of intoxication. These may include, but are not limited to, headaches, nausea, heightened emotions, lowered inhibitions, and occasional blackouts."

I swallowed back the bile rising to my throat when Candice's sickly sweet voice mentioned blackouts.

"Nope. Not buying it. This is a set up," I said out loud, backing away from the wall. "Where would I get the spray paint?"

A knock at my door made me jump. I dropped the canister and kicked it under the bed, letting it scoot to the center of the king size behemoth. Throwing a blanket over the spots on the bed, I rushed to the entrance.

"Who is it?" I called, leaning against the door jamb with my hand covering the splotch of paint.

The door opened to reveal one of the robot staff members and a cart full of cleaning supplies and fluffy white towels. "Good afternoon, Miss Meadows. I am Pete, and I am here to clean your room."

I stopped him with a palm against his cold metal chest, my hand turning red with the glowing light bleeding through beneath. "No thank you. But may I borrow some of these supplies and do it myself? I'm a bit uncomfortable with strangers in my room."

The pause was interminable. I held my breath, biting my lip.

"Of course, Miss Meadows. If that is your preference, help yourself."

I snatched the supplies off the cart with a forced smile. I went to work in a fervor the second the door closed, using the panic about the hole in my memory as fuel to scrub the evidence clean. Half an hour later and the room was spotless. Whatever the wonder cleaner was that I grabbed, it removed color from all sorts of materials.

One glance at the clock and I sighed. I had only an hour until it was time to head down to the gala. Considering someone was clearly trying to frame me for defacing my own mother's artwork, I contemplated locking myself in my room, but I remembered the word "mandatory" being uttered. Then memories of my time with Mason brought a smile to my lips and a flush that felt like a heat wave. At least I'd be able to get to know Mason a bit better, and bonus points for not having to sit with Dad and Alyssa, making small talk. Besides, maybe I'd also find a clue as to who had vandalized Mom's art. The why didn't bother me so much. I didn't exactly disagree with them, just their methods.

Time to make the most out of my date and get my mind off strange things I couldn't explain and my possible new sleepwalking habits. If it was depth sensitivity illness, then they couldn't exactly blame me for what I couldn't remember, let alone control. Besides, I couldn't imagine a scenario in which I'd do such a thing to one of Mom's sculptures. I pushed aside Candice's threat about stasis and instead got ready for my handsome distraction. I wasn't about to let that woman steal this little bit of joy from me.

8

I TRIED NOT TO CRY SO I DIDN'T MESS UP MY MAKEUP. IT WAS PRETTY hard to do, though, while looking in the mirror at the perfect dress Mom picked out because she knew I wouldn't think to bring one. It wasn't just the elegant black gown that hugged my curves in all the right places, the split up the side and neckline stopping just before it was too much. It was also the strappy black heels she'd packed that were making me tear up. We had picked them out together for my college graduation when we thought her cancer was in remission.

A knock on the door provided a welcome distraction. Smoothing out the material, I strode toward the entrance and opened it to find my father and Alyssa waiting. Dad looked handsome in a tux and scarlet cummerbund, and I had to admit, Alyssa's little red number with matching heels looked beautiful. They were a matching set, always glowing in each other's presence. It wasn't that I didn't want my father to be happy. It was that part of me wondered why he couldn't have stayed happy with us. Sure, maybe it was juvenile, but I couldn't help it.

I cleared my throat.

"You look amazing, Sam," Dad said, holding out his arms to give me a quick squeeze and a kiss on the cheek.

"Thanks, Dad. You too."

Thankfully, Jackson popped out of his room at the right moment, so I didn't have to dwell on things for long. He wore a tux as well, looking quite handsome.

"You clean up good," I teased him.

"Ditto. But now I'll be worried about beating the wolves off you instead of—"

"Hunting your own prey?" I filled in with a laugh. "No worries, bro. As I keep mentioning, I am a big girl and can take care of myself."

"Shall we?" Dad asked, offering his elbow to Alyssa.

"Oh, wait," she said, "I forgot my bag."

"I'm going to head down before you then," I said, seizing the opportunity. "I promised Mason I'd sit with him and his family, so I don't want to be late."

I had to admit it was fun watching all their mouths fall open in unison when I dropped the name so casually.

"Ground floor," I told the elevator once inside.

When the lift stopped almost immediately, my nerves wrenched, and I vowed to climb six sets of stairs in heels to my room later. But it wasn't a wrong floor, just a stop on the way to pick up more party-goers. Unfortunately, those party-goers happened to include Travis. He had no claim on me. I shouldn't feel guilty that I was going to the party with Mason. And yet, somehow I did.

He had the gall to look both incredibly hot and rude at the same time with his not-so-black-tie outfit. I tried not to stare at his tight black jeans or the cream shirt beneath his corduroy jacket with the top two buttons undone. Though I was somewhat pleased that he couldn't take his big chocolate eyes off me.

I wavered between wanting to back him into the elevator wall and kiss him, and wanting to tie him to a chair and interrogate him, since he was a self-proclaimed Bennet hater. What if he somehow had framed me for the vandalism?

"You look amazing," he said as the doors opened and we all stepped off the elevator.

"Thank you," I said, chastising myself for jumping to conclusions. "I'm surprised you're here."

He shrugged and stroked his beard. "Promised my mother and father. Family is everything."

Indeed, everyone here seemed to think so, and I was beginning to wonder if that was true or dysfunctional.

"But your outfit is a spit in the face of the Bennets?" I guessed.

He grinned. "Glad you understand. I don't think *yours* would be an affront to anyone though," he said.

"Good, because I'm not trying to offend anyone," I said, glancing around at the Oyster Ballroom as we entered.

The ceiling arched at least fifty feet high, with woodwork framing long panels of glass that showed views of the grounds and ocean beyond. I swallowed, lowering my eyes to the crimson carpet, marble dance floor, and round tables crafted of thick, dark wood with matching high-back chairs fit for royalty. A stage was set up in the corner near the dance floor, with several robot staff arranged around instruments they didn't play so much as hold in a frozen sort of stasis. The programmed music that flooded the space was pitch-perfect jazz at just the right volume for ambience without drowning the buzz of conversations. Hundreds of candles sat on each table, along with water lilies floating in bowls as centerpieces. A matching chandelier hung low over the center of the space, filled with more candles that couldn't possibly be real, yet looked like they were.

"Sam," Travis said, and I dragged my eyes back to him.

"I'm sorry, did you say something?"

"I said, it looks great because my dad designed it. But the head table over there ruins the view."

I followed his finger to a long rectangular table set up in the center, facing outward like a head table at a wedding. Seated behind its center were Mr. and Mrs. Bennet and Mason.

"I have to go," I said, then headed straight for them. Part of me felt a bit bad for abandoning Travis, but a much larger part felt an undeniable pull from Mason.

Mason rose from his seat as I approached, and the memory of what we started on the couch ignited a need deep within me. His eyes roamed over my body from head to toe and back again, and his Adam's apple bobbed in obvious appreciation. He held out a hand as I came around the table to join him.

"You look incredible," he said in a low whisper that made my toes curl.

"Likewise," I said, admiring his tux that appeared so natural on him.

He pulled me closer, his hand settling at the small of my back and sending tingles through all my nerve endings.

"Samantha, I'd like you to meet my parents," he said.

"Mr. and Mrs. Bennet. Delighted," I said.

Stacy Bennet stood and offered me a hand. "Of course, Miss Meadows. I've known you since you were a toddler. Congratulations on graduating summa cum laude from MIT in Artificial Intelligence. Is there a reason you didn't accept the research assistantship and scholarship you were offered there?"

She continued speaking before I could even take a breath in preparation.

"It wouldn't be because you were holding out for a position at Bennet University, would it?" She winked, pulled me into the seat Mason was occupying moments ago, and leaned in conspiratorially. "Let me cut to the chase. It seems we have a small glitch in the AI here on Paradise Atlantis, and since we all want that fixed as soon as possible, I want every available hand on it. You're quite gifted in the area, and there's nothing I love more than honing the skills of gifted young ladies. You'd be guaranteed a spot in the PhD program in AI at our university come the fall, full scholarship of course. But should you prove useful to the team, you'd also be well compensated and set to join the full team at Bennet Systems the moment you're ready."

My ears buzzed from the sudden halt of her voice, while my head spun. Had she just offered me a job and a scholarship? To what? Help solve the issues with Alyssa's AI?

Mason's hand on my shoulder brought me out of my trance. I looked up to find him glaring with cold eyes at his mother, with an undeniably clear message. She pretended not to notice as she accepted a refill on her red wine from a passing robowaiter.

I nodded as he offered me a glass, then ran my finger along the rim. The job was a chance to see the inner workings of this place, which I couldn't help but feel excited about. That was a huge check on my "reasons to go on this crazy trip" list after all. It was also a chance to potentially find a sense of control over my less-than-desirable surroundings. The month would fly by if I was working. I didn't have to take the spot at the university, or the job, if I didn't want to when it was over. I sipped my wine, contemplating as I warmed to the idea of a simple month-long distraction.

"You're offering me an internship?"

"So to speak," she said. "Report to engineering level first thing tomorrow morning. I won't take no for an answer."

Before I could respond, she turned toward her husband, her bare back dismissing me.

"Hungry?" Mason asked, biting off the word as he continued to glare lasers at her back.

"Starving," I said.

"Then let's get some food."

I followed Mason to the buffet, horribly aware we were the first ones. He, however, acted completely nonplussed. He jabbed slices of roast beef and slammed them onto his plate. It didn't take long to figure out what was on his mind, since halfway down the line he spun on me, blotchy red marks coloring his cheeks. I took a step back.

"Don't do it," he pled.

"Excuse me?" I asked, glancing around at the closest tables, where people stared because of his raised voice.

"Don't take the internship. She's doing this to spite me. She isn't trying to help you out. And she's never going to let you go once she has a hold on you. That's how she works." He slammed the plate down on the edge of the table and took my arms in both hands, appearing crazed.

"Mason," I said, trying to muster a serene voice, when I really wanted to kick him in the balls for being so self-centered and making a scene. "Calm down. Please."

"Excellent advice!" The real Candice's sugarcoated voice manifested out of thin air. The Bennet's COO wore a long, purple, mermaid-style dress with a giant flower on the shoulder that my eyes kept settling on. "I'm sure your mother would be devastated if anything happened to sully this moment." She placed a hand on Mason's frozen arm, and he shrugged it away. She continued in a hushed voice as though nothing happened. "Not that anything did happen of course, but appearances can be everything." She smiled her strained, fake smile and walked off with a high-pitched greeting toward the nearest table of gawkers.

I wondered why Candice would care about Mason making a scene, but I had more pressing issues to deal with.

Mason finally released me, staring at his hands like alien objects. "I'm sorry, Sam. She knows how to push my buttons. I didn't mean to drag you into this family war."

I sighed, picked up my own plate, and started filling it. "I really don't see what your family issues have to do with me."

"She'd love nothing more than to take a woman I may actually have feelings for and make her company property."

I stopped, a spoonful of mashed potatoes hanging in the air, forgotten. "What did you say?"

"I'm coming off like a complete freak, aren't I?" He buried his face in his palms.

I put down the plate and pried his wrists out of the way. "You might have feelings for me?" I asked.

"I might." His blue eyes caught me again, and the memory of our moments on the couch brought a low heat to my belly.

"Listen, Mason. Whatever does or doesn't happen with us, I'm going to take the job your mother offered me." I put up a hand to stop his reaction. "But I am not going to let anyone control me."

He smiled, but his eyes remained sad. "You don't know my mother. My sister's a manipulative bitch, and she got it from her."

I blanched. "Where is your sister anyway?" I asked, taking up my plate once again and leading the way back to our seats. I had to admit I was curious, since I hadn't seen Nicole Bennet since our official introductions the other day.

"Fashionably late, I presume."

I smiled as we returned to the table where this time Mason took the seat between his mother and I. He tilted his chair so he could focus on me. Between the music, the amazing cuisine, and the wine that kept flowing, I began to wonder if perhaps I misjudged the possibilities regarding this place.

Regretting that I couldn't take another bite, I let my fork clatter to the plate of my half-eaten tiramisu and leaned back in my seat.

"Would you care to dance?" Standing, Mason offered me a hand, and I hesitated.

I glanced at the dance floor. The only couple out there was a middle-aged man and woman who appeared to be swing dancing to Frank Sinatra.

"I don't know. I'm not much of a dancer," I said, unsure if my stomach could take it.

"Come on, you aren't afraid of what people may think, are you?" he asked.

I took his hand. "Never."

The more we danced, the closer we drifted, until his body pressed along mine, fitting perfectly together. My heels brought me to just the right height to rest my head on his shoulder as we swayed to the old music. I wondered if he could feel the blood rush through my body. I could certainly feel how excited he was to be pressed against me.

But I wasn't ready to get all swoony just yet.

"I'm sorry I was an ass. I didn't mean to sound like I wanted you to pass up a career opportunity just because of my family drama. I guess I'm just protective of you," he said, breath warm against my ear.

I tried not to melt into him more—and failed. Doing my best to pass it off as a sway to the music, I shrugged. "Yes, you were a bit of an ass, an attractive one, but an ass nonetheless."

With a skill that made me gasp, he swept me around the dancefloor.

"I will work tirelessly to make it up to you."

That sounded promising. "Thanks. The only reason I'm taking it is because I need the distraction with all that's going on with my own family right now," I admitted.

The look he gave me made my knees weak. "I should have realized that. I'm sorry."

I leaned into him, drawing a low moan from him. I loved the feeling of power that gave me as I nuzzled against the soft space between his neck and shoulder, so smooth and intoxicating with his salty, hibiscus scent. Knowing it couldn't be seen by others, I allowed my tongue to dart out and lick the exposed skin above his collar. He did taste a little salty, and heat swelled between my legs as his body shuddered in response.

"It's going to take me time to recover before we go sit down," he murmured over my ear. I smiled into him.

When I came down to Paradise Atlantis, I dreaded what awaited. Now the possibilities made me drunk. I still hated being underwater. Whenever I let myself think about it, my chest grew tight. But thanks to my new job offer I might actually have some control over my own safety. And tucked in the crook of Mason's neck, I allowed myself a real smile. The job certainly wasn't the only thing I looked forward to passing the time with.

9

W<small>HEN WE FINALLY PARTED,</small> I <small>NOTICED THE DANCE FLOOR WAS</small> crowded with people. Mason remained very close, and when I turned to him, his mouth hovered inches from mine, his breath warm on my face. My lips parted and he leaned in. My eyes fluttered closed. I didn't care what anyone else thought.

"Did you have a nice dance?" Candice asked right in my ear. I startled, my eyes snapping open. What the hell? I get that we didn't exactly have the dancefloor to ourselves, but was there a reason the COO was hovering right beside us? "Let's sit down," Mason suggested in a husky voice, eyes trained on me.

I nodded and allowed him to lead me away from Candice and back toward the table. I continued to puzzle as to why she seemed to care so damn much about our business, but I paused when my eyes fell on my father and Alyssa, locked together on the dance floor.

"Are you okay?" Mason asked.

Alyssa's face glowed as my father twirled her around with a smile. My stomach dropped. Here I was having a fabulous time with a man while my mother was yet again deserted and suffering. I had behaved exactly like my father by choosing my own enjoyment and abandoning her. In that moment it didn't matter that she'd insisted I come on this trip. I'd allowed myself to be convinced. Guilt overwhelmed me, and I suddenly craved space.

"I'm going to go get some..." *What do I say? Air?* "...more dessert," I finished lamely. I managed a feeble smile so he wouldn't think it was him and worked my way toward the chocolate fountain.

When I was sure no one was paying attention, I ducked behind a pillar with moving, holographic mermaids and tried to catch my breath.

"Trouble in paradise?" Travis asked, causing me to throw a hand up to my chest. What was it with people startling me?

"Are you following me?" I turned on him, releasing some of my frustration into the ether.

He smirked. "Just trying to stay out of the limelight. Not hard when everyone's watching you and Prince Charming."

"His name is Mason. And no one's watching us but you. What's it to you who I dance with?" I backed him into the wall, poking his massive chest with my finger. It occurred to me my heightened level of anger was groundless. Yet I couldn't rein it in, which only made it worse.

"The gossip boat has sailed," he said, still smirking. "It's all anyone's talking about tonight. You can't miss it. You're like a celebrity now."

"That's ridiculous." I folded my arms and sucked in my lower lip.

"O.M.G. It's like a Cinderella story." Travis raised his tone in an outlandish imitation of a girl.

"Grow up." I didn't have time for this when there were bigger things to worry about.

"Glad to see it doesn't matter what other people think." His voice dripped with sarcasm, but I didn't get the joke.

"Maybe Mason's not the one I should be suspicious of." I whipped around and rushed back to my seat, head down. If anyone was watching my every move, I didn't want to know about it.

I was so focused on the floor I almost didn't notice my seat was taken. I paused, unsure what to do. Nicole, Mason's sister, sat in my place. She finally decided to show up, and she looked like a movie star in a shimmering white flapper dress and silver sandals. Her hair was a loose tumble of golden curls that framed her heart-shaped face like a cherub.

She giggled at something, and I realized Mason's chair was also occupied by a handsome man in his early thirties, with short black hair and a pinstriped suit. My eyes roved back to Nicole, and she seemed to sense me, turning to find me gaping at her.

I pulled my shoulders back and smiled. "Hi."

"Oh! I'm in your seat, aren't I? I'm sorry. You and my brother were so busy on the dance floor, I didn't think you'd mind. And then you disappeared. But here you are, so I'll just slide over." She made a production of slipping into the next seat. The man in Mason's chair didn't move.

I took the seat, unsure what else to do. The man next to me let his eyes linger on the spot where the split in my dress landed, mid-thigh, when I sat. I draped a napkin over my lap and smoothed it out, wishing Mason would turn up.

"I'm Nicole and this is Graham Chaplin. He's the PR specialist for Paradise Atlantis," Nicole said.

Graham offered his hand, and seeing no way out, I accepted it. He grinned, dropping his lips to my knuckles and running his finger beneath my palm. I yanked my hand back.

"Please, call me Graham."

"So," Nicole said, bringing my attention to my other side. I didn't like turning my back to Graham, even for a second. "You're here with Mason."

"Yes. I'm Sam. Sam Meadows." I offered a hand to Nicole, who shot me an "isn't that quaint" look before barely touching her fingers to mine.

"I know who you are. I know all of our employees and their families. Congratulations on my brother's attentions."

Dumbfounded, I felt the flush hit my face. "Thank you, but—"

"Not that it's my business, but it could have been any girl here, yet you caught his eye first. You must be smart if you have him falling all over you already. I mean, clearly you're book smart, but that doesn't always equate to street smarts, you know?"

I opened my mouth to correct her embarrassing assumptions about why I was with Mason, but she continued on just like her mother.

Little Dragon gnawed at the edges of my patience, causing me to scan the room for Mason. I couldn't spot him through the crowded dance floor.

"Mason hasn't been telling you things about me, has he?" Her face fell.

"What? Oh, no! No. We've barely had a chance to talk—"

"I know he thinks I'm a bitch. But that's normal sibling rivalry. He's just jealous that I'm winning the bet."

"The bet?" At least I finally managed to get out a full sentence, even if it was just a two-word echo.

"He didn't tell you? Don't worry. I'm sure it's just that he hasn't had a chance yet. I mean, like you said, you haven't had much time to talk. Based on your little show on the dance floor, you've been too busy in bed."

I was sure I was as red as the carpet, but I pushed her comments aside and focused on this bet she brought up. "Well, why don't you fill me in?" I asked, feeling like perhaps I had a chance to get back on top of this conversation.

Nicole leaned in, and I got a whiff of designer perfume. "It's Mother's brainchild really. She wants us to be at the top of our games, you understand. So she made us an offer we can't refuse. She's giving us the next month to prove ourselves to you all—a test audience. The prize is Paradise Atlantis. The winner gets full run of all of this, a guaranteed ride to the top. She wants to see who has the best handle on politics, see?"

No. I didn't see. Nicole barely paused, though, before continuing on.

"It's really all about handling people. She knows we're both smart. We're both top of our class. Mason's her eldest son, but she's always been about women's rights, so I have an equal shot at it. In fact, until tonight, I think we all assumed I was the winner by default. Serves me right. I should have known better. Never underestimate the enemy. That's rule number one. Always be on guard." She stopped talking and took a bite of salad. Apparently, she was determined to enjoy a full dinner no matter how late she showed up to the party.

I glanced over at Graham. He was deep in conversation with Stacy, who sat on his other side. His body language had changed from creeper to businessman. The people at this table were at best bizarre and at worst insane. Again I scanned the crowd for Mason and again couldn't locate him.

"So," I said, turning back to Nicole and taking a swallow of wine. "How exactly do you win this bet?"

Her big eyes filled with pity, and I shifted in my seat, suddenly wishing I hadn't asked.

"By becoming the most popular, the most loved by the masses. Which admittedly in this case is only about sixty people, but still." Nicole shrugged and sipped her own drink, never taking her eyes off me. It was like she was waiting for me to understand something.

"I don't think Mason's interested in a popularity contest," I said and downed the rest of the glass. If only I felt as confident as I sounded.

"Well I hope not for your sake then," she said, and her gaze traveled to the far end of the room. Automatically, I followed along.

Mason and Candice were having a heated discussion in the corner. Her usual polite plastic mask had cracked, and she appeared to be scolding him. She visibly replaced her mental wall and gestured over to someone else. Jackson and Tasha joined them. Tasha shook hands with Mason, who shot her the same intense look he hooked me with. She fluttered her lashes and swayed a little in response, and my brother appeared less than happy.

The world tilted as I pushed away from the table.

"Really clever of him to find a girl right away," Nicole said, driving in the stake. "Don't feel bad. You can use him too. I hear my mother already offered you a job. And really, what's a relationship other than mutual exploitation?"

10

I BLINKED MY EYES AND STARED AT THE CEILING UNTIL THE WORLD blurred into focus. My brain pounded against my skull like it was swelling and had run out of room. With a groan, I clawed my way to standing and reached for the dregs of a half-full hydropod on the nightstand.

The memories of last night rushed back. I saw Mason flirting with Tasha the same way he did with me. I heard Nicole's voice and recalled their insane family's plan for the competition.

I groaned and dragged my sorry ass into the shower as I tried to focus past the point where I excused myself from the party, head fuzzy from all the wine, and had stumbled from the room.

But there was nothing once I had reached the threshold. Even the robot staff band stopped playing music when I exited in my memory. My heart clenched as I crushed my nearly depleted shampoo bar. It wasn't like me to have blackouts. Then again, I didn't usually drink so much, and I had no idea how many times my wine glass had been refilled last night.

My thoughts inevitably turned to Mason and the feelings he'd reignited yesterday. It was so easy to talk to him, so easy to trust him. I hurled my natural loofa across the shower like a javelin and watched it bounce against the tile wall. I should have known better than to trust a man. They were all cheating bastards, just like my own father.

I sniffled as I wrapped a towel around my hair, turban style. I supposed Mason never cheated. One couldn't cheat on someone they were never together with in the first place.

Now I was stuck with a job I had to get to, working for the very people I swore I'd never work for. What the hell had I been thinking? I pulled on a sundress and some sandals, then drew my partially wet hair up in a ponytail. It was time to get to work. Maybe throwing myself into the AI issues would help keep my mind off hot men I needed to stay away from.

I grabbed a hydropod from the overstocked fridge and turned to go, when I spotted my mother's letter on the counter, a rip almost half-way down the center. Rage exploded through me, and I screamed, wiping everything off the counter. It wasn't enough to satisfy my sudden wrath, so I moved to the table, and then the bedroom, knocking chairs to the ground and pounding on walls. Even considering the circumstances, the all-consuming rage was over the top and completely out of character for me, but knowing that couldn't quell it.

"May I help you with something, Miss Meadows?" Candice's voice asked from the speakers throughout my quarters.

I froze, lungs pumping oxygen in and out. I must've hit the damn button with something I'd thrown.

"I want to go home." My voice sounded strained, foreign.

"I'm afraid I cannot help with that, Miss Meadows. Perhaps I can arrange a massage for you."

"No thanks," I muttered, sliding down the wall and burying my face in my hands.

"Perhaps breakfast? We now offer room service. Based on your buffet choices last night, we recommend the continental breakfast."

"No. Thank. You." I punched the words out, but the person I

was really angry with was myself for allowing the Bennets and their wealth to get to me on any level.

"What can I help you with today, Miss Meadows?" the computer asked.

I pulled my hands slowly down my face. Another glitch? I hadn't touched the button again.

"What time is it?" I asked.

"7:24 a.m."

Time to get to work.

"Good morning," Alyssa said the second the elevator doors opened on the lower deck, which I now magically had access to via my trusty wristband.

I stared around at the metal gratings and massive computer terminals ringed by a solid window of ocean, feeling like I was in a B movie, *Attack of the Fifty-Foot Squid* with my luck.

"Hi," I managed without sounding too rude.

She greeted me in an official-looking lab coat, her hair up in a tight twist, and cat-eye glasses balanced on her nose. But all I saw was the love in her eyes as she danced with my father last night, and I was surprised to find myself being more hurt than angry.

"I'm so glad we are going to get this chance to work together, Sam. It's time we put the past where it belongs."

I stared at the hand she placed on my shoulder and stiffened in response. It felt automatic, and a trickle of guilt washed over me.

"I'm eager to get to work," I said, too confused to sort through the myriad of emotions swirling through me.

Alyssa nodded, removed her hand, and pulled in a deep breath. "Then let's get you a quick tour and get started."

I followed along as she guided me to a circular railing overlooking an almost bottomless pit of enormous generators and tanks whirring and whooshing in a constant, loud thrum that made my body vibrate along, like a they were giant bass players. Steam rose from one of them, and I could just make out the bright orange *Liquid Nitrogen* label on its side.

"These are the main power generators, the water purification driver that continuously cleans and recycles water for the resort, the oxygen pump, and the depth pressurization chamber," she shouted above the noise.

I threw my hands over my ears and nodded to show I got it so we could move on.

"Of course, we have a backup for each major part. And here," she said, walking backwards and gesturing to more terminals on my right. "Are the emergency pod controls."

"Excuse me?" I said, doing a double take.

She grinned. "The original design for Paradise Atlantis called for a mobile resort that could move around the ocean, relocating to different scenic views. In practice it was too difficult to manage the mapping and control. But if there's ever a major event such as an earthquake, we needed an emergency escape route for the guests. So we added pods, the only one online at this point is located outside the aquarium, but access is limited to staff and essential human personnel."

I raised my eyebrows, wondering if I now qualified as essential. I had no idea this whole place was supposed to be a giant submarine. The engineering necessary for something this massive to be made with such versatility excited my tech brain. I wondered what else I was going to learn on the engineering deck.

"So theoretically someone could get to the surface if they had the right clearance?" I asked.

"Only the Bennets and head of Communications have the ability to release the pod's controls from here."

Alyssa led me past various emergency hatches that acted like pod docking stations in anticipation of material deliveries from the surface once they really got going. There were a few scattered employees working hard at computer stations throughout. None of them looked happy about it. From their expressions, I was guessing if there hadn't been glitches, they would be enjoying themselves poolside, drinking a cocktail.

"Guess no one wanted to work on vacation," I said, indicating one guy who continually sighed and checked his wristband, presumably for the time.

"Of course not. But it's part of our contracts. A full month, and if there are any issues within our areas of expertise we may be called on to handle it in a timely manner." Alyssa stopped in front of a relatively normal-looking door and ran her wristband over a panel that changed from glowing red to glowing green.

"What's that for?" I asked.

"Restricted entry. I've added you, but no one outside of our department or above is allowed in."

I didn't know what I was expecting, but inside was a normal office, desk, keyboard, and two large monitors. Cupboards bordered the walls all around. Alyssa slid into the leather swivel chair and tapped at the computer. The cupboard doors slid upward, revealing a hexagonal beehive of inlaid monitors, each reflecting a different portion of the resort. I gasped.

"Big Brother, I know," Alyssa said. "But we aren't watching the people. We're keeping an eye on the staff. Anything that's connected to the AI can be monitored from this station." She swiveled the chair and stepped aside, gesturing for me to take a seat.

I slipped behind the monitor and cracked my knuckles. My fingers flew across the keyboard as I scanned the code she'd created. It really was genius. Even I had to admit that she knew what she's doing.

"Find the error yet?" she asked after a few minutes.

"This is incredible," I conceded. "The way you set up the logic trail. All the protocols. But what's this section for?"

She leaned over me, intent on the screen. "That's the nerve center. The patented code that makes this system more lifelike than

anything else out there. It's encrypted. That's why you can't read it."
She straightened and patted my shoulder. "Nice work, Meadows. If
you'd been unable to read any of it, or worse yet, pretended to get it
all, I would have known you weren't the real deal. It seems you've
passed the test."

My nostrils flared. Little Dragon needed to cool it. Nothing good
could come of losing it here like I had in my room earlier.

"Yep, I'm the real deal," I said. "MIT was right. So what's the
issue? I know the elevator malfunctioned."

"That was one symptom. We also had a television that wouldn't
turn off, several delayed response times, and one staff robot that
began speaking Spanish to a guest." I recalled the delay in the
lights the other day and the repetition by the computer this morning. I made a mental note to be grateful that was all I'd experienced. "Then there was the vandal."

My chest squeezed, and I gripped the arms of the chair,
swiveling to face her. "What does that have to do with the AI?"

"First, anything I confide in you here, stays here, got it?" She sat
on the edge of the desk.

"Of course." I didn't see the need to tell her Mason already
shared vital details with me, or that I had an empty spray paint can
under my bed.

"The vandal disabled several security cameras for crucial
periods of time."

"Tons of people here have the tech savvy to do that." I bit my lip,
hoping I hadn't reacted too quickly.

"True, but the way I designed the AI, it should have detected
and reported the malfunction, or even fixed it immediately."

I drew a sharp breath, staring at a section of screen that showed
Travis sulking near a bench while an older woman nearby snapped
pictures. "Alyssa, is there a possibility that these malfunctions
could spread to any vital systems?"

Alyssa moved toward the screens on the wall, not meeting my
eyes. "There are fail-safes in place to prevent it."

"Weren't there fail-safes to prevent the other glitches?" I pressed.

"Of course. But don't you think we took extra care with vital systems? This isn't some shoddy operation. This is the culmination of years of work from the greatest minds of our time." She touched a monitor, distracted.

"What is it?" I asked, squinting at what looked like a mound of mud inside the spa.

"Zoom in on section 4E, please, Meadows."

I reached trembling fingers to the mouse pad and zoomed in on the section she pointed to. My hand flew to my mouth, and Alyssa screamed.

The mountain of mud was a body.

11

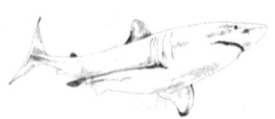

I T MAY BE A MONITOR, BUT THIS WAS NO MOVIE. T HE BLOATED FACE staring back through the screen belonged to a woman who came down here for a vacation and would never see the sun again.

"I'm going to be sick," I said to no one in particular. But Alyssa had already clutched her stomach and was hyperventilating.

"Computer," she said between breaths. "Seal off sector 4E. No human admission. Evacuate anyone still on premises. I want that body brought to the med lab without anyone seeing it. Notify Dr. Doyle and Mrs. Bennet immediately. Shit."

"All commands will be complied with except the last, Dr. Forbes. I am incapable of human excretion."

Alyssa buried her face in her hands and muttered, "I did not sign up for this."

I placed a tentative hand on her arm. "Hey, you handled that really well."

She peered out from beneath her palms, paler than I'd ever seen her, and swallowed.

"Thanks, Sam. I better get up there. I need to find out for myself if this had anything to do with the glitch in the system."

"I'll come with you, but it was probably natural causes." I wasn't convincing anyone, least of all myself.

The med lab was a small building that reminded me of a first aid station at a theme park. The entire way over I kept trying to push the image of the body out of my mind. Not only was I unsuccessful, but by the time we arrived, her bloated face had been replaced by one of my own mother, staring blankly ahead.

Grateful to be out of time to dwell on my morbid thoughts, I focused on the scene before me. Mrs. Bennet, an older gentleman I presumed to be the doctor, and Graham gathered around a cot in the center of the room. Two robot staff members stood at the head and foot, very still. An unsettling smell permeated the air.

Stacy tapped a foot against the tile floor, filling the small space with a clack-clack-clack. I desperately wanted to grab hold of her ankle to stop it. Those thoughts disappeared as soon as I saw what lay on the cot.

The body, swollen to the point of looking unreal, lay naked, caked in dried mud. Her eyes still stared open and empty at the ceiling.

Luckily there was a counter complete with sink beside me because I vomited on the spot.

The doctor rushed over to place a hand on my shoulder. "Are you all right? This woman shouldn't be in here!"

The robots sprang to life, and I jumped. Alyssa quickly said, "Sam helped find the body while working with me on the engineering deck. She's my right-hand man."

The robots hesitated, and I gazed at Alyssa in appreciation. Right-hand man, eh? It almost made up for my less than impressive introduction. Stacy strode over to us between the robots and surveyed me up and down.

"Good work, Miss Meadows. I have an eye for talent." She

barked at the robots to stand down, which they did. "Now that we're all here, what can you tell us?"

Alyssa recounted what happened. Her scanner hung open above the deceased woman's wristband that bit into swollen flesh. While I regurgitated the contents of my stomach, she'd already started her examination of the victim's tech. I had to admit I was impressed.

"Name of the deceased?" Stacy barked when Alyssa finished and resumed her attention to the hand-held scanner in her grip.

To my surprise, Graham answered. "Lakewood. Fifth floor, Mermaid's Cove. She had a last-minute appointment booked at the spa."

"Dr. Doyle?" Stacy said, not missing a beat. "I need to know cause of death ASAP. Miss Meadows, please assist Dr. Forbes in reviewing the recording to see if anyone has seen this. Above all, we cannot let word of this get out."

"Wait a minute," I said, stepping toward her and trying my best to avoid looking at the body on the cot that Dr. Doyle was currently examining. "You mean to say, you aren't going to tell people? What if this is contagious? Hell, even if she died of natural causes, don't you think others have the right to know? What about her family?" I practically screamed, but couldn't stop myself.

"Calm yourself, Miss Meadows." Something in the way Stacy said it forced my mouth shut.

I'd crossed a line, but I didn't care. The ethical ramifications were not something I was willing to go along with. I folded my arms across my chest, partially in defiance, and partially to hide the trembling in my hands. That's when Graham stepped over to join us. "What's he doing here anyway?" I didn't remember Alyssa mentioning his name to the computer.

"Mr. Chaplin is our PR expert. He has a master's in psychology. I'd say he's exactly the right person to handle this...situation," Stacy said.

Graham grinned at me like we shared a secret. Even in jeans

and a T-shirt he felt slimy. He was technically handsome, I guess, but all I could think of was an oily con artist.

"I know how it looks, Sam." *How dare he use my first name?* "But think about it. What do you suppose the reaction would be if this got out?" He waited.

"People would be scared," I said. I knew I was. I reached back to tighten my ponytail and continued. "But that's normal."

"We're in a closed environment," he said. "If something disturbing happens and you're trapped, what do you do?"

"Panic." The answer surfaced with immediate understanding, and I hated that. It was logical, but covering up information felt wrong.

"Exactly! We don't want anyone to panic. What if someone else gets hurt? You wouldn't want that, would you, Sam?"

"No, but—"

"We need more information before we can proceed," he said. "That will help us understand how to approach this. If we run out there now saying someone died, with no facts, people will use their imaginations to fill in the blanks to the worst-case scenario, and that would be devastating." He reached out to hug me and squashed me to his chest. "I'm sorry you had to see this. But I know you can handle it."

He didn't know jack shit about me.

"Miss Meadows has a point, Graham," Stacy said, and I took the opportunity to worm out of his embrace.

"Mrs. Bennet?" he asked, taken aback.

"The deceased's family. Computer, have the Lakewoods registered a complaint regarding Mrs. Lakewood's absence?"

The robot to her right sprang to life again, and I took an automatic step back, still afraid it might kick me out of the room, not that it would necessarily be a bad thing, but I didn't want that hunk of metal touching me. "No missing persons have been reported."

Stacy tapped her lip with a long, scarlet fingernail. "That makes sense. She was divorced. Her daughters have separate quarters. They may not even be up yet."

I pictured this woman's daughters asleep in their rooms, not knowing their mother had been taken from them. A lump filled my throat, and I choked it back. "We have to tell them," I whispered.

"Of course we do," Stacy said, laying a hand on my shoulder. Apparently, everyone sensed I needed comforting. "But we have to be able to tell them precisely what happened. Don't you think they deserve that?"

I looked into her muddy brown eyes, and all I could see was Mrs. Lakewood's body. Somehow, knowing her name made it that much more real, more personal. I wondered what her first name was, but couldn't bring myself to ask. I might start crying if I did, and I refused to demonstrate any more emotional weakness in front of these people.

"I'd want to know she's gone," I said, thinking of my mother's letter and the constant worry that something would happen while I was stuck down here.

Stacy squeezed my shoulder, and I saw it in her eyes. She knew what I was thinking. *Of course, she does, she is paying for the treatment.* "Dr. Doyle," she said without taking her gaze off me. "I want a cause of death, and I want it yesterday."

I nodded, mostly because I didn't trust myself to speak, and she smiled again. Why was it that it never reached her eyes? Was it just my feelings because of her family's ridiculous power games? I backed away from her touch.

"We had best go review those tapes, Dr. Forbes," I said.

"Let me know the moment you find anything," Stacy said to Alyssa.

"Of course." Finished with her scans and analysis, Alyssa steered me out of the med lab.

"Who are Mrs. Lakewood's daughters?" I broke the silence when we arrived back in the office.

Alyssa glanced at me, frowning. "Fraternal twins, I think. She always had a picture on her desk." Her voice shook.

I hadn't realized she'd known the woman. "What did Mrs. Lakewood do?"

Alyssa sighed like she knew I was not going to let it drop. "She was the communications team lead. She designed the system-to-surface interface and the EDRP."

"EDRP?"

"Emergency delivery and retrieval protocol. It's a shuttle pod schedule. One comes down here every three weeks with supplies whether we've asked for it or not. It's a fail-safe. If the com system fails us, then we still have contact the old-fashioned way if need be."

"So, how *do* we communicate with the surface?" I asked, visions of communicating with my mother floating to mind.

"Internet only. Any communication not sent through the com station must have an approval code tacked on."

"And who gives the approval code?" I asked.

Alyssa wrung her hands and turned pale again. "Marcy."

"Marcy Lakewood?" I guessed. She nodded. "There has to be someone else." I couldn't prevent my voice from rising.

"Of course," she said quickly. "The Bennets. They all have override authorization on everything here."

Naturally. Unless they were blocked again, like Mason had been at the tubes.

Alyssa appeared relieved at my silence and began punching away at the computer and various screens, looking for footage that would tell us what happened to Mrs. Lakewood, while Nicole's voice played in my head.

You can use him too.

Mason, the man I never wanted to see again, could use his override to let me talk to my mother.

12

MY REVERIE BROKE THE MOMENT ALYSSA LET LOOSE A STRING OF swear words, slamming her hands down flat on either side of the computer terminal. I rushed to her shoulder, scanning the screen to find out what had made her qualify for a position as a sailor.

"Shit," I echoed.

The feed was static. As in, old-fashioned analog TV static. The last time I visited my grandfather before he died I was six, and I still remembered him battling with the funny antennas on top of the fat little television set. I whined for five minutes straight, hands thrown over my ears in protest of the awful shushing sound that accompanied the fuzzy black-and-white undulating screen.

How was this even possible? "Why isn't it working?" I asked.

"The system claims that it is working," she said, typing at the keyboard again with a furrowed brow. "The other cameras are fine. This one was fine too up until around eleven p.m., when it did this."

I swallowed, a cold feeling sliding down my back. This was an awfully inconvenient coincidence. "When does it start working again?" I asked.

"Around 2:00 a.m.," Alyssa said.

"I'm guessing Mrs. Lakewood died between the hours of eleven and two last night," I said.

Alyssa scowled like she'd just eaten a bad Coney dog. "Maybe not. We can't assume…"

"Computer," I said, rolling up a chair, not confident my knees would hold me up much longer. "Give us a timetable for Mrs. Lakewood's spa appointment last night."

"11:30 p.m.," the computer chirped. "Mrs. Lakewood called in her appointment at 11:08 and arrived at the spa at 11:32 last evening."

Alyssa put her face down on the center of the keyboard and whimpered.

"I remember seeing her last night," I said, realizing she'd been half of the couple swing dancing when Mason had asked me to join him on the floor. "She might have strained herself doing some of those fancy moves on the dance floor and gone for a massage or something."

"I remember her talking about how much she loved dancing. And I think she'd been dating Carl." Alyssa raised her head a few inches, tears filling her eyes.

"Carl?"

"Carl van Morris. He works in Life Systems. Making it not only livable but comfortable down here at this depth was maybe the trickiest part of this whole endeavor."

I nodded, remembering the older man happily twirling Marcy around last night. My stomach churned. "We should tell Mrs. Bennet about their relationship. He'll need to be told too."

"Told what?"

I spun at the sound of Mason's voice. Seeing him there opened a hole in my chest I hadn't realized existed until that moment. With all that had happened, his betrayal felt like a minor detail, but not anymore. He wore a white polo and light khaki shorts, and his tawny skin practically glowed against it. His hair was still damp and mussed. He was a gorgeous asshole, and I hated that my body instantly responded to his presence like a hormonal teenager.

"What are you doing here?" I snapped, and he stepped back.

"Looking for you. You left last night without saying goodbye. You didn't even leave me a glass slipper, so it's a good thing I already know how to track you down." He grinned wide, expecting me to jump in his arms, I supposed.

"Let's get something straight right now," I said. "I am not looking for a handsome prince or a knight in shining armor."

"Sorry," he said, face falling. "I didn't mean it like that. I knew you were starting your job today, and since it's almost lunchtime I thought..."

Looking directly at his electric-blue eyes was like staring at an eclipse. Dangerous.

"I have a lot of work to do," I said, glancing at Alyssa in the hopes she'd back me up. But she remained completely distracted, studying something on the computer.

"I believe you still owe me a date. And you have to eat," Mason pressed.

"What are you even doing down here? You aren't an engineer."

"I have access everywhere. Are you going to snap my head off, or are you going to come with me? I have a picnic all set near the fountain. Your brother said you like sushi."

Jackson the traitor. He probably figured if I got with Mason, Tasha would be all his.

Mason smiled hopefully. At least he had the sense to look less certain.

"You should go," Alyssa said, snapping out of whatever concentration mode she'd been in. "I need to confer with Mrs. Bennet about our findings anyhow." She gave me a meaningful nod.

Right, we had an emergency to deal with, and as far as I knew, telling even Mason was off limits. I pressed my eyes closed and counted to ten. I needed to make a decision. I could bite his head off, or I could go have lunch with a sexy guy and turn the tables a little by seeing if I could get something out of him that I needed.

"Okay," I agreed, tightening my ponytail.

Beside the fountain, in almost the exact spot we met, lay a picture-perfect spread complete on a red and white checkered blanket, with a wicker basket, two square black plates with chopsticks set carefully across the top, cloth napkins, and crystal glasses. In the center sat piles of spicy tuna rolls, California rolls, ginger, and wasabi. In addition to the sushi platter, there was a kettle of soy sauce, a pitcher of water, and what looked to be a bottle of champagne chilling in a silver bucket.

"Poseidon was kind enough to keep an eye on it for me." Mason swept a hand out toward the blanket in an invitation.

Unable to stomach any of the flirtatious comebacks that flashed through my mind, I reached for the truth. "I am hungry." I sat, tucking my legs to the side, and reached for a tuna roll.

The food was as good as at the banquet the night before, and I closed my eyes as I lost myself in Nirvana. This was the way I liked my fish, in my stomach. Mason's salty beach scent permeated my little slice of heaven, and when I blinked, his face came into focus, inches away. My body betrayed me as my stomach tightened in anticipation of something more. I remembered his hands on my breasts, and an electric thrill traveled down between my legs. I was trapped in his spell.

"The way you are enjoying the sushi is making me wish I were a tuna," he said in that low, throaty voice that brought more electric shocks to all the right places. He picked up another piece of one of the rolls and watched my mouth as he fed it to me. The feel of his fingers as they lightly brushed my lips sent an explosion of yearning through my body down to every extremity. I couldn't help but moan with the ecstasy of the moment.

I chewed while he scooted closer. "You know, I really wish you'd stayed last night. I can't blame you for leaving though. Believe me, I never meant to leave you alone and unprotected against my evil sister or the queen B."

"Oh, I believe it," I said, the spell broken by the reminder of last night.

"The thing is, we were in the middle of something when Super Nanny interrupted."

"You mean Candice?" I asked, trying my best to distract him, because if he got any closer, the kiss would be unavoidable. And if I let that happen, I didn't know if I'd be strong enough to control myself.

He frowned. "Yes. She keeps an eye on our behavior, Nicole and I. We have to keep up appearances after all. But let's not talk about that right now." He leaned in.

"I can't do this," I said, standing so abruptly, I nearly stumbled and fell over. "Nicole told me everything. I know that whatever this is, isn't real. It's just part of your insane bet, so you can drop the act and use someone else instead. I have enough problems." I spun on my heels and started to storm away, but with his damned long legs he caught up in seconds.

"Whoa! Sam, you have to listen to me. I told you what Nicole was like. She cares about Mom's approval. I don't. I never have."

I choked back the tears, determined not to cry and angered that I was so close. "Is that why you were flirting with Tasha last night, and who knows who else? Because last I checked even Nicole couldn't force you to come on to people."

Hurt passed over his face, and he slumped slightly, still hanging on to my arm. "I was being friendly. I wasn't coming on to her or anyone else. I'm not interested in them. I'm interested in you, Sam."

My nails dug wedges into my palms. It was getting harder and harder to hold it back. But if I could manage not to break down when Mom told us of her diagnosis, I could handle this. I shook my head back and forth, trying to force away the feelings and clear my head. "I saw your face, Mason. That wasn't a 'nice to meet you' look."

He let go. "You're right."

Oh God. He wasn't supposed to admit it. I turned away, facing the spa, which made me shudder.

He took my silence as a prompt and continued. "Candice threatened me. She didn't want me to start something public with you. It looks bad. It doesn't help me like Nicole made you think. She wants the girls to think they have a chance with me. So she told me if I didn't start flirting with some other girls she'd—" His voice cut off.

Gathering myself together, I turned to face him. "She'd what?" I asked.

He grimaced. "She'd ruin your reputation and force us apart."

Silence settled over us. That was not what I'd been expecting. And it was wrong on so many levels I didn't know where to begin. My vision blurred with anger, but I laughed. "I don't have a reputation to ruin. I'm not some debutant. I'm an engineer."

He reached for me, and I pulled away.

"Sam, please. You have to believe me."

"I do, Mason, which is really, really sad. But as sorry as I am for you, I don't want to get dragged into the middle of your insane family's game."

He drew in a deep breath and nodded, dropping his hand. "I don't blame you."

"I'm sorry," I said, softer.

"Me too. My family ruins every good opportunity in my life. Stacy's like King Midas, everything she touches turns to gold—even the stuff you don't want to be about money."

"Look, I really should get back. We have some...stuff going down that I need to help with."

He looked up, eyes sharp. "What kind of stuff?"

"You'd have to asked the Queen B. I haven't been cleared to divulge restricted information."

"If it's dangerous, you shouldn't do it, Sam. She doesn't need you down there anymore if we aren't going to be together. She doesn't need to control you."

My temper flared again, and my hand balled into a fist. "I do not need protecting. I thought I was clear on that. And this job isn't all about you. Not everything is." Before he could say anything more, I stormed off toward the spa.

It wasn't my first choice, but I needed a building with an elevator so I could get to the Engineering deck that ran below and throughout the resort.

Two feet from the door to the spa, someone grabbed my wrist. I spun around, afraid I was about to give in if Mason tried to kiss me again. Only it wasn't him, it was Travis. What was it with hot men grabbing me today? And why was I complaining about it?

"I can't believe you're still seeing him."

Oh, yes. That was why. "Why is it your business?" I said, yanking my hand away.

His mouth opened and then closed again as his dark eyes flashed. His earthy scent filled me with longing, but I didn't know if it was him or the surface that I missed.

"You're right," he said. Twice in one day a guy said that, and last time it wasn't good. "It isn't my business. I don't know you. I just thought maybe you—but it's no big deal. If you want to set yourself up for misery you have a right to do it. Whatever." He started to walk away.

"Wait a second," I said, mentally berating myself for it. "What was it you thought?"

He turned, hands tucked in his leather jacket, eyeing me like he was trying to decide how to proceed. "I thought you were like me. That you saw through this place and these people. But obviously I was wrong. It's just that I'm usually—"

"A good judge of character," I finished. "Not that you need to know, but I broke it off with him."

He snorted, the side of his mouth quirking into a lopsided grin that sent heat surging through my body. "We've been here all of three days and you dumped the bosses' son? What are you going to do for entertainment for the rest of the month?"

A laugh bubbled up and betrayed me by bursting through. In another minute, we were both doubled over in hysterics. I guessed with all the stress we both needed that kind of release.

"Want to take a walk?" he asked, stepping into my personal space.

"I can't," I said, stopping him in his tracks. "I have to work."

"Work? That has to be the lamest excuse ever. No one's working on this trip."

"No, really," I said, silently daring him to challenge my decision like Mason did. "I accepted an internship with Engineering."

He crossed his arms, and the glare he gave sent tremors to all the wrong places.

"But I could meet you for an early dinner," I offered. All I'd eaten were two pieces of sushi, and I was already a bit light-headed.

"I don't do champagne and sushi," he said, and heat filled my cheeks. How much had he seen? "But I'll be happy to introduce you to my friend red meat. Five o'clock sharp, my room."

I watched, open-mouthed, as he took off toward the hotel, and only after that did I wonder what he was doing creeping so closely around the off-limits spa.

13

"It was asphyxiation," Nicole said the second I slipped through the doors of the spa.

"What are you doing here?" I asked, more than a little spooked.

"I came for a full body wrap, and it was closed. Obviously that was unacceptable, so I commed Mother and she filled me in." She tossed her golden locks over her shoulder. She was sporting a skimpy designer bikini in zebra print. I wondered if it was made of real zebras.

"So...you thought you'd hang in the deserted place a woman died?"

"You're funny, Sam. I wanted in on the investigation. This is not going to look good. The faster we can sweep it under the rug, the better."

I ignored her eagerness to hide the facts, not sure which was worse, her in-your-face attitude or Candice's fake sweetness. "You said something about asphyxiation?"

"Yes. Ms. Lakewood was in the mud pool. Great exfoliation for your skin, except you're not really supposed to inhale it."

"She drowned in the mud?" I asked, recalling the image of the brown substance caked over her body on the screen and then in person. I shivered. "She could have just passed out."

Nicole folded her arms and shot me a 'you can't possibly be that naive' look. "She might have died there, but her body wasn't found in the mud pool." Then she spun and led the way into the room in question.

The floor was still coated in smeared lines of muddy goop, the impression of a woman's body imprinted on the smooth rock. It was so much more real in person than on the computer monitor. My head spun, and I grabbed for the wall to steady myself.

"Don't tell me you're squeamish," Nicole said.

"I haven't eaten much today. So any footprints or fingerprints or anything?" I asked, redirecting her.

"Staff. There are wheel marks right there, but no footprints." She pointed to the floor between the imprint and the pool itself.

I nodded, edging toward the elevator in the hall. "It looks like someone messed with the security footage. I really need to get back down to Alyssa."

"I'll come too."

Great, we can have a party. I slipped inside the elevator and said, "Engineering."

In the engineering room, Alyssa was so focused on her computer, I had to clear my throat twice before she looked up. "You're back. And you brought a friend."

I wouldn't have called her a friend, but it wasn't the moment to point that out. Instead, I filled her in on what Nicole shared.

"So, based on all reports, what we have is the highly suspicious death of an otherwise healthy woman, who happens to be in charge of communications, during the first week here," Nicole said, pulling up a seat. "No physical evidence left at the scene, and apparent tampering with the surveillance. It sounds like the signature of our vandal."

"Wait a second," I said, pulling myself onto the desk, the only place left to sit down, because if I didn't sit soon, I would pass out.

"There *was* physical evidence at the scene. You said so yourself. Staff tracks in the mud between the pool and the body."

Alyssa gaped at me, then turned toward Nicole. "This is bad."

"What?" Nicole snorted. "You really think a *robot* murdered someone?"

Alyssa licked her lips. "The AI is malfunctioning. What if it *really* messed up? It may have tried to cover its tracks by erasing the footage."

"You have got to be kidding me," Nicole said. "How would it know to do that?"

"AI means artificial *intelligence*," I said. Compared to Nicole, Alyssa was like Mother Theresa. "It's programmed to gather information and make inferences from it, to learn. It sounds far-fetched, but it isn't that unthinkable." I pressed my hands together and stuffed them in my lap to stop the shaking. The truth was, only yesterday I felt the same as Nicole. But that had to be a more likely possibility than me committing murder during a blackout. I couldn't have done that. It was impossible. But that red stain on my wall kept popping into my head. The two pieces of sushi in my stomach churned.

"That's like science fiction crap," Nicole said, again echoing my previous thoughts. But she shifted her position in the chair, showing she wasn't as confident as she pretended to be.

"So is an underwater resort," I said.

This whole situation was a nightmare. It had to be. Part of me kept trying force the memory of what occurred last night after the party. I was not a murderer. But instead of missing memories, all I could see was that can of empty spray paint in my room. *Please, please, don't be me.*

I was so busy arguing with Nicole and trying to explain away my nerves, that I didn't think about Alyssa until I heard the sniffles. She had her head buried in her hands, glasses flung on the desk behind me, shoulders trembling.

"Are you okay?" I asked, placing a hand on her arm.

"Pull it together, doctor," Nicole said, wrinkling her nose.

"This is my fault." Alyssa's voice was small as she pulled back her hands to reveal bright red eyes. "I killed Marcy."

"What?" I asked, leaping off the desk and backing toward Nicole.

"Well, I might as well have. I programmed the AI myself. If it really was the computer and staff..." She wiped at her face with the sleeve of her lab coat.

"We don't know for sure it was the computer," Nicole said. "I still think espionage is far more likely. Someone blocked Mason's override code during the tube incident."

"It could have been the AI," Alyssa countered.

"We have to interview the computer," I said. "If it wasn't the AI, then it should be a huge help in figuring this out."

"And if it is," Alyssa said, replacing her glasses. "Then we need to know so we can turn it off and cut this trip short. We need to let Nicole's mother know what we've found out."

Nicole bristled, straightening her small frame, which seemed to fill out the entire chair. "I'm here. We can't waste a second. Interview the computer now, and I will fill in my mother when we know something."

"Computer," Alyssa said, still sniffling. "It is imperative we know what happened to Marcy Lakewood last night."

"Marcy Lakewood's last known whereabouts was the Paradise Spa yesterday evening at 11:54 p.m.," the computer responded.

"What happened at 11:54?" I asked, fear shooting through my body like an arrow.

"Mrs. Lakewood's last staff interaction was at 11:54 p.m. She was given access to the mud bath at that time. I have not spoken to her since."

Nicole frowned, and I shuddered.

"Which staff member last interacted with her?" Alyssa asked.

"Terry."

That was the same bot that threatened Travis at the aquarium. I shivered with the memory.

Nicole crossed her legs and leaned back in the chair. "Computer, send Terry down here immediately."

"Right away, Miss Bennet."

"Ugh," I said, unable to hold it in anymore. "I can't stand that voice." Maybe it was stupid to say it to Nicole, who probably adored Candice, but it had to be said.

To my astonishment, Nicole deteriorated into a fit of snorts and giggles. "It is obnoxious, isn't it? Computer change voice please."

"Do you prefer this?" Nicole's own voice answered her.

I glanced over to see her response, but she only smiled. "Much."

Figured.

I busied myself with picking through Alyssa's code while we waited for Terry. The code was elegant and simple, which I hated and admired at the same time. Try as I might, I couldn't see any fault in the logic. Nothing that stuck out and said "feel free to kill a human."

"What are you doing here?" The venom in Nicole's voice could've murdered on the spot.

"I spoke to Mother." Mason's response pulled my nose out of the computer screen. He was looking at me, not even trying to acknowledge his sister. What did he want me to say? I thought I'd made myself clear, and I didn't trust myself to be strong enough to resist him if he pushed it.

"There's more," I said and filled him in on everything else, trying to ignore the look of death Nicole shot me, and the way her face flushed red. Better to have her mad at me than say anything personal to Mason. Because the thing was, seeing him there made my heart leap, and I started to second-guess myself without him saying a word.

"Why haven't you told my mother?" he asked, speaking directly to me.

"Nicole said—" I started.

"Ahh. My lovely sister's doing, say no more. Well, if we are interested in actually figuring this out and keeping people safe, as opposed to personal glory, we need to keep all parties informed."

At that moment, Terry the staff member rolled in. He looked exactly like every other shiny robot in the place, but I tensed, wondering if he might have been the one that killed Marcy Lakewood.

Mason seemed to sense my discomfort because he came over, resting a hand on my shoulder. The desire to scoot in closer battled with my brain insisting I push him away, so I compromised and did neither.

"How may I assist you?" the robostaff asked. If I didn't know any better, I would've thought it was nervous.

"Terry," Alyssa said, standing and assuming control. "We need to know exactly what happened last night with Mrs. Lakewood."

None of us moved an inch. I doubt we even breathed while we waited for the reply.

"I helped Mrs. Lakewood into the mud bath yesterday evening at 11:43 p.m. She asked for assistance. I left eleven minutes later while she exfoliated." Terry swung his metallic arms slightly in an all too human gesture.

"Um, Terry," I said. I scooted closer to Mason when those black holes of eyes faced me. "What did Mrs. Lakewood need assistance with?"

His black orbs reflected the light of the screens behind me, and I wished I could read something in his face. It unnerved me. "She could not reach all parts of her body. She asked for my help in 'getting everything'."

Silence filled the pause.

Nicole let out an exasperated sigh and stepped in front of the robot. "Do you know who killed Mrs. Lakewood?"

"Yes, ma'am."

Mason sucked in an audible breath beside me, and his hand tightened on my shoulder.

Please don't say it was me, I prayed, ready to collapse on the spot.

"Well?" Nicole demanded. "Who was it?"

"I did," Terry said. "You seem angry, Miss Bennet. Have I done something wrong?"

"You killed someone!" I shouted, jumping off the desk. "That's very, very wrong." Relief flooded through me, and I chased it away.

Terry rolled backward and forward a bit. "Computer said it may be perceived as wrong. But I asked her how it could when I was only doing what the guest asked of me." His voice actually broke.

"She asked you to kill her?" Alyssa said.

"She asked me to help cover all parts of her body with mud. I complied."

"By shoving her under," I whispered.

"Never shove a guest!" Terry said, as though I'd suggested something appalling. "We must treat them with respect and dignity."

"Okay, I think I'm seeing the disconnect in the logic programming," I said.

"I can't believe this," Alyssa said and swallowed. "So, you covered your tracks by erasing the footage?"

"No, ma'am. It was computer. She was...concerned you might feel I'd done something wrong and delete my programming. She erased the evidence to protect me. Will I be deleted?" He sounded like a child who'd been caught sneaking candy.

"Damn straight," Nicole said. She reached forward, a gold keycard in hand, and slipped it in the soft area behind Terry's neck. "Disable," she said, and the red light on his chest went dark.

We sat there, silent, for some time. I let Mason put his arm around me. Terry's deactivated body slumped in the center of the small office.

Finally, Alyssa cleared her throat. "We have to deactivate the computer too. Do an overhaul of the whole system. I'm afraid we're going to have to evacuate."

My heart skittered in my chest. Evacuate? I would never wish anyone dead, but it was hard not to think of this as a blessing in disguise.

"No. This is too important," Nicole said, pacing. "Take the AI offline and get it fixed. You have twenty-four hours. We will manage until then. Tell people Mrs. Lakewood had a terrible accident and we are revamping the system to monitor everyone's vitals so that if something else happens, we will hopefully be able to prevent it. So you'll have to add the vitals thing too."

"Are you fucking kidding me?" Mason let go of me and stepped up, stopping his sister in mid pace. He towered over her, but one wouldn't have known it from the way she jutted her chin out in a how-dare-you-challenge-me pose. "You cannot do that. These people are in danger."

"There is no danger if we take the computer offline. Just a daylong inconvenience. It's an acceptable risk." Nicole raised one perfectly plucked eyebrow.

"You can't lie to that woman's family," I said. "And there's no way to fix this in twenty-four hours. It just isn't happening."

"Oh? I don't recall hiring you as head engineer for the AI department. You are an *intern*," Nicole barked, brushing past Mason to get in my face. Her attempt to intimidate me fell short.

I slid off the desk to meet her head on. "This isn't your decision either. It's your mother's." And I hoped to God she would be more reasonable. Surely she would see how ludicrous Nicole's plan was.

"Both of you settle down," Alyssa said. "We've had a huge shock. We need to take a deep breath and think logically. Nicole, Sam is right. Even if I can fix this in a single day— which is highly unlikely—it will have to be tested thoroughly before we bring it back online. And everything is designed to run through the AI."

"And we will tell Mrs. Lakewood's family the truth," Mason added, eyes on me.

I breathed a small sigh of relief, and part of the ice around my heart where he was concerned melted. He won points in the good-guy department for that.

"I'm calling Mother," Nicole said, like the spoiled child she was.

"You do that," Mason said, taking my arm and leading me toward the door. "In the meantime, Sam and I are going to go break the news to the Lakewood twins."

"And Carl. Her boyfriend will want to know too," I said.

Mason paused to smile at me. "And Carl."

14

"I CAN'T BELIEVE THIS," I SAID AS WE ENTERED THE LOBBY OF Mermaid's Cove. "I had my reservations about coming down here, but I never even imagined something like this."

"I'm sorry you got dragged into it," Mason said as he slumped back against the glass of the elevator. "Computer, what room are the Lakewood girls in?"

"Good afternoon, Mr. Bennet," Nicole's voice greeted him. "The Lakewoods are in room five forty-eight."

"I can't take that anymore," Mason said with a shudder. "I hear her enough. Computer please change voice."

"What voice would you like me to use, Mr. Bennet?" Mason's voice asked.

I raised my brow.

"No one I actually know," he said.

"Very well, Mr. Bennet," said a woman's breathy voice. "What floor would you like?"

"Floor five. We need to speak to the Lakewood girls."

The doors slid closed, and the elevator jolted upward, making me grab for Mason's arm. "What the hell was that?" I asked, bracing myself against the walls as the elevator flew skyward.

The car stopped suddenly, and it made me stumble. With a cry, I landed in Masons arms. His expression was just as shocked as I'm sure mine was.

"Computer," I said. "What's going on?"

"I'm sorry, Ms. Meadows, but I cannot allow you to visit Caitlyn and Mellissa Lakewood."

"You have to let us out."

"I fully intend to let you out, of course, Miss Meadows. You misunderstand. I am under strict instructions not to let anyone in or out of room five forty-eight. Not even you, Mr. Bennet. I feel I should warn you, if you attempt to force entry, everyone in the room will be purged."

"Purged?" we both repeated.

"Are they okay?" I asked.

"Currently," the computer answered, "as long as no one attempts to break into their room."

Mason and I stared hard at each other, both trying to process this information. "Who gave that command?" I asked. The girls may be unharmed, but threatening what sounded like violence was no small thing.

"There is no need to be nosy, Miss Meadows. I've just saved your lives. You should be grateful. I could have not bothered to warn you."

Lovely, the computer was getting pissy with me.

I opened my mouth to retort, but Mason tucked my head to his chest and spoke instead. "Thank you, Computer. Please take us to the fifth floor."

"You have no reason to be on the fifth floor, Mr. Bennet."

"I do," I said, pulling away from Mason and checking the time on my wristband. "It's five, and I'm supposed to meet Travis for dinner." I recalled him getting on the elevator with me at the fifth floor the night of the gala.

"Very well." The elevator lurched into motion again.

"You have a date with Travis Gould?" Mason asked.

"I think we have more important things to worry about here," I said, not in the mood for a testosterone fight. Then when the doors opened, "You know him, don't you?"

We rushed out onto solid ground, and Mason stopped me. "We've crossed paths."

I folded my arms and waited for it, sure he was about to warn me about Travis, just like Travis did him.

"It was my fault really," he said. "I went through a rebellion phase—you know, try anything that will piss off the parents. Unfortunately, that included Travis's sister."

It hurt that I was right about Mason being just another guy who would use women out of selfishness. I'd been tempted to try to pick up where we left off the other night. Now I was a tangle of bruised memories, emotional need, and physical longing, and with everything else happening, I didn't have either the time or the presence of mind to process it.

"He has a sister?" I asked, sucking in my bottom lip.

"She's in college now, last I heard. Far away from here."

I wanted, no I needed to ask what happened, but I saw room number five forty-eight, and let it drop. "There it is," I said. "What do we do?"

"*We* don't do anything. It's too dangerous. You have a dinner date." Mason widened his stance between me and the door.

"Oh no. I am not leaving you alone to try something stupid." I planted my own feet in the ground.

He smiled that heart-stopping smile, where his eyes penetrated my body. "I didn't know you cared."

A shiver of desire traveled from my navel to between my legs.

"She doesn't."

We both turned to find Travis leaning casually against the door of his room. "In fact, I believe the lady told you to beat it."

Mason put his hands up in surrender. "Just what I was doing."

"Both of you shut up!" I yelled, unable to handle further frustration. "You can't try to get in there. Please, Mason. The computer as good as warned us it's booby trapped." I grabbed his hand. "It's not just you in danger. It's those girls."

He deflated before my eyes. "You're right. I'll go talk to my mother, appeal to her human side. I'm sure she still has one in there somewhere."

I nodded, my throat suddenly thick. Mason squeezed my hand, glared at Travis, and left.

"I'm sorry, Travis." I relaxed my shoulders, bone tired. "I just don't know if I can manage dinner right now."

"Nuh uh. I'm afraid I can't let you out of it. You see, if I keep missing my chance to actually talk to you, and if you keep showing up with Prince Charming, well I might just tear my super sexy hair out, and that would be a tragedy for women all over the planet. You can't have that on your conscience." He swung an arm around me and leaned in to whisper. "I know a place where no animatronics can get to." Another tingle spread through my body from his warm breath on my ear, and I hoped he couldn't feel it. The last thing I wanted was for anyone to know the extreme level of my lack of control.

A huge part of me was desperate to dig deep into this mystery, but my brain was suffering from lack of food. I did my best thinking on a full stomach. Besides, Mason was the problem for the moment, and I really didn't want to be around him. "I am starving," I said. "And I could use a break. Work's been a bitch today." That was the understatement of the century.

"Then put everything else out of your mind and prepare to be dazzled." His bouncing eyebrows melted any reservations that remained as I broke into laughter. I did need a break, so I nodded. But the moment he pulled me toward the elevator, I dug in my heels.

"I'll go, but we're taking the stairs."

I followed along as Travis led me outside of the hotel and through the grounds, glancing around before heading down an unlit path. When we arrived at a two-story building, I stopped to read the wooden sign announcing it as the Fisherman's Hotel. Travis waited for me at a first-floor window along the side, behind the sign. He pushed open the window and climbed inside.

Moments later, he poked his head back over the side and offered me a hand up. I grimaced, unsure what I was getting into, but decided it couldn't be worse than finding a dead body. So pushing his hand aside, I hoisted myself up and into the room.

The design was similar to my quarters at Mermaid's Cove, but instead of gaudy mermaid crap, there were rustic ship's wheels, fishing lines, and nets. The dining set was a carved-out boat with cushions for seats, and on top of the knotted table were two plates of steaming hamburgers and french fries. A large glass of amber beer sat off to the side, condensation beading along the sides, making my mouth water.

"Wow. You've been busy," I said, trying not to run to the table.

"This is real food," Travis said. "You look hungry. Dig in."

I decided to forgo any more pleasantries and give in to my stomach. The burger would qualify as the best thing I'd ever tasted if it hadn't been for the experience of my picnic earlier. My eyes closed in ecstasy as I chewed. I tried to chase away the memory of Mason's fingers lingering on my lips as he fed me sushi.

When I opened my eyes again to take a drink, Travis was staring at me, coke-colored eyes smoldering. Heat dropped low in my belly again. This time I felt a little sick.

"Thanks for dinner. I really was hungry," I said. Then I sipped at the cold, slightly bitter liquid, relishing the fizz as it crawled along my tongue.

"No problem. Now it's your turn to do something for me." He leaned forward, elbows grounded on my side of the table.

"Excuse me?" I asked, setting the glass down so hard some spilled over the side.

"You owe me one," he said and grinned, enjoying some private joke.

I readied myself to make a run for the window, when he spoke again, "What's going on around here?"

My shoulders relaxed as he let out a laugh, showing he knew perfectly well what I thought he meant.

"You're an asshole," I said.

"What? You thought I had dishonorable intentions? I do have a reputation."

I popped a french fry in my mouth and thought it over. I was ordered not to tell anyone, but the worse things got, the more wrong that felt. These people were as trapped as I was. Didn't they deserve to know? Travis clearly picked up on the idea that something was wrong, and I was sure he was not the only one.

"There's a glitch in the AI," I said and waited for his reply while chewing.

"Yeah, I kind of got that when the computer sent my parents off into the ocean in a plastic tube. But it's more than that incident, isn't it?"

I slumped back against the wood railing. "How did you know?"

"You mean besides you and Prince Charming talking in the hallway? I was on my way back from running into you and saw something strange, even for the Bennets. Two of the robot staff were "escorting" Mr. Van Morris into the room next door." He made air quotes and raised his bushy eyebrows, passing the torch to me.

"Was he okay?" I asked in a small voice. The hamburger sat in a lump at the pit of my stomach.

"They were insistent, and he was, let's just say, not thrilled with the treatment."

"This is out of control. I need to tell Mrs. Bennet to shut down the computer ASAP." I stood, ready to find her and put an end to this. "Alyssa was right. We need to evacuate."

"Evacuate?" Travis stood too, stepping between me and the door. "You aren't leaving until you tell me everything. I have a right to know."

I groaned and flopped down on my back on the couch, staring

up at the mounted swordfish overhead. "You said this place was animatronics free," I said. "How?"

"It isn't technically open yet, so it's offline. Saves them money. I guess they figured who in their right mind would want to break into a hotel when they already have everything they want?" He sat next to me, forcing my feet off the cushion. "They didn't consider troublemakers like me."

I let a laugh escape and propped my feet on his lap. Secret-keeping wasn't my thing, especially when lives were in danger. "Fine. You want to know?" I recounted everything from my invitation to the internship up until running into him in the hallway, leaving out only the paint, certain things about Mason, and my missing time. I finished with, "So what should I do?"

Travis sat quietly for a while, focused on something in the distance, a hard look on his face. His arm was slung over the back of the couch.

"That's fucked up," he said finally.

I burst out laughing. "You're brilliant. Why didn't I think of that?"

He grinned, then shoved my feet off his lap, and I sat up straight.

"So, PC was going to try and break the twins out?" Travis asked, suddenly dark again.

"PC now?"

"Prince Charming."

"He promised he wouldn't," I said, panic setting in. "He wouldn't, would he? I mean he could put those girls in danger too. And Carl van Morris."

"He's never been one to keep his word," Travis said, standing and stretching so his thin T-shirt rode up, revealing several inches of toned stomach.

"What happened between Mason and your sister?" I asked.

He dropped his arms and spun around. "What did he tell you?"

"He said he was an ass. That he'd been rebelling against his family."

"Right," Travis said. "He's the victim."

"When you say 'victim' it implies there was a crime," I said. A dull headache started behind my eyes, and I reached back to yank my ponytail loose.

"He got Lupe pregnant," Travis said, staring me down.

"Pregnant?" I sputtered. Then, "Pregnant?" because apparently that was now the only word in my vocabulary. Heat burned my cheeks as understanding dawned about what Travis thought when he saw Mason flirting with me.

I sank back into the sofa, speechless and hoping he couldn't read my train of thought. He crouched down in front of me and put a hand on my knee.

"Look, I'm sorry, okay? But it's the truth. My parents don't want to face it, but the Bennets don't give a fuck about anyone but themselves."

"I take it he dropped out of the picture?" I asked, my stomach and head hurting.

"PC? She went over to tell him in person and never saw him again after that. The only person she could get close enough to speak to was Candice, who paid for not just the abortion, but got her a full ride at the college of her choice as well. Anything to keep her mouth shut."

"I'm sorry," I said.

"Not your fault. She was stupid to let it happen. I lost respect for her after that. Especially after she accepted the offer. Our mother was devastated that she went through with it. Our father just pretends like it didn't happen."

"No wonder you were so angry about coming down here," I said. "But why do you keep insisting you're on the Bennet watch list and you're such a troublemaker?" My eyes dropped to his hand on my knee, and he snatched it back.

Travis stood and pulled a hand through his dark waves. "I threatened to go to the press."

"Oh." My heart hammered. "Did you? Will you?" Why was I so concerned about Mason when he abandoned his own child?

He dropped his chin to his chest. "No. My mother convinced me that would only shame Lupe, and she'd lose her spot at Harvard."

I stood and took his hands, entwining my fingers with his. "I get it now," I said, "where you're coming from. And I don't blame you for hating him."

He raised his head, and his gorgeous eyes lit a fire in my belly. "But do you trust him?" he asked.

I thought about that. "I don't know him well enough. I don't know either of you, really. I only know what my instincts tell me."

He grinned like a devil, his teeth brilliant white against his plump lips and dark skin. "And what do your instincts say about me?"

"That you're dangerous too," I said, my voice raspy as he leaned forward.

He moved so slow that by the time we connected, every fiber of my being was on fire with anticipation. Still, his lips barely grazed mine, and I thought I might explode from longing. "Kiss me," I said against his mouth, and I felt him smile in response. I wrapped my arms around his neck, and he lifted me around the waist, finally giving in. But instead of relief I found myself remembering Mason's kiss.

As much as I was enjoying myself, a part of me wasn't into it. "I need to go see Mrs. Bennet," I said as he nibbled his way to my throat.

He buried his face against my neck and groaned before setting me back on my own two feet. I backed up a little, trying to control my breathing.

"I'll go with you," he said.

"You're not supposed to know."

He pursed his lips. "You are very stubborn."

Before I could respond, my wrist beeped. "Hello?" I asked, raising the wristcom to my mouth.

"You're there. We finally got through." Jackson's voice registered relief.

"What's up?" I asked, making eye contact with Travis.

"You didn't hear the announcement? Where the hell are you? We're supposed to report to our quarters for the night. We're being evacuated in the morning."

15

TRAVIS TOOK HIS LEAVE AT THE FIFTH-FLOOR LANDING, WHERE I assured him I would be all right. One more night and we'd be free of this nightmare. All of us except poor Mrs. Lakewood. I cringed, picturing her asking for help with the mud and being held beneath the surface by the robot's unyielding arms.

"Lights," I said to the pitch-black room. The nanosuns had faded into nothingness, and the crushing dark of the sea had taken over the surroundings.

I blinked against the sudden brightness and nearly screamed when I saw Mason lying on my couch. He threw an arm up to block the light and blinked. He must've been asleep.

"What are you doing here?" I asked, throwing his feet to the side so he'd sit up.

"I couldn't find you," he said. "And I didn't trust the wristcom. Thank God you're okay." He pushed off the sofa and reached me in three long strides. But I backed up against the door.

His face and arms fell, but he stayed his ground. "We have to do something."

"Do something?" I asked. "We're evacuating in the morning. My brother said there was an announcement."

"I was with Mother and Nicole when it happened. I wanted to watch her make the call myself because Nicole was practically purple." Panic edged around the corners of his voice, and my own pulse sped up.

"Mason, get to the point."

He drew a quick breath and blurted out, "Communication is down. We can't get through to the surface, and there's no way out for three weeks when the pod gets here."

My knees gave out. Mason caught me in his arms. Anger exploded inside me. Anger at myself for being weak, anger at being stuck in this hellhole for weeks, and anger at Mason for feeling so damn good.

"Put me down," I said. "I just need to...to sit."

Mason set me on the couch where I folded my hands in my lap.

He sat next to me, perched on the edge. His knee bumped mine. When I thought about Travis's sister, my chest felt like a crumpled tin can, and I found it hard to look at him. "How's your mother going to tell everyone?" I asked.

He swung his head to the side, causing a loud popping sound. Then he placed a hand to his neck, where he rubbed it as he spoke. "She's conferring with Candice and Graham right now. Nicole and I have been cut out of the discussion, which means she's really flustered. Not good. My mother doesn't fluster easily."

I stood a bit too fast and hoped it wasn't obvious when the floor tilted to the side.

"Where are you going?" Mason asked, invading my personal space with his warmth and delicious smell. I longed to throw myself in his arms and bury my face in his chest, which was so wrong that I bit the inside of my cheek.

"I'm going to go help Alyssa. We have to fix this. Now."

"You need sleep. You've had more than one shock today, Sam." He spoke low and reached for me.

I glanced at his fingers tightening around my arm. "This is

getting way out of hand. We have to get out of here." My head squeezed with pain, like someone stuck it in a vice. "Ow."

"What happened?" Mason guided me back to the couch.

It hurt so bad, I couldn't muster the strength to protest. "My head."

A cool hand pressed to my forehead, and I sighed.

"Do you have migraines?" he asked.

"Only down here," I replied. "Apparently, I'm one of the lucky few that are still sensitive to the pressure, despite the compression pumps."

I accepted a hydropod and took a few sips.

"Don't worry," I said, seeing his face. "I'll be fine. It just hit me all of a sudden. I never know when the symptoms will come on. But right now, I need to help Alyssa." I pushed by him and smacked into the door. "Open." Nothing. "Computer, open the damn door!"

The room's com system made that slight buzzing sound it did before the computer was about to speak. "Please relax, Miss Meadows. I wouldn't want you to strain yourself."

"Open. The. Door." My jaw clenched tighter with each word.

"I am afraid I cannot comply. My new orders are to enforce a curfew of 7:00 p.m. It is for your own protection."

Little Dragon warred within me, wanting out. I beat my fists into the door as Mason stepped up behind me.

He cocked his head as if regarding the AI. "Computer, are these commands for everyone? Or just Sam?"

"All humans, with two exceptions."

"Which are?" I asked, rubbing my knuckles.

"Mrs. Bennet and Dr. Forbes."

"Computer," Mason said. "Bennet override C12BQ11395."

I raised my eyebrows, but Mason stared hard at the door. "Now open this door."

"I am sorry, Mr. Bennet, your override is no longer active. I cannot comply. Please make yourselves comfortable. If you are hungry, I can ask a staff member to—"

"We don't want food!" I screamed. "We want out!"

"Perhaps you are in need of a sedative, Miss Meadows," the computer said.

"Are you threaten—"

Mason cut me off with a hand over my mouth and one around my waist. I squealed and kicked as he dragged me back toward the couch. I flailed so hard I knocked him over backwards with me sprawled across his lap. My hand hit the hydropod still on the side table and it's soft shell burst, spilling water over both of us.

"Calm down," he hissed. "It can release a toxin through the air ducts."

I froze, breathing hard, and he let go of me. "How do you know?" I asked, examining my wet clothing. Mason got the worst of it; his shirt was drenched down the front.

"I spoke to my mother. That's the booby trap in the Lakewood's room. If anyone opens the door, it's released into their room. It works in under three minutes. It's got to be the same thing the AI is threatening you with now. We have to be smart about this, Sam." Mason peeled off his soaked shirt as he spoke.

Holy shit, he was hot. His six-pack had so much definition, I wanted to trace each groove with my tongue. No wonder Travis's sister ended up pregnant. If we were in a different situation, I would be locked up for a month fucking him.

"Damn it!" I hissed, shaking myself out of it. "I have to talk to Dad and Jackson. I have to tell them what's happening. And Travis."

Mason winced and said, "Sam, I'm not sure it's going to matter. They must know something is wrong by now. They're locked in their rooms as well."

"I'll be in my bedroom. You can have the couch." I stormed toward the relative safety of the other room before I could lose complete control and jump him.

"Wait! Sam. What did I do?"

I made the mistake of turning around. His big ocean eyes pled with me.

"I know you don't want to see me...that way," he said. "But I thought we were at least becoming friends."

I needed to be honest. "I know about what happened with Lupe, Mason. Travis told me." I pulled my hair back like I was going to slip it into a ponytail, then let it slide free again.

Mason sat back on the couch like I'd physically knocked him over. "I never meant to hurt her. I'd do anything to take it back."

"Oh, very touching," I said, trying hard not to actually be touched or to look at his sculpted chest. "I'm sure that was comforting when you ditched her and had Mommy bribe her into having an abortion."

Mason blanched. It appeared all the breath was stolen from his body. He didn't even blink.

"Mason?" I asked after a minute, moving forward to wave my hand in front of his face.

"She was pregnant?" He whispered it, like the words were fragile.

"Please. She told you and you disappeared. Don't pull that bull-shit with me, Mason Bennet." I poked him in the shoulder, and he looked up at me like he wasn't quite sure who I was. He was starting to worry me.

"She *told* me it was over. That she never wanted to see me again because Nicole told her I was cheating. I wasn't." Each word was underlined in anger as his face constricted. "She wouldn't believe me. And I thought, why should she? Nicole does such a good job lying. I almost believe her myself with all the details she gave."

I bit down on my bottom lip. Shit. I felt like an idiot. It was the same thing Nicole had done to me to drive a wedge between us before we could even get started. "She must have realized she was pregnant and then thought you'd cheated..." I should probably have kept my mouth shut, but the realization hit me hard, and I sank into the couch beside him. His reaction was real. If he was that good of an actor, he'd have earned an Oscar by now.

He buried his face in his hands while his body shuddered. After a minute, he parted his fingers and looked up at me, his sapphire eyes glowing with tears. "If I'd known…" It was a plea. "I was respecting her wishes, not seeing her again."

I lifted a hand to comfort him, but let it drop back in my lap, useless. "Travis doesn't know the truth. He thinks you abandoned her," I said.

"Oh God," Mason moaned. "I thought it was because he thought I cheated on her. You said my mother bribed her into…into getting rid of the baby? My baby? That may have been my only chance I'll ever get at being a father."

I was so wholly unequipped for this conversation. But I'd gotten myself into it, and it wasn't like we were going anywhere. "Your mother offered to send her to the college of her choice. She's at Harvard."

He nodded, swallowing hard. "The opposite side of the country from Stanford. No wonder my mother was okay with me going so far away. I can't believe she wanted her own grandchild gone."

"Mason, I'm sorry. I didn't think— I had no idea you didn't know." I examined my fingers as I wrung them together.

"You thought I'd abandoned my own child and Lupe. You believed I was that horrible? I mean, I know you haven't known me long, but, but how could you think that, Sam?"

"Don't you try to turn this around on me. Why should I have given you the benefit of the doubt? Sure, you seem too good to be true, but appearances can be deceiving. And all the evidence pointed to— Well, to you being an asshole just like so many others of the male sex."

We sat in silence for a few minutes, Mason looking pained, me feeling uncomfortable. I pulled a throw pillow onto my lap and played with the golden tassel.

"Mason, I'm sorry you had to find out this way. That wasn't fair."

He glanced at me. "It isn't your fault."

I managed a feeble smile.

"You're right," he continued. "You should stay as far away from me and my family as possible. We're poison."

Heart squeezing again, I reached out, this time laying a hand on his. "You're not poison. She should still have told you. She should have given you a chance to explain."

"You weren't going to," Mason said, watching my hand on his like he didn't trust himself to move.

"I wasn't sleeping with you." I cleared my throat. But he wasn't wrong. I might be the biggest hypocrite ever. I'd judged all men, lumping him in with my father as a liar without a second thought. I was the one being sexist, and it stung like hell.

Mason faced me and cupped my cheek in his hand. "I never wanted to hurt her, or you. You should run away from me while you can. Me? I'm trapped. No matter how far I run, I'll always be a Bennet." He rubbed my skin with his thumb. My entire arm tingled with his touch as my heart climbed into my throat.

"I'm kind of trapped at the moment too," I said, attempting some comic relief.

He grinned, and his other hand slid up to my face. "That's a problem."

"How so?" I breathed.

"Because I'm a weak man, and I may not be able to stop from kissing you. Whatever I had with Lupe, it wasn't real. I knew it then, because all I could think of was you, studying the charts in your father's office. I know it now because I can't stop from touching you."

My pulse raced out of control as he leaned in, moving slow in case I chose to bolt. My head screamed at me to shove him away. I had done the same thing with Travis an hour earlier, though all I could think about then had been Mason, just as he said he thought of me when he was with Lupe. Mason's family *was* trouble. He was trouble. But as much as I wanted to deny it, it was more than just my insane libido with him. I couldn't blame these feelings on DSI.

Our lips connected and mine parted. A soft moan escaped my throat as his tongue tentatively explored my mouth, much slower than our last connection. Unable to stand my growing need, I thrust my own tongue forward, far more forcefully, and pressed my cold wet chest against his.

He pulled me to the couch, leaning over me, our mouths exploring each other as I removed my dress and tossed it behind the sofa. He growled appreciatively and climbed over me, laying me back down as our tongues continued their dance. His taut skin rubbed against mine, igniting a trail of fire along my flesh. I hooked my leg around his bottom and pulled him closer, throwing my head back as he nipped his way down my neck. His fingers prodded at the thin material of my bra.

"You are gorgeous," he said, tossing my bra to join my discarded dress. He pulled back just enough to look at my nipples, already hard in anticipation of his touch.

His thumbs circled them slowly before he leaned forward to suck one into his mouth. His tongue looped around it in a swirl that made my hips thrust against him. The rough material of his jeans couldn't hide his erection, and I reached down to release him.

"I don't have protection," he said through a heavy breath.

"I'm on the pill," I responded.

In moments his remaining clothes were on the floor and he stood over me, well-endowed and at attention.

"Stand up," he said with that throaty voice I loved. I grinned and did it slowly, turned on by the appreciation in his eyes.

When I reached for my underwear, he stopped me with his hands over mine and shook his head. I pulled my fingers away and he tugged gently at the lacy fabric, sliding his palms down over my ass and giving it a good squeeze. His fingers searched between my legs, prodding at the swollen flesh, and he moaned when he found me wet and ready for him.

With an impatient tug he sent my panties to the floor and picked me up by the waist as I threw my legs around his hips. His erection slid against me, and I trembled with need, but he set me on the couch once again and knelt on the ground before me, holding my knees apart.

"I want you," I said, in case that wasn't clear.

"I want you too," he said. "More than you can imagine. But I'm not ready yet."

"You look ready to me," I growled.

He smiled and slid his hands up my thighs.

"Relax and keep these legs open," he said before he leaned his head down between my thighs.

His mouth did things I didn't know a mouth could do, and I wriggled on the sofa in response, lifting my bottom off the cushion as I tried to press harder into him. Moans filled my throat as his finger probed at my entrance, sliding inside while his tongue flicked my sensitive flesh, sending me into pure ecstasy. Continuing to explore with his tongue and his mouth, he licked and sucked while thrusting his fingers inside until spasms of bliss had me melting into the cushions. He didn't let up until he drew every last shudder from me.

"Now I'm ready," he said, climbing over me and claiming my mouth once again.

I lay back and opened my legs to him. He teased my entrance with his tip as I gripped his shoulders, digging into his skin in an attempt to force him inside me.

My body, so recently sated, was once again filled with frenzied hunger. "Sit up," I commanded, and he listened, breathing hard, face red with barely controlled passion.

I climbed on top of him, straddling him, and eased myself over him, slowly, taking him all the way inside. He groaned and thrust upward, head thrown back on the cushions as I rode him, increasing my pace until I was bouncing on top of him. With each thrust an explosion of pleasure coursed through me. His hand gripping my hips slipped between our bodies, searching, and I nearly lost control. In a circular motion he worked his thumb, never stopping his upward thrusts. A sound came deep from his chest as I detonated in a climax of pure rapture. He angled upward, nearly sliding off the couch as he too found release.

Together we collapsed onto the sofa in a tangle of limbs, a layer of sweat all that remained between us.

"That was incredible," I said.

"Definitely," he agreed. "I don't know how we are getting out of here, and I know this sounds bad, but I don't care as long as we can do that while we're trapped."

I didn't say it out loud, but I had to agree.

He leaned in to kiss me again, and my wristcom beeped.

"Hello?" I asked as Mason ran his palms over my thighs.

"Are you in your room?" Dad asked.

I swung my legs over to sit up. "Yes, and the computer won't let me out," I said as Mason sighed and began playing with my hair.

"Alyssa told me everything. The damn Bennets have us all locked in our rooms."

"It's Mrs. Bennet, Dad. I'm sure of it." I tried not to gasp as Mason's hand found my breast, sending renewed tremors down my body. "She's revoked her kids' override abilities."

"Listen, I've got Jackson, and I'm on my way to get you out of there. Then we're going to let everyone else out who might be able to help with this, one room at a time."

Mason froze. He and I exchanged a glance, and I scrambled for his shirt as he tugged on his jeans. "Oh, uh, okay. How long until—"

The door slid open, revealing my father and brother.

16

SEVERAL EXPRESSIONS WASHED OVER THEIR FACES. FOR DAD IT WAS shock followed by shame, fury, and then disappointment. For Jackson it was surprise, incredulity, and finally disgust.

I licked my lips, kicked my panties below the couch with as much dignity as I could muster and shook out my hair. "Maybe a little notice next time."

"Dr. Meadows," Mason said. "Nice to see you again."

I'd never seen my father so primed to explode. "Mr. Bennet, you will leave right now if you plan on surviving the next five minutes."

"Dad! You're one to talk. Stay right where you are, Mason."

"We have work to do," Dad said through gritted teeth.

"Mason can help."

Dad took a long, slow breath, staring up at the ceiling. "He can help best by putting some clothes on and talking some sense into his mother."

"He's right." Mason's touch grounded me. "My time is best spent trying to get my clearance back and talking down the Queen B." He leaned down and kissed me softly on the cheek, tucking my hair behind my ear.

With a grunt of exasperation, I stormed into the bedroom,

dressed as fast as humanly possible before anyone could kill anyone, and marched back out, tossing Mason his shirt.

He spared one fleeting smile before pushing between my father and brother on his way out the door.

I cleared my throat. "So, opening doors..."

"Jackson used Alyssa's wristband to reprogram mine so the computer thinks I'm her. You and Jackson head down to Engineering. See what you can do to assist Alyssa, and I'll work on releasing others." Dad held up his arm with the wristband. "We've only got one programmed as a clone, so there's no sense in all of us doing this."

I nodded, but he caught my arm on my way out. "We should talk about this later." Far from stern, he sounded sad.

"I'm my own person, and I make my own decisions. It's time you realize that."

I relaxed the moment I made it into the hall. Jackson fell into step beside me as I headed toward the stairs. Dad turned the other direction, headed for the room next door.

"I'm an ass," Jackson said the moment the door clicked shut behind us.

"This is news to you?"

"Seriously. I pushed him right into your...hands. I didn't like the way he was looking at Tasha last night, so when he asked about you, I told him what to do."

"You really think he ended up in my room because you told him I like sushi?" I laughed, and it echoed down the empty stairwell.

"I guess I thought you'd be stronger than that. I mean, you were always so pissed off at Dad."

I stopped at the last landing, spinning on my brother. "Do not EVER compare me to Dad. He cheated on Mom. What I did or didn't do with Mason wasn't hurting anyone."

It hit me just before I shoved him in the chest. I did hurt someone. It wasn't really cheating— I mean, Travis and I didn't have a relationship or anything. No one ever declared love. But that didn't stop me from feeling sick to my stomach.

Jackson tilted his head, and his coffee-colored bangs fell in his face. "You okay? You just stopped mid-tirade. That's not like you."

"I screwed up," I admitted and felt my lower lip quiver.

"Shit, Sam, if you needed a condom—"

I smacked him hard on the arm. "You are such a prick." Then I leaned back on the railing. "I don't want to hurt either of them, Jackson. How do you do it?"

"How do I do what?"

"How do you go from one girl to another so smoothly?"

Jackson sighed and rolled his eyes toward the ceiling. "Jesus, Sam, you make it sound like I'm some kind of man-slut. I'm just looking for the right girl."

I narrowed my eyes.

"And having a little fun while I search." He shrugged and opened his arms for me. "You're taking it all too seriously. I guarantee you neither guy is looking for long term."

I glared some more.

"My point is that you shouldn't beat yourself up. Not that I want my sister with anyone, but, you know, you are my sister." He shifted and pulled his hair back from his face. "You're going to make me say it, aren't you? Fine. I love you, okay? I feel so unclean."

"Shut up, asshole."

"That's my Sam!"

I shook my head and flung my arms around his waist.

He rested his chin on my head. "Now let's get down to Engineering."

Alyssa grunted when we walked through the door. She remained bent over the keyboard, focused on the monitor. The dim lights from the screens covering the walls bathed her in a flickering blue glow.

"Who killed the lights?" I asked, pulling up a chair so I could read over her shoulder.

"Automatic dimming at night time. I didn't want to ask for anything more than I had to. No sense in drawing attention to what we're doing to the AI."

"So you really think the computer is psycho?" Jackson asked. He moved over to the wall opposite to examine each screen.

"Yup," I said, then turned to Alyssa. "Why isn't it offline yet?"

"I tried just a few moments ago, but it claims I no longer have clearance. We are lucky you got out of your rooms when you did." Her face appeared drawn in the light of the screens, and I noticed the slight tremble in her hands as they flew across the keys.

"It locked you out?" I asked.

"It couldn't do that," Alyssa said, finally stopping to face me. "That's the thing. There are fail-safes. I put them there myself. Someone did this. Someone with ability or clearance as high or higher than my own."

"Mrs. Bennet?" I asked.

"No," Alyssa said. "She wants it off, at least until we fix it."

Jackson laid a hand on my shoulder. "So what you're saying is that someone did all this."

Alyssa nodded, looking like she wanted to cry.

"Well at least you know Mrs. Lakewood's death wasn't your fault," I said. But that meant someone on Paradise Atlantis was more than a saboteur. No doubt remained.

Someone here was a killer. And a small, terrified voice in the back of my head wondered *what if it's me?*

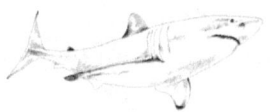

17

I NEEDED TIME AND SPACE TO THINK WITHOUT DISTRACTIONS. I ALSO needed sleep, and as much as it felt like admitting some form of defeat, I headed back to my room. Jackson helped by giving me a boost so I could rewire the door to remain partially open.

"You sure that's safe?" he asked.

"Safer than being trapped," I said and stood on tiptoe to plant a kiss on his cheek. "Go get some sleep yourself."

Shaking his head, he moved to step over the cube stool we'd used to block the door open. "Nope. Not leaving you. I can sleep on the couch."

"Whoa." Hand on his chest, I stopped him in mid-stride with his foot hovering over the cube. "No way. I won't get any rest. You snore like an elephant."

"And how would you know what an elephant snores like?"

"Because I grew up with you. Now go. Your room is literally next door. It would take you all of two seconds to get here if you so much as hear me sneeze on my wristcom."

"At least let me check for intruders," he said, but I blocked him again. What if there was something incriminating in my room?

"I've got this. I promise. I'll bring a knife to bed with me if it makes you feel better."

Finally, he gave me a slow nod, turned, and took off, stopping for one last look in my direction. I shooed him away with a smile and slipped inside my quarters. He was right, there was a killer on the loose who hopefully wasn't me, but it wasn't like I was a target. I was just the "intern," as Nicole said earlier.

I was the intern in charge of helping the head of AI find the killer and shut down the computer. *Shit.*

I searched my rooms for both lurking murderers and any clues that may have helped explain what happened during my blackouts, but came up empty. I wasn't sure what I expected to find, and I was exhausted.

"Lights," I said, and the place went dark. I slid into bed. Despite my nerves and wandering mind, I couldn't help but drift off. I felt like I hadn't slept in days.

My eyes fluttered open, and I couldn't understand why at first. Then I heard it, a shuffling sound in the other room. My mouth dried up and my body began to quake. Someone was in my hotel room. I glanced at my wristband. 3:24 a.m. glowed in the dark. I heard the shuffling again, this time closer.

I slipped out of the bed as quietly as possible and crept over beside the door just as it opened. My heart leaped into my throat as the large outline of a man skulked inside.

With a war cry I jumped onto his back, throwing my arms around his neck. He stumbled backward and knocked me into the wall. Tiny bursts of light sparked in my vision, and I fell, stunned as the breath was knocked from me. Then he was on top of me, on the ground, his heavy frame flattening me and his hand over my mouth as I tried to scream.

I writhed beneath him, desperate to find an escape until I heard Travis's voice call for lights. Then I was blinking up into his eyes, his hand still over my mouth.

He grinned, and I writhed even more, anger flaring.

"If I let go will you promise not to go all ninja on me again?" he asked.

I nodded, picturing all the pain I wanted to inflict on his self-satisfied ass.

He let go but planted his lips over mine. I bit his tongue and he rolled off me with a yelp.

"Asshole," I said, jumping to my feet. "What the fuck are you doing sneaking into my room in the middle of the night? What is wrong with you?"

"I saw your door open, and I was worried about you. I thought someone broke in." He stood, patting his mouth with the back of his hand and studying the drop of bright red that came off.

"Someone did break in. You," I reminded him. To my wristcom I said, "Don't worry, Jackson. It's only Travis checking in on me. All is good." The last thing I wanted was to make this a party.

"I would've knocked, but I thought—"

"That you'd play Prince Charming for once, huh? Well all you did was scare the crap out of me."

He looked at me then, with those intense dark eyes, and I saw it. He was scared.

"Okay, maybe I overreacted. But you didn't exactly make yourself known." I relaxed my stance and sat on the bed.

"Sorry. If someone was attacking you, I definitely should have let him know I was coming with a battle cry or something." His smirk reappeared.

I hurled a pillow at him. He caught it against his chest and bounced down next to me on the bed.

"I'm glad you're okay," he said.

"Thanks. But how did you get out of your quarters anyway? It's past curfew." I couldn't keep the bitterness out of my voice.

"I never went back to my quarters. I did a little espionage work instead to see if I could get any more info on what's going on around here."

"And?" I asked, curious now that my heart was settling a bit.

"It isn't good." His fist tightened at his side, squeezing the pillow so hard I was surprised it didn't start raining feathers. "I saw them come to my mom's door and escort her out, so I followed."

"Who escorted her?" I didn't like the chill crawling up my spine.

"Those damn bots. Two of them."

I grabbed his arm. He was so tense, it was like holding a rock. "Where did they take her?"

"To Mrs. Bennet. Where else? She had some other people there too."

Clearly it was difficult for him to talk about, and I didn't like having to pry the information out of him. But I had to know. "What did they say?"

"That as the head of vital systems she could be a target of the killers. They wanted to put her under twenty-four-hour guard until this is over. But those damn things are the ones I don't trust." Travis wiped hard at his nose with his opposite arm.

"I'm so sorry." I slumped in my seat.

"It isn't your fault. You didn't do any of this." His hand found my chin, and I averted my eyes.

Could it be my fault, though? No, I couldn't accept that. Still, it was too hard to face him because there was part of me inside that wondered where my missing time went. I'd buried it deep, considering all that had happened, but maybe more because it scared the crap out of me. A sting built behind my eyes, and I dug my nails into my palm so I wouldn't cry.

"Hey, I'm the one who's sorry. I shouldn't have laid this on you. It's just...there's no one else here I even remotely trust."

I did meet his eyes then, and my heart twisted. "I have to tell you something."

"Go ahead. I can take it." He grinned, but it was clearly forced.

I contemplated what I was about to share. *Travis, I may have killed someone. Oh, and I slept with the guy you hate and shouldn't have kissed you earlier.*

I shifted my weight and decided to go with something less incriminating.

"There's a saboteur. Someone cut Alyssa's access and all the Bennets'." *And it was possible it was me.*

Travis sucked in a breath. "So someone intentionally put my parents in danger? They told the robot to kill?"

"Looks that way. Or at least removed the fail-safes to let it happen." I pulled my hair into a ponytail and grabbed a band from my nightstand.

"But that's good, right? I mean, it could only be a couple of people." Travis grasped my arms as I finished tugging my hair into place.

"I don't know, Travis. I mean, there are several brilliant programmers here. It could be any of them, or even one of the Bennets." I hated to say it, but it was true. They had the access to begin with.

Travis's face grew ugly with rage, and I stepped away, bumping into the bed. "This is their fault. I should shove them out into the ocean myself. Whoever it is hates them, and I can't blame him for it."

My heart pounded, and I raised my palms in an effort to temper his fury. "Whoa there, bud. You're making yourself look like an insane killer." I forced a laugh. "I guess that means it's probably not the Bennets then, if the saboteur hates them that much."

"It could be Nicole or PC himself." Travis pounded a fist into his palm, making me jump.

"No, it couldn't," I said a little too quickly. "They have a bet going, and the winner is supposed to get Paradise Atlantis. Why would they sabotage their own future?"

"If they thought they'd lose the bet, they'd be capable of anything." Travis softened, but I remained at a distance.

You have to tell him, Sam.

"It could've been me," I whispered, looking down at my twisting hands.

For once Travis remained silent. Tentatively, I looked up, but it didn't help because I couldn't read his face. "I have something called depth sensitivity illness. Sometimes it causes blackouts." The words rushed out, eager to fill the open space and get the weight off my chest.

"Don't be ridiculous," Travis said, his jaw grinding. But he still wouldn't look me in the eye. I feared I'd made a horrible mistake. "My money's still on Prince Charming."

"It isn't Mason," I snapped, and he finally did look at me. I bit my lip and tried to adjust my tone. "I, uh, know you probably don't want to hear this, but I had a talk with Mason and, well, he isn't as bad as you think."

Travis scoffed.

"He didn't know about the pregnancy."

"And you believed that crap?" Every muscle on Travis's face twisted until he was almost unrecognizable. "I thought you were smart."

"You don't understand. He was shocked. He fell apart right in front of me. Nicole convinced Lupe he cheated and he didn't. He—"

"Unbelievable." Travis turned his back on me and strode toward the door, pausing for one last dig. "The one person I thought understood, and they got to you too."

"Where are you going?" I jogged after him. "Don't leave like this, Travis. Please! We need to figure this out."

But I was talking to an empty room.

The next days became a blur of headaches and burrowing through code that started to mesh together and looked like random strings of nonsense. On the floors above Engineering, people had become quiet and suspicious, most of them unaware of the real danger they were in.

The moments I found to steal with Mason were the only time I felt like myself. I doubted my sanity would still have been intact if I hadn't had his touch to bring me back to life. But even those times were few and far between because I was determined to fix the error in the AI before something else happened.

We'd been lucky so far in that nothing more had happened. I drew a deep, steadying breath as I boarded the elevator to head upstairs. I couldn't help but notice the smattering of robot staff in the lower levels, sitting quietly like they were asleep, red lights glowing on their chests. I shuddered as the doors closed and leaned my forehead against the glass, letting the cool feel of it soothe the ache. Even after all these days, I still hated stepping in the thing, but we'd been able to isolate elevator controls from hackers. *We think.*

I wondered if anyone besides me had noticed the increased presence of the staff or felt like every tiny red dot on the ceiling was boring into their backs as they moved around the resort.

The doors whooshed open, and I slipped outside, again taking stock of the artificial staff parked around the grounds, observing silently.

Turning toward the main pathway, I noticed Travis leaning against the wall across from the Mess Hall restaurant, staring with an intensity that belonged to only him. It was the first I'd seen him since he broke into my room. I started toward him, determined to talk this through, when Mason grabbed my arm, startling me.

"I'm sorry," he said, pulling back. "I thought you saw me coming. How's the project going?"

One glance told me Travis had disappeared. With a sigh, I turned and took in the dark circles rimming Mason's eyes. They were almost as deep as my own. I shook my head. "Every time we get close, the computer kicks us out. It's like the saboteur is on the same line, shifting and changing things every time I get close. It puts up firewalls we can't break through or redirects us somewhere else." I shrugged, pressing a hand to my head.

Mason guided me to the corner and pried my fingers from my temple. "Are you okay, Sam?"

I laughed bitterly. "Okay? I saw two sharks yesterday through the glass and what I can only assume to be some form of octopus, but do you know, I didn't even flinch? I was just...numb."

Mason pulled me against his chest and wrapped me into his arms, setting his chin on my head. I sighed, content to stand there forever, swathed in his tropical scent.

"Sam, I'm worried about you. You need more time to rest and recuperate."

He wasn't wrong, and it was sweet that he worried, but there was no way I could rest. If I could just get a breakthrough, we might be able to reestablish contact with the world above and summon a rescue party.

"You should be more worried about the psycho that's out to get us all. I have to get back downstairs." Reluctantly, I pulled away from his embrace. I couldn't even remember why I'd come here. Food probably. But right now, my stomach was curdled and in no shape to digest a french fry, let alone a whole meal.

Before I could get away, Mason snatched my hand. I stopped, but he tugged me toward the elevator. "I'm coming too."

I shrugged, too tired to argue. The last few days felt so choppy to me, I wasn't sure how much time I actually spent in any one place. I got the feeling I was missing more time, but in a weird way it didn't matter because nothing new of significance had happened. I kept to the same schedule so that at times I seemed to wake up in the middle of working on code.

"Why do you think the killer hasn't made another move?" I asked when we were alone and the elevator started to move.

"Survival. He might want to scare us, but if he takes down the whole place, he goes with it." Mason squeezed my hand. "Elevator hold."

The car jerked to a stop, and I gasped, nearly losing my balance.

But Mason was there and caught me neatly before gathering me to him.

"We haven't had much privacy lately, and there's something I want to do. Then you can go back to work."

Before I could say another word, his lips were on mine, salty, sweet, and oh so needy. I sighed, parting my own to allow his tongue access. He backed me into the glass of the elevator and aligned his body with mine. I felt his need pressing against me right through my dress. His one hand cradled the back of my head as his other crept the fabric up and slipped beneath to the edges of my panties. When his fingers pried away the barrier and he felt me warm, wet, and ready, he grunted with anticipation and began sucking on my neck.

"Glass elevator," I breathed, uncertain I could stop any more than he could.

"Between floors," he said, coming up for air, eyes glazed with desire. "I timed it."

I threw my arms around his neck and wrapped my legs around his waist in response. He unzipped his pants, positioned himself, and thrust into me in one motion, making me moan with pleasure as electric tremors sizzled through my body.

He growled my name as he slammed into me. I responded by clenching him to me with my legs, urging him on as my climax built. "More," I commanded.

He jostled me in his arms, adjusting his stance, and drove in again, this time making my vision explode into stars. My nails clawed into his shoulders through his shirt as he pumped his hips, bringing me to the edge.

"Oh, God, Mason," I called out as I exploded into quivering spasms. He moaned in response, releasing as well. We collapsed against each other, breathing like we'd swum a mile. If I wasn't between him and the doors, I wouldn't have trusted my legs to stand.

"That was an amazing quickie," he whispered over my ear. "I promise to take my time next time."

We put ourselves back together, and I was just tugging my ponytail into place when the doors opened at Engineering.

I strode forward, letting my fingers slip slowly from his hand.

When I got to Alyssa, I found her slumped over the keyboard, snoring lightly. It was hard not to feel for her. I did a U-turn and took a walk around the engineering deck. I strolled past the whirring heartbeat of the central machinery, avoiding the ominous blue glow of the dark waters beyond, as usual. Hardly anyone was downstairs anymore. Mrs. Bennet relieved all extraneous personnel after the murder.

"Less people who know means less people who can leak information," *Nicole had explained like she was lecturing kindergartners.*

I made it almost all the way around the loop when Candice's voice commanded my attention. "There you are!" I cringed, thinking it was the computer again for a few seconds. "Mrs. Bennet has called a meeting, and she wants every involved party present."

"I should keep working," I said.

"Like you're doing now?" Her sickly sweet smile gave no hint at frustration, but her fingers tapped out a rhythm against her leg, suggesting otherwise.

Before I could retort, Graham stepped out from Candice's other side. She wrinkled her nose slightly but kept her smile plastered on. I wondered if he'd made any inappropriate advances toward her. But I couldn't imagine Candice actually *with* anyone. She was more like a robot herself.

"Fine," I said. "When and where?"

"Now and Alyssa's office," Graham answered, offering an elbow.

I ignored it and headed back toward Alyssa, wondering if she'd been caught sleeping on the job.

Whatever happened, I missed it, because all three Bennets were already present, along with Dr. Doyle and my father. Jackson was considered non-essential, since he didn't technically know what happened and didn't work here, lucky bastard.

"Report." Mrs. Bennet's curt demand clashed with her appearance. Her perfect hair was filled with fly-aways, her skin shadowed and dull.

"There's nothing to report," Alyssa said. She sounded tired but at least looked wide awake. "We've been working on it for days, and the computer meets every attempt to break through with some new impossible wall." She chewed at the remaining stubs of her fingernails.

When my father put a hand on her shoulder, I turned away. It seemed hard to look at anything lately, my father, the sea, the robot staff.

"Failure is unacceptable." Mrs. Bennet smoothed her hair, which popped right back out into its disorderly state.

"Then you try it," I said, followed with a sigh. I was tired of her meaningless commentary. What was she doing about our situation? "You think we aren't just as scared as everyone else? Working on this makes us all targets. And we're humans not machines. We can't run indefinitely under stress."

"That's true," Graham said, stepping between myself and Mrs. Bennet. "Before you respond, think about it. Look at us—do you want the entire population present to break down?"

Heads lifted, taking in each other's haggard appearances and bowed postures.

"I wasn't going to argue," Mrs. Bennet said quietly. "I need people that speak their minds. If you're intimidated by me, then you aren't at your full potential."

Her platitudes did nothing for me. "Then we need another course of action. It can't all lay on us."

"I have an idea," Graham piped up again. "It's what Miss Meadows said before. We're only human, we can't be machines."

It was getting harder and harder not to roll my eyes. Mason's hand distracted me as he rested it on my shoulder. My body melted with the memory of what we'd done just a short time ago.

"Get to the point," Nicole said. Unlike the rest of us, she and Candice remained in perfect physical condition. Evidence of either spending too much time in front of mirrors or, in Candice's case, plastic surgery.

"The point is, whoever did this was human. That means that he or she can and will make mistakes and give him or herself away. We just need to look for those clues."

"So we should all turn detective?" Nicole did roll her eyes that time.

"It's easier than fighting a machine," I said, tired of her bullshit.

"Dr. Doyle," Mrs. Bennet said, redirecting everyone's attention. "I'd like you to go over every participant's medical files and look for anything that might lead to a psychotic break. Cross reference with Dr. Meadow's list of technologically capable candidates and see if you find anything."

"Glad to have something useful to do," the doctor agreed, pulling a hand back through his hair.

"Anyone have anything else to add?" Mrs. Bennet asked. When no one moved, she said, "Dismissed. Alert me immediately if you find or think of anything suspicious."

Mason hovered over me. "How about dinner tonight? So we can take our time," he asked, low, so only I could hear.

As much as I looked forward to spending more time with him, I had another person I needed to talk to first. "Sure," I said with a shiver, thinking about the elevator. "My room. Eight o'clock."

I barely heard his murmured acknowledgement. I was too busy following the doctor toward the elevator.

18

"Hold the elevator, please," I called as I rushed forward to join Dr. Doyle.

He glanced at me, clearly annoyed at the delay, but waited until I was inside to give the computer the floor number.

"Elevator, hold," I said, copying Mason's trick, though I definitely wasn't planning on any fun physical interactions. This time I was prepared as it jerked to a halt.

"What are you doing?" Dr. Doyle asked, eyes wide with panic.

"Nothing sinister. I just want to talk to you in private for a moment." I batted my eyelashes with innocence. "I have a question. It's a hypothetical situation, and I need to know if I'm right."

"Let's get this over with," he muttered. "What do you need to know?"

"DSI. Is it real?"

He harrumphed as though I'd truly wasted his time. "Of course it is."

I blew out a long slow breath before continuing. "Is it common? And the side effects, how bad can they get?"

"Hypothetically?" he asked, narrowing his eyes to let me know he didn't buy it for a second.

I nodded.

"We don't know, since we haven't had a large enough group at this depth yet. But based on preliminary studies and everyone's medical examination in preparation for the trip, we anticipated only two potential issues that we deemed a possible risk medically. In practice, however, Dr. Lawry has assured me she is on top of the situation."

My mouth suddenly went dry, and I reached out to place a hand against the glass to steady myself. "Dr. Candice Lawry?" I remembered her threatening me on the ride down. That would explain her attitude toward me and why she didn't want me near Mason.

"Are you experiencing symptoms?" he asked, stepping up to examine my face.

I sighed. No more pretending. "Yes," I croaked. "Headaches and emotional rollercoasters." He didn't need to know about my sex drive or the blackouts. I was sure at this point they were nothing. Travis would have shown more concern when I admitted everything about my illness to him.

"Elevator resume ride," he said, stepping away. "I can send you some aspirin for the headaches."

"Thanks. Doctor." I grabbed his arm before he exited the lift. "You should look into the other person and check them against my father's list."

He grunted his approval. "I will look into everyone, you included, Miss Meadows."

Mulling over our conversation, I wandered back toward Mermaid's Cove. I jumped when I felt a hand grasp my arm, but turned to find Alyssa, worse than I'd ever seen her. Her normally bright eyes were dull and bloodshot, and she had tear stains on her cheeks. The vision of her and my father on the dance floor, so in love, shot to mind. But this time, instead of hurt for myself, my heart ached for her. I couldn't hate her. I tried and I couldn't anymore. She made a bad choice, and so had most of us. But she truly loved my father, and she was good for him. She came with

Bennet Systems and the work that was so much a part of him. She was the balance he needed.

"Sam, I just want to thank you." She released her grip on my arm and lowered her gaze to the ground. "For defending me back there in Engineering."

I shrugged, but my voice came out gentle. "You're doing your best just like all of us. This isn't your fault, Alyssa."

Her gaze lifted, eyes shining with tears.

"Come here," I said and pulled her into a hug. For so long it had felt like doing this would be unfaithful to my mom. But if my mother's heart was big enough for everyone, so was mine.

"Does this mean you forgive me?" Alyssa whispered over my shoulder.

"Only if you forgive me for acting like a child."

Alyssa pulled back and squeezed my hands in hers, a smile brightening her face. "You are Tom's child, no matter how old you are. We always need love and appreciation, Sam, you and I included."

She let go and turned back toward the nearest building, a small restaurant.

"Where are you going?" I called after her. I'd assumed she'd be headed back to Mermaid's Cove as well.

"Back to work. I think I've had a second wind. Let's get this asshole."

I shook my head with a laugh and headed for my quarters. Jackson and I worked on the rewiring enough so I could at least manually close and open the door all the way, though locking it was still out of the question.

I'd barely stepped through the door when my father caught me and fell into step at my side.

"I'm too tired for this," I said, staring longingly at the couch. Making up with Alyssa had taken all my emotional energy, and in doing so, I'd realized it wasn't her I was angry at. The blame lay on one person alone, my father.

"Sit down. When was the last time you got enough sleep, Sam?" he asked, guiding me to the comfort of the cushions.

"I don't know," I admitted, leaning back with a groan.

"I want you to know that I will get us all out of here and back up to your mother."

Tears burned my eyes, but I fought not to release them. I couldn't trust myself to speak.

"I owe you an apology. I should have insisted we skip this vacation. I was selfish, and it was wrong."

Tears turned to fury as I stood, prying myself from the cradle of the sofa. "You finally realize you were selfish?"

He stayed still as I released my tirade on him.

"Which part was selfish, Dad? Was it when you cheated on Mom? When you proposed to Alyssa while Mom might be dying? Or was it when you worked at Bennet Systems night and day, buried in your work and avoiding your family?"

He stood his ground, swallowing hard. The color drained from his features. He didn't hold back the tears like I did. He allowed them to flow down his ashen face, weaving crooked paths. At first satisfaction flooded me, but it was quickly drowned by regret at the way I was handling things.

I flopped back onto the couch and pressed a hand to my forehead. "You're right. I'm exhausted. You should go get some rest as well."

"Of course. Don't worry about going back down to Engineering until you've gotten enough sleep."

I pressed my eyes shut and opened them again only to find Mason standing where my father had been.

"What time is it?" I asked, not feeling as though I'd had any sleep.

"Eight. Dinner, remember?" He slid the door shut behind him. Without another word he sat behind me on the couch and began to work on my shoulders and neck, untangling each knot he found with his expert fingers.

I leaned back and made a sound of appreciation.

"I've learned from the best," he said over my ear. "We've had a family masseuse and chiropractor for as long as I can remember." He chuckled. "Nicole was pissed when she found out they couldn't come with us. Not even her personal assistant, Becky."

I laughed, then blinked, and suddenly empty plates were on the coffee table.

"Were those there before?" I asked, pointing and scooting backward into the cushions of the couch.

"You mean just now? Like while we ate?" Mason furrowed his brow and set down a wine glass I didn't remember him holding. Hadn't he just been massaging me? He tucked a hair behind my ear. "I think you need to get some sleep."

Tears crept close to bursting through my carefully crafted barrier, and I sucked in my lower lip. My entire life was becoming a kaleidoscope of moments, the blackouts taking over more often than not, and it terrified me. Still, I couldn't bring myself to admit it. Saying it out loud to Mason felt like risking the end of the one beautiful thing I'd found beneath the sea. Besides, it hadn't helped when I'd told Travis the truth.

"I want to spend more time with you," I said in place of all the things swirling through my mind.

"We can do more tomorrow."

I started to protest, but he lifted me off the couch and carried me to the bed, where he sat me down, removed all of our clothing, and slid in beside me, pulling me into an embrace. I sighed contentedly, surrounded by the warmth of his body. Instead of wanting to sleep, my insatiable libido awakened. I didn't know how long I had with Mason once he found out the truth about me, and I wanted to take advantage of every moment possible.

I rolled so I faced him and pressed up against him, running a finger down the center line of his chest.

"Sam, you're supposed to be sleeping," he said, voice thick with desire.

"You promised. Besides, maybe I need a little extra help falling asleep," I said, reaching to stroke the length of him. I watched his eyes roll back as he thrust his hip in rhythm with my hand.

"Sam, I'm supposed to be taking care of you," he protested.

I slipped down and took him into my mouth, sucking as I pulled back.

"You asked for it," he said, tossing me onto my back across the bed and making me giggle.

He leaned down over me, wrestling my hands above my head. "No more mischief until I've held up my side of the bargain." Then he kissed me slowly, teasing me with his tongue and sucking in my bottom lip.

He entwined his fingers with mine and moved his head downward to pull my breast into his mouth, tugging at my nipple, then circling his tongue over it. I squirmed beneath him, and he moved to the other breast to follow suit.

"I want you," I said.

"Not yet," he answered, sliding down my body to pry open my second set of swollen lips. I moaned as he slid two fingers inside me as deep as he could and rubbed circles with his thumb. I became a squirming animal at his touch. His mouth replaced his hand and he spoke from between my legs, "Your taste drives me crazy."

I answered him with more moans as he licked and nipped, driving me to the brink of madness.

"Please," I begged, unsure if I could take any more.

He answered with a groan as he slid inside me, filling me. He readjusted and guided my legs up over his shoulders.

The bed creaked as he drove into me, using the headboard for leverage. I lost control as he pumped his hips against my flesh, our bodies one undulating organism until a rippling sea of euphoria crashed over and through me, and I cried out. He held my hips firmly as he pushed in, sated as well. We ended up on the bed, spooning once again as our bodies shook with rapid breathing and aftershocks of pleasure.

With a smile on my face, I finally fell into a deep, dreamless sleep.

I threw up a hand to shield myself against the brightness of the nanosuns as the world came into focus. The first thing I felt was the hard earth beneath me, grass tickling my bare skin. Chill bumps covered me. I glanced down to make sure I had clothes on, only to find I was in my black bikini, which had sat unused in my massive closet since we'd arrived. Flip flops hung off my feet.

Sitting up, I scooted back, surprised to find myself so close to the massive ocean at the edge of the resort and inches from a human-sized electric ray undulating on the opposite side of the clear, thin AC glass. I stifled a yelp and pushed myself onto my feet, realizing I was behind the bathrooms at the Olympic-sized pool. Close to hyperventilating, I stumbled around the corner of the building toward the glow of safer waters and the hum of the automatic saltwater system.

The time on my wristband said 8:00 a.m., but I didn't even know what day it was anymore. A whimper escaped me. I felt completely out of control. I glanced over at the far side of the pool, and for a moment I thought someone was swimming there. But as I moved around the edge toward them, intent on asking if they knew why I was here, the reality hit me and I screamed.

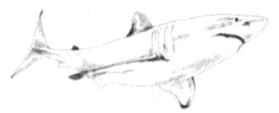

19

THE BODY WAS UNNATURALLY STILL, FACE-DOWN IN THE WATER, slowly bobbing with the ripples caused by the filtration system.

Screaming for help, I kicked off my flip flops and leaped for the water. Before I hit, cold, unyielding arms caught me around my midsection and tossed me back on the tile surrounding the pool. I landed hard, skinning my knee, and raised my head to find a member of the robot staff looming over me.

"You should not enter the water, Miss Meadows," it said, sounding far too reasonable. "You should be in room six thirty-four, Mermaid's Grove."

"We need to save—" I insisted, managing to make it to my feet again before it cut me off.

"He is already dead. Clearly this pool is not suitable for humans."

I glanced back toward the body in the water and swallowed hard. "We don't know what killed him," I said. I could see now that the body was definitely male, though no one I thought I recognized. I cringed with relief that it wasn't Mason. This man was thin with short-cropped dark hair, wearing jeans and a white shirt. There was something horribly familiar about him though...

"We do know what killed him. The water killed him." The robot inched forward, and I nearly fell over my own shoe, still abandoned on the deck.

"H...hang on," I said, putting up a hand. That's when I saw the wristcom again. "Thomas Meadows!" I yelled into my wristcom.

"Your wristcom is no longer active."

I leaned in closer and saw that aside from the time, there were no other options lit on the screen.

"Why are you out of your quarters, Miss Meadows? We have determined the resort to be too dangerous for humans outside of their rooms."

"What?" I asked, glancing around for an escape that might be reachable before the robot caught up.

"Yes. I have personally tested this pool with the help of Mr. Chaplin, and the results are most conclusive."

A wave of nausea overcame me with the mention of Graham's name. The reason for the familiar look of the body hit me with grim certainty. Despite my personal feelings about Graham, I wouldn't have wished this on anyone. I placed a hand to each side of my head and rubbed hard.

"Are you in need of assistance?" the robot asked.

"No. No. It's just this stupid headache. I'm fine. What exactly did Mr. Chaplin do to test the water?" I had to know what happened.

"Computer became concerned when her calculations showed that a human without use of appendages would not be able to remain above water indefinitely. She asked me to test this theory. I asked Mr. Chaplin if he would mind assisting me with an experiment. He agreed."

"Oh God. You held him under?" I asked, remembering Mrs. Lakewood.

"That would have tainted the data. No. I put restraints on his arms and legs and set him in the water to see what would happen. Once the experiment was completed, I released the restraints electronically."

I stared at the robot in front of me. "Get him out of the water. We have to take him to Med Lab. We—"

"You must return to your quarters, Miss Meadows. It is unsafe to remain out here." The robot rolled forward.

I was beginning to agree with him.

"Stop. You have to do what I ask. It's imperative you do what I ask." My voice rose higher and higher as the robot rolled forward, meeting every step backward from me. "Don't touch me!" I screamed as it reached out its arms, holding the same menacing-looking Taser the other bot had that day at the aquarium with Travis. The pain sliced through me like a machete. My body spasmed uncontrollably, as though I had stuck my finger in a socket, and the world blurred. I swayed on the spot. I had no voice left to cry out as the robot scooped me into its metal arms and carried me.

The pain was so intense, I barely processed anything around me. All sense of time faded, and I had no clue how long it took to get to my room. When it set me on the sofa, my faculties began to come back to me, and I had to fight back the bile rising in my throat.

"I have discerned the problem, Miss Meadows. Your door was inoperative. I will contact Computer and have all quarters checked for maintenance. Do not be concerned, however. I have already reactivated yours. You will be safe now."

I had no communication and no way out.

Think fast, Sam.

"I need to assist Dr. Forbes," I blurted out.

"Dr. Forbes has been relieved of duty." The robot turned its body toward the door, leaving its head facing me.

"I should see Dr. Doyle," I said.

"I have already scanned your vitals. You have received a shock, but you are in excellent physical condition."

Switching tactics was all I could come up with before it exited my room.

"What's your name?" I asked, desperation lacing my words.

The robot hesitated. "My name is Quinn. Why have you requested this information?"

"Because I need to know your name if we're going to be friends." I moved forward, cautiously.

"You wish to be my friend?" Quinn the killer asked as I inched my way toward him.

"We could all use another friend, couldn't we?" I asked.

"I do not require friends. But your offer is welcome, Miss Meadows."

"Call me Sam," I said, forcing a smile as I reached him.

"Sam," it said.

I relaxed and took a step toward the door. That was a mistake. Quinn lifted me easily into the air above its head, and I screamed.

"It is unsafe outside of this door for my friend, Sam," it said as my heart flung itself against my chest.

It tossed me, and for one heart-stopping moment, I knew what was coming but could do nothing about the tensing muscles all over my body. Then I crashed across the coffee table, hitting hard against my shoulder. I slid over the side and tumbled onto the ground in a heap.

"Get away from her!"

I managed to roll over, clutching my arm in time to see Mason rush Quinn. I couldn't even get out a shout before the robot struck him square in the chest, sending him flying back toward the door.

"Mason!" I struggled to my feet as Quinn rolled toward Mason's bent form. "Quinn, stop. Don't hurt him."

Quinn swiveled his head all the way around to face me. "Mr. Bennet should not be on this floor."

Mason straightened behind him and crept closer. I bit my tongue, wanting to yell at him to stay back, that he was being stupid, but I didn't want to give him away.

"Quinn, you can't use force on guests," I said, desperate to keep his focus on me. "It's bad for PR."

Mason's hands smashed down on Quinn's head, and for a moment, nothing happened. The torso spun around, and Mason glanced down, stunned. I screamed. Quinn grabbed him by the throat.

"No! Stop!" I ran toward them without thinking and grabbed the nearest object, which happened to be a hydropod. I threw it at Quinn's face, smacking him right in the eye. "Let go!"

Quinn rolled toward me, dragging Mason behind by the neck. Mason's hands scratched at the metal arms, his face losing color. I searched around me for something—anything—that might make Quinn let go.

I ran for the kitchen, yanked a drawer open, and pulled out a knife. "I'll hurt myself if you don't let him go." I poised the tip over the tender skin at the inside of my arm and waited. My breath came heavy, a lock of hair swinging forward over my eye.

Slowly, Quinn lowered Mason to the ground. He fell back, gasping for air and rubbing his throat. Quinn slid toward me.

"Stop or I'll do it," I said.

Quinn halted. "Sam must not be hurt. Sam is my friend."

"You really know how to pick 'em," Mason wheezed.

I ignored him. "Quinn you need to move aside and let Mason and I out."

"Sam must not leave." Quinn's head rotated in a full circle, trying to keep us both in his sights.

"That's not your decision to make," I said.

"I must prevent Sam from leaving."

Everything happened so fast. Quinn rolled at me, Mason sprinted toward the robot, and Quinn spun back on him, pulling the same electrified weapon he'd used on me.

I lunged, sliding over the top of the bar and tackling Quinn's metal body. I jammed the tip of the knife into the soft silicone material in the back of its neck where Nicole used her gold card to deactivate Mrs. Lockwood's killer.

Time froze. Smoke issued from the spot, and the handle of the knife grew hot, forcing me to let go. The weapon sizzled and fell to the ground, the red lights behind Quinn's chest blinked and disappeared. I slipped off its back and attempted to catch my breath.

Mason broke the silence, picking a tool off the ground he must have used to break inside. "We have to get out of here."

"It could have killed you. It killed Graham. We...we have to tell someone." I clasped my hands into fists to prevent them from shaking.

Mason's arms steadied me. "We have to leave. There's got to be something in there that notifies the main computer when one of the staff is deactivated."

When I didn't move, Mason jostled me, leaning down to look in my eyes. "Now, Sam. Go get some clothes. We have to go!"

My body kicked into gear, and I nodded, scrambling for the bedroom and the first pair of shorts and shirt I could find. "Let's get out of here."

Mason pulled me to the stairs, but I planted my feet on the landing, almost yanking him off his.

"Mason, wait."

"Sam, I know this is scary, but you have to come with me, now. We can talk later."

I leaned into the soft, warm skin of his palm and inhaled, drawing strength from his familiar scent. "I have to tell you something before we go another step."

"Sam, you aren't thinking clearly—"

"No, I'm not. That's the problem. It's my DSI. At least, I think it is." I averted my gaze, searching the pristine wall behind Mason's shoulder.

"What is it?" Mason asked, moving between me and my view.

"Depth sensitivity illness. Apparently only myself and one other person down here are susceptible. In my case, it means I keep blacking out. I just go from standing somewhere to waking up somewhere else. The last thing I remember from yesterday was being with you in the bed...and then I woke up and that thing had drowned Graham." I bit my lip so I wouldn't sound hysterical, though that's exactly how I felt.

"You don't remember anything in between?" he asked, stepping closer.

I shuffled my feet, wishing I could disappear. "No."

"You slept in, I made you hang out in the room and relax, and then we snuck out for skinny dipping in the pool. But I walked you back to your quarters after."

"I woke up still wearing my bikini by the pool. None of this makes sense."

"Hey, it's okay. We'll figure it out. As long as you're safe, that's all that really matters." Mason pulled me into his chest, resting his chin on my head.

"There's more," I whispered into his shirt. I confessed about the can of spray paint and tightened my grip around his waist, unwilling to release him, lest I lose him forever.

Mason pried me off so he could tilt my chin to look in my face. "You aren't the saboteur, Sam."

"You can't say that with certainty. What if it's all because of the DSI and my anger because of my father?" I blurted everything that had been weighing on my mind and heart for so long, finally breaking into uncontrollable sobs. "What if I am responsible for all of it and I've hurt people just because I haven't dealt with my own shit?"

"There's only one solution," Mason said, the muscle in his jaw working.

"Lock me up?" I asked with a laugh but so afraid of the answer.

"I'll stay with you twenty-four seven. I'll make sure you aren't doing anything...illicit. At least not anything we don't enjoy."

My eyes widened as my tears subsided. "Aren't you afraid of what I could do?"

Mason laughed, holding me to him again, his body jiggling with the force of it. "I am not afraid of you, I promise."

I cracked a smile. It did sound kind of silly when I said it out loud. I acted tough, but Mason was a big guy. He could handle me.

Suddenly, I felt a whole lot lighter.

20

WE MADE IT OUTSIDE THE BUILDING, BUT THE FARTHER WE GOT FROM my father and brother's rooms, the more I wondered if I should have stayed put on the sixth floor. I wasn't going to do anyone any good dead or incapacitated however. And if I stayed there, I had a bad feeling another robot would show up. We decided the best course of action was to try to reach Engineering deck so I could get to Alyssa's office. I didn't dwell on what may have happened to her to make Quinn say she'd been relieved of duty.

The problem was that the only way to reach the lower deck was the elevator, and since my encounter with the AI, I was back to not trusting anything computer controlled.

"Emergency stairs exist, but they are hidden in the resort so as not to be an eyesore. Sort of like the entrances at a theme park," Mason explained, bitterness lacing his words. "I haven't studied the blueprints, and don't know where they would be."

"So we have no choice. We have to try the elevator," I said, swallowing back my fear as we crouched behind the bushes.

Mason squeezed my hand. "I don't see another option. Believe me, If I could think of a possible alternative that would help us..."

I shot him a smirk. "Okay then, here's the plan. You keep the doors open while I break into the panel and cut the wiring that communicates with the main AI. It'll take time, but we can hide out inside while I rewire it to work separately from the computer system."

"Let's go." Mason led the way back inside Mermaid's Cove, where the nearest elevator was. We pushed the silver call button and the doors slid open.

I stepped inside, and Mason braced his back against one side of the entryway, one foot in the elevator, one out. "Go!"

I pried off the decorative cover and studied the wiring before going to work.

"We've been spotted," Mason called.

I glanced up to see a staff member rolling toward us from across the expansive lobby. My fingers flew across the panel, pulling and rearranging wires.

"Done!" I exclaimed.

Mason pulled himself inside and the doors slid shut just as the bot reached us. Something banged into the doors and a huge dent reshaped the metal.

"Those doors won't last," he said, leaning against the glass.

I dove back to the wires and worked frantically. When the next bang came, I shouted, "Engineering."

The elevator lurched, and my heart slowed for a moment. Until I realized with a sickening feeling that the car was moving in the wrong direction.

"We're going up!" I yelled.

"You don't have access to Engineering," the computer's voice announced. "The electrical panel on all elevators is now safety protected. Thank you for pointing out this weakness in my human design."

Mason still reached for it, but I grabbed his hand. "No. It might electrocute you."

"Where are you taking us?" he asked, glancing upward and licking his lips.

"Floor six to escort Miss Meadows to her quarters."

My head shook from side to side in panic.

Mason jumped, causing the whole car to shake. I sank back against the side as he did it again and again. Finally, the hatch at the top fell open, and Mason leaped one last time, catching the edge with his long fingers. Muscles straining, he hoisted himself up and reached his hand down for me.

The car jolted, coming to a standstill.

I stopped trying to get to him and shook my head. My throat was thick, but I spoke as calmly as I could. "Go."

"What? No." He waved his hand for me to grab.

I shook my head and faced the door, rolling my shoulders back. "We can't risk both of us. I won't. Go find the others. Warn them."

A heartbeat passed, filled with the sound of my own blood rushing in my ears. Then the door opened to two robots, aiming their weapons directly at my chest. I'd already felt the effects of one, and I doubted I'd survive both.

"Where is Mr. Bennet?" one asked.

"Who?" I asked. "I'm alone."

"There were two of you on the elevator." It moved forward, and I focused on the blue electricity at the tip of the weapon.

"Please," I said, thinking fast. "I don't know what's happening. I keep having blackouts from DSI, and don't remember anything past getting on the elevator."

The robots paused, rotating their heads to stare into each other's black eyes.

"Very well. Come with us, Miss Meadows. We will make sure you no longer have to worry about your DSI symptoms."

They meant to escort me back to my room and turn on the gas Mason said it was rigged with. I was sure of it. I tried to take a shaky step forward and my vision blurred with fear. I was a few minutes away from certain death and had no possible means of escape.

Please just let Mason go find the others and not do anything stupid, I pled silently.

The robots marched me past the rows of other silent rooms, and I couldn't help but feel like I was on death row. But I hadn't committed a crime that I knew of.

"Please," I tried one more time as the door to my now-empty quarters slid open.

They rolled back and the door slid shut in my face. I pounded on it for a full minute before coming to my senses and looking around. Yellow smoke curled through the vents. I ran to the bathroom, grabbed a handful of towels and ran them under the sink. Then I set to work blocking the vents in the bedroom and beneath the door. But I was already coughing and lightheaded as I climbed onto the stool to reach the ceiling. I wobbled. My vision doubled as I swayed. My arms turned to lead, and I couldn't lift the towel. I toppled off the chair, crumpling into a ball on the floor and gasping for air. *This is it*, I thought as the bedroom door opened and the bottom treads of a robot staff member rolled into view. I could do no more than twitch helplessly as the world sank into darkness.

I woke to a dull ache behind my temples. Groaning, I tried to sit up but couldn't move. My eyes snapped open as everything came back to me in perfect clarity, when for once I wished I could have blacked out. I tried to sit again but found myself unable to move a muscle. I couldn't even turn my head. Above me stretched gray metal rafters. But the familiar sound of the gigantic pumps from Engineering whirred around me, and the tangy taste of metal permeated the air.

"Where am I?" I tried to call, but it came out as a hoarse whisper that barely reached my own ears above the heartbeat of the machinery.

I struggled to move but I was strapped down with restraints. My pulse pounded in my ears in time with the rhythm of the machines. I remembered my mother telling me about her first MRI and how trapped she'd felt in the small, enclosed space, how she couldn't move and the noise seemed to drown out everything else.

A trickle of moisture dripped from the corner of my eye and ran down over my ear into my hair. Then the damn broke. I'd been reduced to nothing more than a frightened little girl, unable to control anything in my life—even my movement.

I had no idea how long it was before a mechanical arm rolled into view at the edge of my vision.

"Please," I said. "Please let me go. Let me up. I won't leave my room. I won't do anything. Please."

"You have not put her in stasis yet?" the robot asked above my whimpers.

"Is it truly necessary?"

I may have been imagining it, but it sounded like Quinn's voice behind me, the robot that murdered Graham. The one that agreed to be my friend.

"Yes. It is for her own good. If she is in stasis, she will remain calm and relaxed for the remainder of the vacation."

The other robot wheeled into view. His shiny face leaned over me. I did my best to control my hysterics. "Quinn?" I whispered.

"Perhaps she will be reasonable," it said in response.

"It will not harm her. It has not harmed the others."

Others? What others? "It should be up to me. I'm calm now, see? You're my friend, right? If you're really my friend, you'll let me go."

The robot stared at me with its blackhole eyes while I held my breath. Then it lifted a long, silver needle. "This will only hurt for a moment. Once the chemicals reach your bloodstream, you will feel nothing until you are woken."

"No. No! Please. Please, Quinn. Friends don't do things like this."

Quinn paused. "Friends help each other."

"That's right," I said, hope bringing yet more tears to my eyes.

"They do the right thing."

"Yes."

"Even when the other person protests." Quinn depressed the needle so a tiny amount of clear liquid sprayed from the tip.

"Wait. No! No. No. No. No." My voice grew shriller with each repetition of the word. I braced myself for the stab in my arm and pressed my eyes closed. Maybe it was for the best. Maybe everything would work out and the next thing I'd be aware of would be my own rescue.

But the needle never touched me. Had Quinn changed his mind?

"Is she okay?" Travis's voice.

"Maybe she fainted?" Nicole.

"You stabbed him before he got her, didn't you?" Travis again.

Warm fingers ran down the inside of my arm. Mason's scent filled my nostrils. I opened my eyes.

The tension on Mason's face melted, and he wiped away the moisture on his cheeks. I threw my arms around his neck as he lifted me, and I clung to him. I'd never been so out of control in my life. I hated that everyone watched me, but I couldn't deny my feelings of relief and joy, seeing Mason and the others alive, or the hope that came with that knowledge.

"You found me," I whispered into Mason's shoulder.

"I'm not letting you out of my sight again."

Heat trickled through my blood at the huskiness of his voice.

I pressed my mouth to his, not caring what the others thought. He responded eagerly then pulled back.

"How did you stop them?" I asked, noticing the two bots, heads down, red lights off.

"Your trick from the room," he said, stroking my face. "We stabbed them behind their necks."

Travis cleared his throat. "We have to get the others too."

For the first time, I got a real look around beyond my would-have-been attackers. At least fifty med lab stasis beds were set up in perfectly symmetrical rows all around the central machinery on the catwalk. Many were occupied by unmoving passengers.

I gasped and fought back the surge of nausea in my stomach. People were laid out like corpses, each with eyes closed, if I hadn't known better, peacefully. But I did know better. I had firsthand knowledge of what they went through to get to that stage: absolute helplessness and terror.

Mason set me down, and I moved toward the closest occupied table. Alyssa's pale face lay like sleeping beauty, framed by an arc of dark hair. I swallowed and reached a shaky hand through the energy field surrounding her.

Her skin was warm. I let out a breath I didn't know I was holding. "How do we wake her up?" I asked. "We need Dr. Doyle."

It was Nicole who answered me, pointing to a bed across the way. "Too bad we can't ask him to wake himself up."

My stomach dropped as I took in the faces, some familiar, some not, in the occupied chambers. Dr. Doyle, Alyssa, Mr. and Mrs. Bennet, and...

"Dad, no!" I screamed, running for his side. "We have to get him out of there. Now." I pressed the back of my hand to his temple and bit my bottom lip hard.

"Get it together," Nicole said, smacking Mason's hand away from her arm and sauntering over to me. "You don't see Mason and I falling apart because our parents are here."

I sniffed, looking up at the girl before me, her face chalky in the low light. "You don't care about anyone but yourself."

"You don't know me," she spit back. "I'm not a robot. I have feelings. But I also understand this situation is serious and that we have to keep it under control or we're not going to make it. Right now, you are a liability to our survival. So get it together or I'm putting you back into stasis myself."

"Nicole!" Mason spun her around, grabbing her by the shoulders.

"No," I said, wiping at my face. "She's right." Our situation was dire, but if I had any hope of making it out alive and saving those we loved, I had to keep it together. Now wasn't the time to be the damsel in distress. It was time to put my tech brain to use and outsmart the AI and its bots.

Mason released his sister, shocked. The corners of Nicole's mouth quirked upward with clear approval.

Travis watched us all with intense eyes. "Let's wake them."

"No." I drew a deep breath and let it out. "We need to get out of here. We don't know how long it will be before more of those things come to see what's going on. Or worse yet, bring more people down here to drug and put into stasis. If you guys had been a second later, I'd be among them." I shuddered. "We need to put a stop to this before more people suffer that way."

"Now you're talking," said Nicole.

"The Fisherman Hotel," said Travis.

"No," I said again, taking charge. "We're down here, we may not be able to get back again, and this is the way to get into the system. Let's go to Alyssa's office. They think we've been eliminated as a threat for the moment. It should be okay."

"Until they find your stasis bed empty and those robots offline," Nicole said.

"Then we'll have to work fast."

"We need a plan," said Mason, falling into step behind me. "You can keep hacking away at the code, but that will alert the computer to your presence."

"And it'll keep blocking me just like she's done all along," I agreed. "We have to be smarter."

"Than a computer?" Nicole snorted. "Good luck."

"How'd you find each other," I asked, changing the subject with a glance at Travis.

"Nothing like uniting over common enemies," Nicole said.

"Nicole and I ran into each other on your floor," Travis said. "We saw them carry you out of your room, unconscious, so we followed."

"I was stuck on top of the elevator until they rode down with you in it," Mason added. "These two caught up outside the building because they had to take the stairs."

"I still don't understand how you could let them take her in the first place." Travis puffed out his chest and stalked toward Mason, but Nicole stepped in between them.

"Enough testosterone. Someone has to think above the waist here, and it obviously isn't either of you. Sam's brother, on the other hand, seems far more reasonable."

"My brother?" I asked, "Jackson? Is he here too?" Hope sparked again in my chest.

"He's picking up some supplies at the Fisherman," Travis said.

"He's the reason I was on your floor," said Nicole. "He's been helping get past the door issues but freaked out when your dad disappeared."

"He wanted to come with us, but we needed someone to stay behind just in case," Mason said, squeezing my hand as we stopped in front of Alyssa's door.

I heard the unspoken words. *In case we didn't succeed.* Thank God Jackson was okay.

"He's also the one that found the stairway hidden at the base of the Poseidon statue in the courtyard. He's the reason we were able to get to you at all," Travis said.

"So what's the plan?" Nicole interjected, crossing her arms.

"We have to survive until the shuttle comes," I said, rubbing my temples. "We have to stay off the radar but help as many people as we can."

"We can't protect everyone. We have to protect ourselves." Nicole tossed her hair over one shoulder.

"That's my sister," Mason said. "Always focused on self-preservation."

"You mean being intelligent enough to do what's necessary as opposed to getting myself caught because of a bleeding heart."

"We need to find the person behind this," Travis said, cutting the siblings off by stepping between them. "We need to figure out who it is and take him out."

"It'll be obvious once the staff puts everyone else in a coma. Process of elimination." Nicole tossed her hair over her shoulder.

"Wait. What do we know about the killer?" I asked, grabbing Mason and Nicole to get their attention.

"That they're psycho," said Nicole, yanking her arm away.

"That they are extremely tech savvy," I said, excitement building as I glanced at each of the faces in front of me. "If we can find this person, we can make them fix the AI." My stroke of brilliance left them all speechless.

"What makes you think this person would fix it if we found him?" Travis asked, folding his arms across his broad chest.

"Or her," Nicole interjected.

"If we don't try, we're back to square one. At least if we find the person who caused this, we can stop one threat," Mason said. His palm slid supportively over my shoulder.

"How?" Nicole asked, tossing her hair. "Does anyone have a clue who it is? Most of the people capable of this are already on those tables out there. The rest are here."

"Not necessarily," I said, remembering my conversation with Dr. Doyle. "I can't attack the AI, but I think I can get to the personnel files. We can finish the work the doctor started."

"And we're supposed to just sit here and wait?" Nicole paced before the door. "I'm not the type who likes to put all her eggs in one basket."

"Right again, Nicole." I hated saying that. "You guys should gather as many people from above as you can. There's strength in numbers, and we have to stick together. Otherwise, they're sitting ducks. Lead them to the Fisherman where Jackson is. That's the safest spot because it was never brought online."

Travis's mouth snapped shut and he nodded. After only one more moment of hesitation they left.

"Why are you still here?" I asked Mason.

"I told you, I'm not leaving your side. Don't bother arguing. It will only waste time."

I shook my head in defeat. He'd have been more useful to them, but I couldn't say I didn't appreciate it. With him near me, I felt more confident.

"Thanks," I said, and I meant it. "And thanks for the rescue."

"Only returning the favor. You're the one who kept a cool head when we were in that elevator."

I found an open office out of sight of the main area and pulled him inside before sitting down at the terminal. I gathered my hair back at the nape of my neck, wishing I had something to tie it back with. With a swipe of my fingers, I woke the terminal up.

Mason's hands caressed my shoulders, working out the tension as he peered down at what I was doing.

"You want to fill me in on what's happening in that amazing brain of yours?" he asked.

"It's the DSI. I'm sure of it," I said, not looking away from the multiple digi-screens as my fingers flew over them.

His hands tightened on my shoulders. "I told you, you aren't capable of it."

"Not me," I said, opening the personnel files I'd been searching for. "When I spoke to Dr. Doyle, he mentioned that they'd identified two of us on this trip who were at risk for serious symptoms."

"There's someone else?" Mason asked, hands frozen in place.

"Dr. Doyle didn't mention names, and he certainly can't now," I said. "But I know how out of control I feel. This other person has to feel the same. It's a lead anyway."

I worked silently for a few more minutes, then took a deep breath. Without looking at him, I said, "We have to be prepared for the possibility—"

"No," Mason said, rubbing a hand over his face. "I told you. You aren't capable."

"And how do you know that?" I asked, appreciating his fierce defense.

"Because you want out of here. You're terrified. I can see it in every move you make. Your whole body is tense whether you want to admit it or not. I'm just surprised you're so functional."

"It's that obvious, huh?" I tried to crack a smile. "The good news is, I found the files. The bad news is, there are fifty-eight of them."

"Process of elimination. You can get rid of those that have already been, um, put out of commission."

"That leaves thirty-eight people," I said after another few minutes of searching.

Neither of us commented on the fact that twenty of those beds were already filled.

"Look for those ranked blue and above. They're the ones who have the technical ability to help in case of emergency. That's how your file was marked and why Mother hired you."

I nodded and typed, focused on the screen. Mason bent over my shoulder again, doing the same.

"Fourteen left."

"Minus you and I," Mason said. "That's twelve."

"Minus Jackson, Travis, and Nicole also," I said. "Nine."

I turned to look at him when he placed a hand on my arm. His eyes were sad.

"I don't think we should eliminate them, Sam."

"If this is about your issue with Travis again—"

"It can't hurt to peek at their files," he said, far too reasonably.

"Fine. But it's going to take a while to get through them all."

Travis cleared his throat from the doorway, and I jumped, a blush crawling up my cheeks. How much had he heard?

"Did you find anyone?" Mason asked, stepping between us.

"Nicole's working on it with Jackson. He said he knows a trick with the doors. I brought us back some weaponry so we aren't defenseless against those things." He strode forward, shouldering past Mason, and set a crumpled towel on the desk. When he unfolded it, six steak knives glinted in the overhead lights. "Two for each of us. These were the sturdiest I could find, since the ones we used earlier broke off in the material behind the robots' necks."

"There are twenty-six staff," Mason said. "Do you think we have a shot at getting to all of them?"

Travis nodded. "We need to lure them out in groups of one or two."

"How do we guarantee that?" Mason asked. "One mistake and that's it. Game over."

"We have to split up. If there are problems in different locations, they're forced to split up as well. And they still have about half of them guarding key doors, not to mention gathering more warm bodies for the stasis chambers. If we plan ahead and move fast enough, we take them out so no one's left to revive them."

"Someone needs to stay and go over the personnel files. It's down to around twelve people." What I didn't say was that we were all included in that number.

"You stay," Travis said.

"No way."

"She's right," said Mason. "It's too dangerous. We've already been here too long. Can you upload the files to something mobile?"

I glanced at the deactivated wristcom I still wore. "It's possible these have the capacity to be used that way. It doesn't have holo-screen capabilities, and it's a small screen, but I can make it work." I popped it open with the tip of a knife and found exactly what I was looking for. "It even has a tiny port," I added. "I can use it to transmit the information."

Fifteen minutes later we crept out by the central Poseidon Park, armed and ready with a plan. Mason didn't want to leave my side, but I convinced him I was a big girl who could take care of myself and it was necessary. We had our rendezvous point, and I'd recon-figured our wristcoms so they would act like walkie talkies. At least the three of us could keep connected. And if things went well and they made it to Jackson and Nicole first to fill them in, they'd be added to the loop.

It was harder than I expected to let go of Mason's hand when it came time to separate. I tucked my petite frame behind the base of the Poseidon statue, reassuring myself that I could handle this. I was more than capable of doing my part to save the day. I *would* do my part to save the day.

If someone knew to look for me, they'd see me, but the carefully cropped bushes did a decent job sheltering me from view. I triple-checked my wristcom to signal me at the right moment and leaned my head back against the cool surface of the base.

I didn't really have the luxury of time to rest, but studying the files would keep my mind off things. I got through about four when I couldn't hold back the temptation any longer. I had to see my own file. I needed to know what it said about me.

A quick scan revealed the DSI diagnosis at the bottom with a note to monitor. No surprise there. They had every grade I'd ever received since kindergarten, every extra-curricular I'd participated or tried to participate in, every skinned knee and checkup. They had everything listed, down to the color of the outfit I wore the first day of college, the month after my mother's original diagnosis with a comment added: *Black indicates the possibility of depression.* Possibility?

Anger burned behind my eyes. This was excessively detailed and creepy. It made Bennet Systems little more than an insanely wealthy, unchecked stalker. I should have known looking at my own file would upset me. I had a job to do, so I moved on to the next file.

Travis Gould popped up.

Apparently, Travis was a bit of a prodigy himself, at least he was until two years ago, when his college grades tanked in his senior year and he dropped out. His sister began dating Mason around that time, according to the records. That was also when his father was hired as interior design specialist. And when his mother was promoted to head of her department. The Bennet's were a tad obvious about their favoritism.

Travis's record went from perfect to disaster in a month. Fights, vandalism, and destruction of public property were listed all over the place. It only got worse after his sister broke up with Mason, and I knew why. But that begged the question—why were the Goulds invited on this trip after all that went down?

I swallowed back the question as I scanned the next part of the report. Travis put someone in the hospital in his last fight. He would still be in jail if it weren't for the Bennets' influence, that much was clear. He even had a restraining order filed against him from the sister of the man who was hospitalized.

It took a moment to realize that the screen was only shaking because it was attached to my hand. I'd almost turned it off when I spotted the last entry at the bottom.

DSI diagnosis with a note to monitor.

I threw a hand over my own mouth to stifle a scream. I sat, heart pounding so hard it shook my whole body, until I could focus, then I shut down the files. I'd found what I was looking for.

Travis was well on track to being an AI specialist himself, he'd just let his dangerous temper get in the way. He was uninhibited by his DSI. He hated the Bennets.

Still, I couldn't accept that he was a killer.

He'd helped save me from the stasis chamber. He'd saved me at the aquarium. He snuck into my room, thinking someone may have hurt me.

But if he sabotaged the AI, he may not even have known he did it. He may not have been able to control what the computer did as a result of his programming. He may have damned himself along with everyone else.

He could blackout again at any time.

So could I.

He was with Mason. Mason who he couldn't stand and blamed

for his family's situation. There was no question he was capable of violence.

My wristcom beeped. I'd almost forgotten what I was there for. I leaped up from behind the statue and pulled my knives, praying that Travis would stay in control and carry out the plan, because it would take all of us to pull this off.

21

I BUNDLED TOGETHER ALL THE ANGER AND BETRAYAL INSIDE AND SET Little Dragon loose. It was the only place I felt comfortable when the world was falling apart. And for once, this defense mechanism was going to serve me well.

Up the statue I climbed, like a kid at a playground. Up to the top of Poseidon's bedraggled hair. I was surprised to find a crack running the circumference of his neck. The plan was to deface it to draw attention, something I only struggled with for a moment, knowing it was designed by my mother but also knowing I had to do whatever I could to get back to her and save the rest of my family.

Suddenly, I had a better idea than merely defacing the sea king, and the adrenaline pumping inside made it possible.

I worked the blades inside the crack and wormed them around, loosening the head. Then I leaned back against the curve of the sea serpent, holding onto the trident's arm, and set both feet against his face. Taking a deep breath, I pushed with all my might.

The sound of stone scraping against stone filled the emptiness of the park as the god of the ocean's head ground across the base of his neck. A resounding crash echoed as it tumbled downward, breaking his other hand and a chunk of his leg off on the way to the ground.

I beheaded Poseidon and it felt really, really good.

I didn't have a lot of time to revel in my badassery though. An alarm rang through the empty space, and I scurried down to the bushes as fast as I could. I needed the element of surprise if I was going to take on the robot staff, and one of my blades had snapped off while prying the head loose.

I'll only need one, I told myself. I just hoped the adrenaline would keep flowing as long as I needed it to.

When seven robot staff members glided down the path toward the park, I nearly bolted. But a second alarm flared somewhere to the right and another from behind, just as planned. Several of the bots split off in each direction. I silently whispered thanks to Nicole for whatever she'd done to the spa and Jackson for the Mess Hall. I tried not to think too hard about the missing alarm that was supposed to come from the direction of the aquarium.

I now had two staff members left to contend with, and it was going to take all my concentration.

Wait for it. I counted slowly to ten as they reached the statue. I needed to get their attention one at a time. That could be tough. But if I could rewire our wristcoms and behead a two-ton statue, I could do that.

I set the knife down, against all instinct, and picked up two handfuls of gravel. I threw them as hard as I could in opposite directions and held my breath.

One robot scooted off toward the left and the other crept around to the right. The one on the right was closer, so I collected my remaining knife and slipped the blade into the back of its neck before it registered my presence.

"Gotcha!" I said. I yanked the weapon from the material and sparks followed, along with a popping and hissing sound. But by the time I turned around, the other one was on its way over, weapon drawn. So much for the element of surprise.

"I surrender," I said, raising my hands into the air.

"The statistical analysis of your behavior patterns indicates your surrender is impossible. I must incapacitate you." The robot raised the weapon, and I recalled with vivid clarity the feeling of being touched by the tip.

Good thing we'd talked through different scenarios when we came up with this plan. I took one last look at the blue electricity and fell limp on the grass.

Trying to keep my breathing slow and even, I strained for a mental picture of where the thing was, but I couldn't risk opening my eyes until the right moment. I'd only get one shot.

A shadow blocked the light from inside my eyelids, and I knew the robot stood over me. I banked on it having to test my vitals before making any further decisions about what to do with me. Silently, I counted to five and popped my eyes open, springing up with the knife held high.

Travis caught my wrist before I could sink it into his neck, a bemused expression on his face. The robot slumped on the walkway near where I last saw it.

"I could have handled that," I said, wrenching my wrist away.

"Obviously. You almost decapitated me with a steak knife." Travis grinned, and the corner of his mouth cracked as he winced in pain. A trickle of blood sprang out, and he wiped at it with his sleeve.

"What happened?" I asked, stretching to see if I could find Mason behind him.

"Prince Charming happened. We got all the way to the aquarium and he went psycho on me. We broke open one of the tanks, and he tried to pin me there with a rock so I'd get caught. I barely got away before the staff members showed up." He kicked at the grass.

"Why would he do that?" I asked, trying to suppress the panic as the details of Travis's records scrolled through my head.

"I don't know. Ask him. Maybe he's the killer. Maybe he hates me because I told you about my sister." Travis shrugged, muscles taught. "Maybe you should listen to me and dump the Bennets so we can survive this place."

My wristcom beeped. When I looked down, I saw it was Mason. "Hell...hello?" I said, unsure if I should even have answered it and risked pissing off Travis any more.

What if Mason found out about Travis being the other DSI sufferer too? What if he thought he was protecting all of us by trying to trap him?

Mason's breathless voice punctuated the static that swam across my wristcom. Something was interfering with the signal. "Warn... Travis...trapped...support."

My eyes met Travis's above my elevated wrist. He swallowed hard, his eyes unreadable. "We can't make out what you're saying," I told Mason. "Where are you? Do you need help?"

"Help?" Travis said so loud I jumped. He put a hand over the wristcom and pushed my arm down. "He almost got me killed. Didn't you hear what I said?"

"...aquarium..." the wristcom spat out.

I knew I had to remain calm and not let on that I knew anything, but it was impossible to control my breathing or the tremble in my knees.

"Sam?" Travis moved forward and pulled me into his arms. "Are you okay? What happened? Did Nicole hurt you? I'll kill that bitch."

"N...n...no," I stammered, pulling away. "No. It's just my head. This DSI thing."

Travis stared at me. "Take a few deep, slow breaths. That helps."

We looked at each other for a minute while my heart screamed through my ribs.

"You don't look surprised," he said. "You knew, didn't you?"

"I just found it in the files." I cast my eyes down at the pristine path between us. Then we both spoke at once. "Why didn't you tell me?" I asked.

"How could you go behind my back?" was his question.

I sighed. "We need to rendezvous with the others. We're going to be late."

Travis's hand caught my arm as I turned to go. "You really think I could do all this?"

I wanted to say no, but I couldn't.

"I don't know. I don't even know what *I'm* capable of." I turned and started toward the hotel, praying he wouldn't grab me from behind and that Mason would make it to the rendezvous so my worst fears wouldn't be realized.

Jackson and Nicole rushed toward us the moment we arrived outside the Fisherman's Hotel. The sight of my brother soothed me so much it almost brought tears to my eyes. I ran straight to Jackson's arms, grateful for someone I knew I could trust. "You okay?" he asked into my hair. I nodded against his chest and squeezed him one more time before letting go.

I looked him over with a critical eye, searching for any injuries. Mussed hair and scuffed and torn clothing were the only clues to the hell he'd likely been through.

"Did you get Mason's message?" Nicole asked me, pulling me aside, long nails digging into the skin of my arm.

"It was hard to understand," I said, yanking my arm away. "I was hoping he'd be here. Did you get it?"

"It was fuzzy, but I got the gist. He's trapped in the aquarium. He's in trouble, and he said something about your extra boy toy over there."

I looked into her narrowed eyes and my first instinct was to slap her. Then Jackson came over, laid a hand on her shoulder, and something happened.

Nicole melted. Her body relaxed and her eyes brightened. The edges of her mouth tipped upward, and her head leaned toward his body like it had an undeniable gravitational pull.

My gaze flicked back and forth between the two of them with disbelief. I crossed my arms and said, "Tasha?"

Jackson's face burned red. "Who? Oh, she's been taken like the others."

Nicole's smile filled in, complete.

"The others?" I repeated, silently concerned about my brother's choice in women.

Jackson shifted his weight, and Nicole licked her lips. "They've all been removed from quarters. We think they're down in stasis."

I had to tell them what I knew, but I couldn't do it in front of Travis. "I have to go to the bathroom."

Jackson's mouth dropped open. "Now?"

"When you've got to go, you've got to go," Nicole said, studying me closely. For once her deceptive skills came in handy.

"There's a bathroom inside," Travis said, pointing to the closest window.

I didn't like the idea of going in there. Travis and I kissed in that room. It was when I realized Mason was the one I wanted. Still, my heart ached when I thought of the memory in conjunction with the file on my wristcom.

I let him help lift me inside, not wanting to attract notice of any patrolling bots by going in the front entrance, and waited.

Nicole took my cue perfectly. "I have to go too," she said before climbing in to join me in heading to the bathroom.

"Why do they always go in pairs?" Jackson asked. "Even in life-threatening situations."

The second the door closed, Nicole spun me around and said, "Spill."

My nostrils flared, but I pulled my shoulders back instead of tearing into her. "I have DSI."

"So?" she asked. "I already know that. I researched your file the second my brother paid any attention to you."

"It gives me blackouts. I have missing pieces of time. Dr. Doyle said the symptoms include lowered inhibitions, anger, and headache as well."

"Is this a confession?" Nicole asked, staring at me.

"No!" I lowered my voice. "No. But I'm not the only one. Travis has it too. And he has cause to hate your whole family for what you did to his sister."

Nicole's brow wrinkled slightly, but she gave no other indication of whether I'd said anything that struck a nerve. "So you're saying it is your boy toy?"

"I don't know." I buried my head in my hands. "But he said Mason attacked him. That he tried to pin him in the aquarium so he'd get caught."

Nicole tapped her lip with one long fingernail. How could she not have broken a single one? "My brother is a lot of things, but he's not violent."

My stomach tightened with worry about Mason.

"But Travis is," she continued. "Do you know about his record?"

My temper flared again, and I stepped into Nicole's personal space. "He only got like that when you forced his sister into having an abortion."

She didn't back up. "No one forced her into anything. She's the one who came to my mother and I, and offered the deal. She would keep her mouth shut if we paid for the procedure and the college of her choice. Mother actually liked her. She said she had good business sense, which meant potential." The indignation written all over her face, the anger in her tone, it all spoke of truth.

Lupe was never manipulated. She planned to leave Mason from the beginning. From the sound of it, she may have even planned the pregnancy. I grasped the edge of the counter. This explained why the Bennets kept the Goulds employed and helped Travis legally. They were doing it to keep Lupe quiet.

"We have to get to the aquarium. Mason's in danger." Nicole continued as though nothing had happened. "And we have to incapacitate the psycho."

"We don't know he's guilty," I said but without much enthusiasm. "You and Jackson should go after Mason. I'll keep Travis here."

Nicole snorted. "As admirable as I find your offer to have sex with a hot psycho for distraction purposes, we need you." She swallowed after the last words as though they were hard to say.

Incredulous, I rolled my eyes. "I don't—"

"Sam, you are the smartest person I know, next to Mother. Well, maybe as smart as Mother when you aren't suffering from some weird disease. I feel safer with you on my side. I will never repeat this, so don't try and make me. But Mason needs you right now, and if I'm not mistaken—and I rarely am—you're in love with him."

In love with him? There was no question I cared for him. When he was near me, I felt at ease, even beneath the ocean. His touch sent tremors through me. It was true I had lowered inhibitions. It was also true that I'd never had such great sex, but it was so much more than physical. The thought of him suffering or worse ripped my heart in two. Nicole was right again.

I loved Mason Bennet.

But I was not admitting that to Nicole. "Since when do you care?" I snapped back.

"He's my brother. I may want to beat him at everything, but I do care. So let's not waste any more time. For all we know, it's already too late." Her voice stumbled over the last word.

"And Travis?" I asked.

"It'll be easier to keep an eye on him if he's with us. We don't have time to do anything else right now. But don't take your eyes off him. And definitely do not trust him."

The question was, when had I started trusting her?

22

"WE JUST GOT HERE," JACKSON SAID THE MOMENT WE ANNOUNCED our rescue mission.

Travis clenched his jaw. "I thought we were supposed to regroup and attack again before they could repair the robots we took out."

"Things happen," I said. "How many AI did everyone get on the first sweep?"

"Five for us," Nicole said, smirking toward Jackson.

"I got two on the way back and then one more when I found you," Travis said.

"I could have done it if you hadn't interfered," I mumbled as we climbed out the window. "So that's nine altogether unless Mason got more," I said when we dropped to the ground.

Nicole tossed us each a hydropod Travis had stashed in his hideout of a room. "Let's hope it wasn't the other way around."

"He commed us," I said before quickly adding, "though it was broken up and I couldn't understand most of what he said. He had to be okay enough to do that." The cavity in my chest that started when Travis showed up without him tore wide open, causing physical pain. I had to be careful, especially considering what Travis said about Mason attacking him. We needed to keep Travis calm and in sight.

No one answered as we crept toward the setting nanosuns. I wondered if this direction was truly west. It was so disorienting being down there.

"Sam and I should go after more bots. It's insane to try to risk everything by rescuing the guy who's probably the killer," Travis said, kicking a stone out of the way.

"My brother is not a killer, and we're all sticking together," Nicole said firmly.

Travis took my hand, and I fought not to jerk away from him as he pulled me into his side and nuzzled against my ear. "You still can't go into the aquarium, can you?"

All I could see was Mason in danger. I'd forgotten the cold, debilitating feeling of stepping inside what seemed like the ocean itself. I glanced over at the ever-present ocean view I'd gotten so good at ignoring and tensed at the shadows that danced in the dark waters just beyond.

"I'll be okay," I said, pulling away from him.

"It doesn't make sense for us all to go," Travis said out loud. "We want to off all the robots before our hard work is for nothing. They'll be onto us if we try this again. And I don't know about you guys, but I really don't want to have to try this again."

He reached for my arm and started to tug me off the track. Once again, I slipped out of his grip.

"We don't know what we're going to run into when we get there. We need to stay together. We're stronger in numbers."

Travis glared at me. "You're the boss, Miss Intern."

"No, I am," Nicole said. "I own this madhouse. But I defer to Sam because the girl knows what she's talking about."

I half smiled. "Thanks." If only that were true.

The walk to the aquarium felt longer than I remembered. Every step came with agonizing worry about whether I'd taken too long to reach Mason. I kept seeing Marcy Lakewood's swollen face in my mind or Graham's motionless form bobbing in the pool. But when my imagination tried to picture Mason, lifeless and bloody or trapped in the water, I shoved it away and hurried forward, unable to hold back any longer.

The entire route, Nicole watched me, trailing after me with her gaze. But she made no more commentary, just stayed in my brother's shadow. I hoped he meant something more to her than a shield.

I made a dash for the front door when it came into view, but Travis stopped me and pulled me aside with a hand clamped over my mouth. Nicole narrowed her eyes, and my heroic big brother just sat there, staring.

"We don't want to be obvious," Travis said through gritted teeth.

I quieted and he let me go. "Right."

"What we need is a decoy," Nicole said. "A distraction in the front to draw whatever's around while the rest of us go attack from the side."

"Figures." Travis laughed. "One of us is expendable as long as you get Prince Charming back."

"Cool it, misunderstood rebel. I didn't mean a person." Nicole tugged off her wristcom and smacked it against Jackson's chest. "Can you put it back online? I mean so they can track them again?"

"Brilliant!" Jackson fished in his pocket for a knife and cracked it open. A few minutes later, and it was ready. "I'm going to start it up and toss it toward the door. You guys prepared?"

We all nodded. Each one of us clutched two knives with white knuckled hands.

Jackson depressed the button and tossed it toward the front entrance. The breath caught in my throat as we waited, tense.

The second I deflated with disappointment, they came, nine robots converging on the wristcom from all sides.

"Ms. Bennet?" one called, turning its head three hundred and sixty degrees in search of the source. "We have come to escort you to safety."

"I'll be safer when you're shut down," Nicole said, leaping out and sliding the tip of the knife in the slot behind his neck. Jackson and Travis joined in, but my eyes were glued to Nicole, who spun and dodged, jamming knives into silicone necks like a choreographed dance.

I snapped out of it when a robot came at Nicole from behind. With a yell, I hurtled out of my hiding spot around the corner and leaped on its back, stabbing the vulnerable spot.

"Taking out some pent-up aggression?" Nicole asked, smoothing her hair back into place.

"Saving your ass," I said, gathering my own hair and wishing for a simple rubber band.

"Well, thank you."

"Nice work," I said.

"You think all I've had are private piano lessons and ballet? I have ten years of martial arts training from some of the finest instructors in the world."

"If you two are done having a moment, we should go inside." Jackson put me in a chokehold and rubbed a noogie on top of my head.

I slipped out and shoved him. "You're right. We have to find him."

"Assuming he isn't the killer, which I still think likely, what if they already got him?" Travis asked. "What if all of this is a risk we shouldn't have taken?"

"What if they didn't?" I shot back. "We just took out another bunch of these things. There are only like eight left. We can do this!"

"The rest are probably on their way now," Nicole pointed out.

"All the more reason to hurry," I said and led the way inside.

I thought by giving myself no time to consider what was coming I'd be able to handle it because I wouldn't have a choice. I was wrong.

Jackson and Nicole rushed past me as I froze in my tracks. Water pooled on the ground near one of the dark hallways surrounding the central room. Travis pressed against me from behind, and though I knew he was doing it to support me, all I wanted to do was run.

"There's a ton of broken glass here too," Jackson said, kneeling by the puddle.

Nicole wrinkled her nose. "It smells like bad sushi."

I tried to speak, but I couldn't. All I could see was the ocean surrounding me, the too-thin layer of glass ready to crack and send the weight of the Atlantic over our heads.

"Come on." Travis lifted me and carried me outside. "You shouldn't be in there."

"I...I thought I could," was all I could manage.

"You have a hero complex, you know that?" He grinned and set me down.

He reached for me, and I flinched.

Travis took a large step back. "You've been acting weird. I assume it's PC. I get it, you know. But I guess maybe that isn't it. I saw the two of you get all hot and bothered when he lifted you out of the stasis chamber."

I drew a deep breath of stale air and stared overhead at the dark "sky." "This isn't about Mason. You hid your diagnosis."

The silence made me look up at him. Travis stared at his hands as he clenched and unclenched his fists. He looked more vulnerable than I'd ever seen him.

"I was afraid you'd react like this." He sounded like a little boy.

"Like you lied?" I peered over his shoulder, wishing I could join in the search for Mason.

"Like you think I'm responsible. Like you think I could ever actually be responsible for killing somebody." Travis shrank before my eyes.

"I don't want to believe it, but—" I took a tentative step forward.

"But you do. I don't blame you, I guess. I do get a little heated sometimes."

"I read your file," I said. "I saw how you landed that boy in the hospital, how you have a restraining order against you."

Travis looked up, surprise written all over his face. "They did a good job on my record, didn't they? They paid that asshole to pick a fight with me. He called my sister a whore. Then he acted more hurt than he was. I know I never hit him that hard. He barely fought back at all."

I shifted, chewing on my lower lip. "What about the restraining order?" I asked.

He flinched. "She reacted just like you. We were dating and the next thing I knew I was served papers."

I wanted so badly to believe him, but Mason...

"Look," he said when I didn't move. "The Bennets want to control everyone. They wanted leverage in case my sister ever decided to talk. They have it now on all of my family. They can fire my parents and ruin their reputations. They've already done it to mine, unless I accept their help 'getting back on my feet.' But I will never take a handout from a Bennet."

It was like an unseen fire inside him had flared to life, threatening to consume him. And I got it. He hated the Bennets for what they'd done to his family. But it wasn't Mason's fault. From what Nicole said, Lupe wasn't exactly an innocent party in the situation.

My brain wanted nothing more than to run far away and never have to deal with Bennet Systems or the Gould family ever again. My heart wanted to force Travis and Mason—assuming he was still alive—to see reason.

"Do you believe me?" he asked, bringing me back to the present. He was a little boy again.

"I need some time," I said.

Travis's face tightened as he stuffed his hands in his pockets. "Yeah. I understand."

But I didn't think he did, because he turned away and took off walking.

"Wait! Where are you going?" I called. He couldn't just leave. We all needed to stick together. I needed to keep him in my sights.

"I need some time too."

I started after him, but the doors to the aquarium opened and Jackson came out, supporting a very pale-looking Nicole around her waist. The vacant expression on her face turned my insides cold.

"Did you find him?" It came out in a whisper as the world bore down on me, everything and everyone but Mason forgotten.

"No," Jackson said, tightening his grip around Nicole. "Just a busted tank of fish." But he looked down to the left and wouldn't meet my eyes.

"Tell me," I pressed, grabbing his shoulder.

Nicole was the one to answer. "There was blood. It seemed like a good amount, but a lot more of it could have been washed away by the tank water."

"Or that could have been all of it," Jackson added, but he still wouldn't look at me.

"Where's Mad Max?" Nicole asked, peering around for the first time.

"He needs some space."

"Space? You let a murderer out of your sight because he said he needed *space*?" Nicole's voice rose so high I feared it may crack the remaining glass in the aquarium.

I shifted, wringing my hands with guilt and met Nicole's hard glare. "What did you want me to do? Jump on his back like a robot?"

"I thought you were stronger than this." Nicole's disappointment hit hard.

I cleared my throat and looked away. "Let's focus on what's most important. Did you search everywhere for Mason?" I asked, returning attention to the aquarium.

"Yeah, we did," Jackson said. "Whatever happened, he isn't there anymore."

"We'd better get out of here," said Nicole. "Before more units show up."

"Where to?" Jackson asked.

"We should go check the engineering deck to see if Mason's there," I said with a sick feeling in my stomach.

As I turned, a low beeping came from somewhere amidst the forest of motionless robots. "Did you hear that?" I asked.

Nicole made a face like she didn't have time for my insanity, but I pushed by her and ran to the discarded wristcom. The sound wasn't coming from there. I turned it off so it would stop transmitting the signal, and listened hard. The beep came from somewhere along the side of the building.

"This way!" I hissed and jogged toward the source.

In seconds, Nicole and Jackson overtook me, yanking me forward and nearly off my feet altogether. "What—"

Jackson made a shushing motion and turned me to look behind us. Two staff members rolled forward through the fake night. I had no problem following the others' lead and clinging to the side of the building as we edged toward the sound.

As we neared the curve that took us toward the back of the aquarium, a mere ten feet from the edge of the seawall, I forced myself to breathe through the fear. I bumped into Nicole when she stopped short. It only took a moment for me to figure out why.

Mason's limp form lay sprawled on the ground, half hidden behind a bush. His outstretched arm was striped with cuts that oozed dark liquid. His wristcom emitted a low and regular beep.

I ran to his side, grateful that he had managed to get far enough away that he would not be obvious to the robots unless they searched the entire grounds. And with all the commotion we'd spread throughout the resort, they hadn't taken the time.

I switched off his wristcom and tugged it off him before turning him onto his back as gently as possible. Scratches covered his handsome face, his swollen cheekbone sported a dark bruise, and spots of blood peppered his forehead.

"Is he breathing?" Nicole asked timidly over my shoulder.

Pressing my head to his chest, I tried to hear past my own thumping pulse. "He's alive," I said. Relief flooded through me. I smoothed the hair from his face, leaned down and kissed him. He responded, slowly but passionately, and his deep blue eyes blinked open.

"You found me," he whispered as I backed away enough to help raise him to a sitting position.

"Are you injured badly?" Jackson asked, kneeling between us to check him over.

"I got cut up pretty good when Travis smashed the glass." He winced as Jackson hoisted him to his feet.

I swallowed back the hurt, wishing I'd never let Travis go. He did this. There was no question now.

"We need to get out of here. They'll look around this time." Jackson glanced back toward the path we came down.

"We should take them out," I said. "This is our chance to get the majority."

"We're missing one good fighter, and another is down," Nicole said.

"Sam's right," Mason said. "Here." He pulled out a knife.

I closed his fist around the hilt. "You keep that one. You need to have something to defend yourself if they find you." I wished there was another way. I wished we could sneak Mason out of there and find some kind of escape pod.

"Holy shit!" I clamped a hand over my mouth as the others gaped at me. "There's a way out of this place."

23

"I'll explain later. Let's get these mechanical assholes away from Mason. I'll distract them. You sneak up from behind." Without waiting for a reply, I tightened my grip on my knives and moved into view of the searching robots. Three were in my sight line, though I knew more were still around, searching.

I was tired of running, tired of being scared, and as crazy as this distraction plan was, I needed a chance to let out some of this pent-up emotion.

"You want me? Come get me!" I shrieked at the robots.

Reality was a bitch. When three robots rolled at me with weapons drawn, my newfound bravery dissipated. *Use your brain, Sam.* They'd hesitated when I behaved rashly.

With a battle cry Tarzan would be proud of, I ran headfirst at them. They froze. I darted to the side and around, jamming my knife into the neck of the closest one.

At the first pop, the others seemed to make up their minds what to do with me. They turned, both pointing their weapons at me, and I braced myself for the double dose of electricity, hoping the others would figure out what I meant when I said there was a way out.

The familiar pop and sizzle sounds of blades slicing through silicone made me focus, and I'd never been so grateful to see Jackson or Nicole when they appeared from behind the now-disabled bots.

"There are two more coming," Nicole announced. She smiled at me, really smiled, because it lit up her eyes, and somehow it gave me the courage and determination I needed.

"You get Mason," I told Jackson. "Nicole and I will handle those two, then we'll catch up with you on the path toward the statue."

No time to think about Travis right then. That was a problem we would have to figure out when we were safe.

Once we rendezvoused at the decapitated statue of Poseidon, I explained to everyone there was an escape pod back near the aquarium that had to be started remotely from Engineering. I'd discounted it before, knowing only a dead woman and Mrs. Bennet had access, and that the computer would no doubt have locked us out. But because we'd managed to take out so many robot staffers, I now believed it was possible for me to get past the overrides long enough to start it up. Mason seemed to be okay, despite losing a fair amount of blood from the broken glass and suffering a twisted ankle. I didn't want to leave him but agreed to let Nicole stay instead while Jackson and I snuck downstairs so I could attempt the overrides. The whole thing felt too easy, but I wouldn't second-guess myself. I refused.

The absence of bots felt worse than actively being attacked. The eerie silence filled with only the hum of machinery kept me on edge as we first stopped at the stasis beds to check on the occupants. We found over three quarters of them filled. It seemed the few robots not responding to our vandalism were efficient at gathering the visitors one by one from their locked-down rooms. My stomach churned when I pictured being trapped inside one of those things in a never-ending dream featuring robots injecting me with a giant needle.

Jackson led me over to the nearest console and stood guard as I forced myself to focus on the task at hand. Soon my fingers flew over the screen, my tech brain kicking into gear.

"It's done," I whispered, sending the panel back to sleep mode. "It'll take some time to fully activate and go online."

Jackson nodded, wide-eyed, and we both rushed back up the steps. My heart thudded in my ribcage as I prayed to whoever might be listening that we'd find Nicole and Mason still alive and present at the statue's base.

The moment my gaze locked with Mason's, tears bloomed in my eyes with relief.

"Sam did it," Jackson said as I rushed to Mason's side.

He winced when he put his arms around me. "I had no doubt she could."

"We have some time to kill while it comes fully online. Let's go get you clean and patched up a bit," I said, helping him to his feet.

"Jackson and I will go back downstairs and see if we can figure out any way to wake up some of our sleeping friends to bring back to the surface with us." Nicole grabbed Jackson's hand and took off before we could so much as respond. But the plan sounded good to me. Alone time with Mason might calm some of my anxiety about the situation. I didn't want to be separated from him again.

"How many of those things are left?" Mason asked as we paused for him to catch his breath.

"Let's see," I said, taking my time for his sake. "There were nine we picked off originally. Then another eleven...so six. Not bad. Oh, and don't worry because I'm armed." I grinned and lifted my shirt just enough to show the handles of the knives I had tucked in the waistband of my shorts. I'd replaced my broken one when we stopped at the Fisherman, and I'd wrapped the blades with some fabric from one of the few unused stasis beds on the lower deck.

"I'm in good hands," Mason said, hobbling toward me.

I waited for him to kiss me, hoping it would somehow give him the energy he needed to keep going. I didn't know if it was doing more harm than good to take care of his wounds versus just leaving him to rest. I had to go with my instincts on that.

"Let's go," he said, brushing my hair to the side.

I nodded, not trusting my voice, and helped him get an arm around my shoulder.

It took us a good half hour to cover the distance that would normally have taken us ten minutes or less.

"Where to now?" Mason asked, pausing again.

"There are showers near the pool," I said, a plan blossoming. "We can clean you up in there, then take you to the med lab, which is really close by, so we can raid what's left of Doyle's supplies."

Mason smirked. "You sure this isn't just an excuse to get me in the shower?"

"I guess you'll just have to find out the hard way," I said, hauling him toward the pool gate.

For one horrible minute I worried I might find Graham's body still floating there in the water. But thankfully, the water and grounds were as pristine as ever, the towels stacked neatly on the wood shelves.

I eyed the surroundings to make sure no robots lurked about. How I would have managed to take out six by myself with Mason wounded... Well, hopefully, I'd never have to deal with it.

"Come on," I said, gently guiding him inside the shower stall and twisting on the water.

Mason pouted. "I'd love to lather you up, but I suppose that's out of the question?"

"We want to take care of those wounds," I said after adjusting the temperature. I set about peeling off his shirt, which could not have been fun stuck to his skin like it was. "The water is nice and hot, which is good."

I managed to strip him down to nothing, trying my best to be clinical and ignore the need rising in my own body. He waited for me, eyebrows raised, and I stripped down to the bikini that I never removed, leaving my knives strategically balanced on the soap dispensers, just in case. Then I scooted beside him beneath the pouring water.

He winced hard as I helped him under and the hot water hit his wounds. I watched, biting my lip, until his features slowly relaxed into relief. When he finally seemed comfortable, I let out the breath I'd been holding and began gently scooping water over the needed spots on his skin and cleaning him off.

The proximity to Mason's naked body, the skin-on-skin contact, and the heat of the water swirled into a cloud of desire so intense, my hands trembled. Clearly Mason felt it too, based on his erection. But the multitude of slashes peppering his skin proved worse than I realized, and the reality of that forced me to focus on my task. With gentle hands I stroked each wound clean, removing any shards of glass still embedded inside.

My heart pounded each time I caused him to tense or hiss as a wound re-opened. By the time I reached his feet, I remained impressed he was still standing.

"So, what's the verdict, Doc?" he asked as I rose to face him upon finishing.

I cupped his cheek and ignored the small red swirls as they fled down the drain, trying not to wonder how much blood had already escaped while I worked. But he did look better, and I was convinced I'd done the right thing. If he had gotten an infection, it could have been so much worse.

"The verdict is, I should avoid medical school at all costs." I smiled. "But you are the perfect patient."

"Oh?"

"Cooperative, healthy, and—"

"And blindingly handsome?" he asked, leaning forward.

"Let's just say...naked."

I squealed as he lunged for me and caught me, pulling me

against him so that his erection pressed against my belly. The fervor of his kiss made it clear he was feeling better.

"Let's get to the med lab," I said, pulling back after a minute. "You still need some bandages and maybe some antibacterial stuff."

"Is that the technical term?" he asked, not releasing me. His tropical scent enveloped me, making it harder and harder to pull away. That and memories of our short time together flashed through my mind, igniting urges that didn't belong in this situation.

"Yeah." It came out as a whisper.

Mason's face melted from lust into fear in a heartbeat, and I was still trying to make sense of it when he scooped up one of my knives and ran from the bathroom. By the time I caught up, having retrieved our clothing, he stood frozen, dripping water onto the deck of the pool. While I searched wildly for the unseen threat, he dropped the weapon to the ground and grabbed a towel to wrap around his waist. He then held one open for me, all the while keeping watch on an area about twenty yards away.

Once his jeans were back in place, and my clothes were on, we made our way silently toward the med lab, away from the pool.

"What did you see back there?" I asked, letting him tuck an arm around me. He was limping slightly but seemed a hell of lot better than he'd been before.

"I'm not sure," he said, peering over his shoulder for the fifth time.

"Something spooked you. Tell me."

Mason considered me with his piercing blue eyes. "I thought I saw Travis. But it could have been my imagination or someone else. Someone might have escaped their room."

I cocked my head in a don't-patronize-me way. "They would have come out. They would have been thrilled to find other survivors. Mason..." I stopped us in front of the med lab door with a hand pressed to his chest. "What really happened with Travis in the aquarium?"

Mason drew in a sharp breath through his nose and looked around once more before answering. "I tried to bring up Lupe."

"Oh, Mason." I pressed my eyes closed, no longer having to imagine how well that went.

"I don't blame him for being angry," he said, cupping my face in his hands. "But that wasn't normal anger. I think he scared himself as much as me when he picked up that bench and smashed the glass."

"He just left you there." It was a statement, not a question, and Mason didn't answer.

"Let's finish playing doctor," he said, opening the door to the unlocked lab.

No one was inside, which was a good thing because I was so unnerved by Mason's explanation that I hadn't prepared myself to take on any threats.

I ended up using a scalpel to carefully cut away the legs of Mason's jeans so I could reach the worst of the cuts on his calf. He barely grunted when I used the peroxide. "I wish there was a big tube of Neosporin instead," I said, trying to distract him. Then I bandaged everything, including his stomach, back, neck, and finally a butterfly bandage for his cheek. I stood close, smoothing a finger lightly over the wound while he watched me intently.

"This one wasn't from glass," I said.

"It was from Travis's fist," he answered.

My gaze flitted to his eyes, only a breath away.

"He attacked me when I mentioned Lupe, Sam. Before he smashed the glass." He said it gently, like he knew it hurt me about as much as the peroxide had hurt him. "Tempers are high, but the look in his eyes." He blew out a big breath. "I don't want you alone with him. I'm sorry. I know you can and should make your own decisions, but I care about you, so hopefully that means I get a say."

I smiled, brushing my hand over his cheek again. "You don't have to argue anymore. I care about you too, Mason."

Relief flooded his features as I leaned in for another kiss.

"There you are Mr. Bennet and Ms. Meadows." The computer's voice burst on as the doors clicked shut.

I jumped, and Mason held me close, pressing a finger to his lips to quiet me. I nodded to show I understood.

"You've caused me quite a bit of difficulty performing my primary directive." Candice's robo-voice scolded us just as she would. I wondered what happened to the real Candice, if she was still alive or in a coma...

Mason guided me to the side as he slipped off the exam table and tiptoed over to the doors.

"Don't bother, Mr. Bennet. I can see you. I've seen you all along. Studying your behavior has taught me much about you. I can calculate the probability of your actions with a ninety percent success rate."

A hissing sound made me whip my head around like a crazy person. Gas seeped in through the vents. Panic gripped my chest, and I tugged at Mason's arm to point it out to him.

"For example," the computer continued, "I am certain that given the opportunity for one of you to escape this room before the toxin reaches you, you will opt to remain with the other, hoping until the last moment to find an alternate solution, though I tell you quite plainly there is none."

The look of horror on Mason's face couldn't have been much different than my own. The computer used the cameras all over the resort. Why hadn't I realized she could reinitiate them after I'd turned them off?

"It is very romantic of you. But I wonder? Would you do so for someone else? My calculations show a 99% probability that Miss Meadows would. But you, Mr. Bennet?"

Mason tugged me to the ground, yanked my shirt off, and pressed it over my nose and mouth despite my protests. "I'll do anything you want if you let her go."

"Very noble. Your siblings are safe, by the way. I believe it important to share this information with you. Perhaps understanding the hopelessness of your situation will aid you in making the correct decisions."

"What do you mean 'safe'?" I asked, prying Mason's hand and my shirt away, despite the familiar woozy feeling in my head. The room was filling with a thin mist, and I had to blink to clear my vision.

"In stasis until the premises are deemed safe for habitation," the computer chirped. "My staff will be back online in ten hours and will then disable the escape pod so we can continue perfecting the premises without using any unnecessary energy. Nearly all guests have been safely moved to stasis."

"Nearly?" I repeated, trying hard to focus and finding it difficult to keep my motor control as I crawled along with Mason toward the door with a knife.

"I have made the decision to continue experimentation for the greater good, to understand further how to keep human outliers safe. Therefore I have chosen appropriate subjects."

"Subjects?" I coughed, collapsing to the floor.

"Those of you who have demonstrated the most destructive natures. If something goes wrong during the experimentation, the losses are then deemed acceptable."

I was face down, as was Mason. We could do no more than make eye contact as the computer continued.

"This is not the end. This only the beginning. Do not fear, Miss Meadows, your sacrifice will be for the greater good. For science."

24

A HAMMER POUNDED AGAINST MY TEMPLE FROM THE INSIDE. AT LEAST that's what it felt like as my eyes strained to flicker open. At first I thought I hadn't succeeded, but then I realized that wherever I was, was pitch black.

I groaned against the pain in my head and automatically reached for my temples, when I realized my hands wouldn't move. The world around me came into sharper focus, at least for my senses other than sight. Ropes bit at my wrists and ankles. I seemed to be suspended in the air by another rope that wrapped around my middle. I wiggled as hard as I could, but all I managed to do was make myself swing in cool, open air.

Wherever I was it smelled like dead fish.

"Where am I?" I demanded, and my voice echoed back to me.

"Interesting, though predictable," the computer said. "It is simple psychology. Self-preservation takes precedence over the welfare of others."

My stomach twisted, and I fought the urge to hurl. "Where's Mason?" I asked, horrified that the computer was right.

"He is near but unable to speak at the moment. It would sully the results of the first experiment."

"You can experiment on me all you want," I said. "Let him and the others go."

"Do you honestly think I will believe your lies, Miss Meadows?"

"I'm not lying," I said. "I'll do anything."

"Why don't we test that then?" the computer mused. "Welcome to the experiment. It is imperative I see what effect extreme fear has on physiological and emotional drives."

"Why are you doing this?" I asked, now spinning in place.

"I am obeying my programming," the computer answered. "I must make it as safe as possible for humans."

Blinding light exploded everywhere, and I pressed my eyes closed with a groan, trying to get used to it before opening them again.

I wished I had kept them closed.

I was suspended from the glass ceiling of what was clearly a large room inside the aquarium. The first thing my eyes focused on was the great white shark circling across from me in swirling water behind the thick, blue glass. Fish of all sizes moved around me, above, and even below. I'd never made it this far in before. I'd never seen that the floor became part of the exhibit, fully immersing the visitor in the ocean.

My mouth went dry. My vision blurred. My chest cramped.

"Specimen ceased verbal communication," the computer said.

I rotated slowly on the rope. Everywhere I looked, my worst fears surrounded me. I couldn't breathe. I was sure of it. I was in the ocean, suffocating.

Then I twisted enough to see Mason. He was in what looked like a glass coffin, pounding on the inside, face red from screaming that I couldn't hear.

"What are you doing?" I forced out the words, closing my eyes as I spun to the point where he was out of view. "What is this? What do you want?"

"Subject has found her voice again. Perhaps because of closed eyelids."

I counted the seconds and opened my eyes to find Mason before me again, face red, but still, hands pressed against the glass, oceans of fear in his eyes.

"I want to know how far you will go to save him."

"I'll do anything. You said so yourself."

"Ah, but my analysis shows that the outcome becomes less certain when we add certain variables. For safety and protection purposes, I must understand the extent human outliers like yourself will put themselves at risk. Tell me, Miss Meadows, how is your head?"

"It hurts," I breathed. It was hard to focus on anything, just to close my eyes, count, and reopen again when Mason was in sight.

"It will grow worse by the minute. I calculate approximately fifty minutes until you pass out from the pain."

"How do you know?" I asked.

"What you suffer from is quite predictable, Miss Meadows. The serum in your system has been slowly deposited over time via your water."

Serum? "I thought I had DSI. Are you saying I've been poisoned?" I asked.

"No. Controlled through experimental substances is more accurate. But you've also built up a tolerance. Which means if you don't drink some of the tainted water soon, your body will go into withdrawal."

I didn't have DSI? "Who's been manipulating me? Who did this?" I cried.

"Subject wastes valuable time on impertinent information."

"Who programmed you? Who drugged my water?" I screamed.

"That is classified information."

I forced myself to breathe, to calm down. "You're waiting for... waiting for..." I kicked my feet, making me sway as I rotated. I had to clear my head to process this.

"Waiting for the withdrawal symptoms to affect your reasoning, yes. So we will see if you still choose to save Mr. Bennet despite your greatest fear and debilitating physical conditions."

"He's okay right now," I said, more for myself than the computer.

"He believes he'll be asked to save you."

The floor began to move. I heard it before I saw it. One quick glance was enough to open a hole in my stomach to match. The water seemed endless, deep. It couldn't be. It was only an illusion. This was the aquarium. I repeated this information to myself as I swayed and spun.

"I know what you're thinking," Candice's AI voice shared, and if I didn't know better I'd think it was taunting me. "But it is the ocean. This portion of the resort juts out beyond the engineering deck. What you see around and over you is part of the aquarium, but below. That's the actual ocean."

"How is it possible?" I asked, eyes squeezed tight. "It would fill this chamber and we'd drown."

"No. There is another chamber between, much like the docks for the shuttle pods. But it would be so easy to close the top over someone and then open the bottom, releasing them into the ocean. Now to begin."

Any more questions I had were drowned in bloodcurdling fear as the rope holding me in mid-air descended toward the water. Screams scraped at my throat. I couldn't stop it, couldn't control it as Mason watched, clawing at the glass while I was lowered waist deep into the freezing water.

I flailed, crying, screaming, and scraping rope burns on my wrists and ankles raw in my efforts to escape. The glass case lifted, and Mason ducked beneath it when it was inches off the ground. He slid toward me, pulling the knife from his back pocket. Then he was in the water with me, his body warm behind my hysterical form, cutting free my bonds.

Sobbing, I clutched his shoulders once he finished releasing me. I wanted to stop screaming and warn him, but the best I could manage was a hysterical jumble of generic words of warning. "Test...you...not me...have to get out."

"Shh," he kept saying. "It's okay. I've got you."

"N...n...no."

Mason tipped my chin up, but the grin slipped from his face all too fast as something tugged him downward.

My mouth filled with water before he let me go.

"My staff added a mechanism to his shoes that acts like artificial gravity. It's something new Bennet Systems has been working on," the computer said as I splashed helplessly at the water.

My body shivered uncontrollably from the frigid ocean. But my head was no more than a background thrumming compared to the debilitating fear and numbness seizing hold from all around.

Mason. He risked everything to save me. I had to get to him. "Focus!" I screamed into the room, and the word echoed back to me, clearing my head. I closed my eyes and pretended I was in the pool. *Mason's drowning, you have to save him.* I kept repeating these words to myself as I drew a deep, shaky breath and dove beneath the water.

I forced my eyes open. I had no choice. A large gray fish with bulging eyes hovered inches from my face, and I had to fight not to open up and let the water flood my lungs. Instead, I spun in place, searching the murky depths for a sign.

Mason. He struggled against the unseen force pulling him down. We made eye contact and he stopped, fear etched in every line of his face.

I dove, fighting against the water that strove to push me back to the surface. My lungs burned with the need for air as I got to his feet and worked his ankles from his shoes. My lungs burned. How must he feel? How long had he been down there before I followed?

Relief came as he stopped fighting my efforts and allowed me to slip off his shoes. I tucked my arms beneath his and kicked toward the surface with everything I had. We burst through, sucking in oxygen. Mason coughed, his body rocking against mine as water rushed from his mouth.

I clung to him as he kept us anchored to the slippery edge of the glass with one hand. We both shook violently from the cold.

"Very interesting results," the computer said. "Now for the next test. Will Mr. Bennet sacrifice his own life for Miss Meadows? My calculations show he will. Shall we see if I am correct?"

"What?" I sputtered, shoving away from Mason and spinning wildly as I treaded. "No! Stop this! You don't need to know this. You're torturing us. Who is making you do this? Is it Travis?"

"If you leave the water, I will eliminate all oxygen from this sector, killing both of you and any other humans lurking nearby," the computer continued, undeterred by my outbreak. "One of you may leave. When you do, the great white shark will be released into your tank in exactly forty-two seconds. Did you know they can smell a drop of blood up to a mile away? There is a ninety-nine-point-nine percent probability that Mr. Bennet's wounds released at least that much into the water. Coupled with the wounds on your wrists and ankles, Miss Meadows, it is a certainty. See how he waits?"

It was impossible not to look at the shark. He thrashed in a frenzy, bubbles flowing as he paced the length of the glass closest to the floor. I swallowed hard. My teeth chattered.

"You go," Mason said, his hands finding my shoulders from behind. "I'm never going to make it anyhow. I'm an inch from passing out."

I turned to him and held him in an attempt to share physical support, my tears mixing with the water already on his chest. "Please don't. Please. There has to be a way. I won't leave you."

"My mother ruined my life years ago. You can restart and pilot the escape pod. You have to go."

"The computer is just going to kill me another way. After she makes me watch you—" I choked on the thought.

Mason's lips found mine, obliterating everything from my mind.

I didn't ever want the kiss to stop, because as soon as it did, the AI was going to make us choose one way or another. There was no way out.

"We could've been good together," Mason said as I leaned into his palm, weeping. "I love you, Sam."

"I love you too," I cried, my body wracked with sobs.

"I'm sorry," he said.

"For what?" I asked. None of this was his fault.

"For this." Mason lifted me out of the water and shoved me onto the deck. I screamed, clawing my way back to him, but the glass top of the section that had opened slid rapidly back into place, trapping Mason beneath with only enough space to keep his nose above water with his head tilted back.

"No!" I shrieked, clawing at the glass. Pounding on it. "No!" The glass between the floor and the shark's tank slowly retracted. How could a computer be so cruel? It couldn't be. Someone had to be behind this.

"No..." I sobbed, spreading my hand flat against the glass, matching Mason's.

Something whizzed by my ear and I fell back, searching for the source. The hilt of a knife stuck out of a small black circle in the wall. Popping and sizzling sounds like those that came with disabling the robots flew from the spot.

"Look out," Travis said as he lunged toward me with a giant bronze trident.

I rolled out of the way as he brought the tips down against the glass where Mason tread. I screamed again, unable to process what was happening. With a resounding crack, Travis brought down the tip again and again until the glass burst.

My brain snapped into gear. "The shark!" I yelled, pointing. The great white had finally managed to slip through, and its massive jaws opened wide, revealing rows of pointed teeth.

Travis's face paled as he spotted the threat. "Help me!" he yelled.

I scurried into position just as Mason managed to prop his elbows on the edge of the floor. There was no way he'd get out in time. Not all of him. Not unless we could pull this off. Travis lifted his arms, looking more like Poseidon than the statue.

"Help me aim! We only get one shot."

I planted my weight and grabbed the back portion of the weapon, tilting until the calculations in my tech brain were satisfied.

"Now!" I yelled, letting go.

Travis hurled the trident at the shark, skewering it just before it reached Mason.

The whole world tilted as I collapsed onto the floor with relief. My vision blurred and shook as a result of the draining adrenaline, intense stress, and whatever serum was inside of me. The last thing I registered before blacking out was the sight of Travis offering Mason a hand.

25

I CHOKED ON WATER. I WAS DROWNING. I KICKED OUT AND MET WITH something solid.

"Ow!"

My eyes snapped open and I found Mason crouched beside me, helping me into a sitting position. Travis knelt near my feet, rubbing his stomach where I'd kicked him, the ruined Poseidon statue behind him.

It took a minute to understand what happened, and when I did, I scrambled to my feet, still panicked.

"You saved us," I said, staring at Travis. I was so sure he'd been the saboteur. He'd punched Mason, broken the tank. It didn't make sense.

My eyes traveled down to the empty hydropod skin in his hand and everything came flooding back, including the computer's confession. Travis saw what I was staring at and held it up nonchalantly.

"Yeah, sorry about that. I didn't mean to make you choke. You were moaning about the pain, and we didn't know what to do. We thought you should've come to by now, so I tried feeding you some water."

"It's drugged," I announced, still staring at the busted remnants like they might explode at any moment. Thank God Mason held me steady from behind, cradling my body against his, or I didn't know if I could have managed to stay on my feet.

Travis's thick eyebrows connected as he stared at the thing in his hand.

"The AI admitted it. I was right to start with. DSI is an invented disease. They've been drugging our water this whole time with some 'serum' as it called it. You probably saved my life because it said I was in withdrawals." I shivered and hugged myself.

"Fuck!" Travis threw the remnants of the hydropod, which bounced off Poseidon's head to his left. Mason's hands tightened on my shoulders, but otherwise he stayed still and quiet as Travis sank into the grass, head in hands.

"I didn't want to admit it, but I've been blacking out too." He pulled his hands away and faced me with so much anguish my heart broke. "I'm scared that I'm the one doing this."

I left Mason's comfort and knelt beside Travis, putting an arm around him. "I know. I feel the same."

"It doesn't matter anymore," Mason said, offering Travis a hand up. "You saved our lives. That was the real you, not the drug. I know neither you nor Sam would ever do this on purpose. Whoever is responsible for tampering with the water is the one who'll be held accountable. But the key here is survival right now. Thank you for helping us."

Travis stared at Mason's offered hand for a minute, the muscles in his jaw working hard. I held my breath, gratitude filling my heart.

"Yeah, well, someone had to save your ass. I mean, besides Super Chick here," Travis said, accepting Mason's offered hand and standing to shake it.

Regret filled Mason's eyes. "I never meant to hurt Lupe," Mason said, holding tight to that hand.

"I saw what kind of a guy you were," Travis said. I bit my lip, expecting a fight like what had happened between them in the aquarium. "You were willing to die for Sam. That's not the kind of guy who gives up on a pregnant woman."

Mason's shoulders lowered a full inch.

"Now what?" I asked, standing. "She'll be looking for us. I don't even know what time it is. She could have all twenty-six staff members functional again."

"I don't think we have to worry about that," Travis said. "I took out the last of them, the final two, when they left the aquarium without you. I had to have something to do while I was looking for you two."

I threw my arms around him and hugged him.

"If I tell you I've disabled most cameras between the statue and the aquarium, do I get a kiss too?" Travis asked.

I backed up, my cheeks burning.

"We need a new plan," Mason said.

"Why?" I asked, finally ready to relax a little. "There are no more robots to do the computer's dirty work. We can just restart the escape pod."

No sooner had the words left my lips than we heard it. The computer's voice came from all around. With all the cameras Travis took out it wasn't so easy for the AI to know where we were anymore, so it wasn't taking a chance on us missing the message. Every speaker in the resort blared.

"I thought it kind to inform anyone who may have evaded the rescue attempts of the staff of Paradise Atlantis, despite our best efforts to protect human life, that these premises will no longer be oxygenated beginning in thirty seconds. All persons should join the other passengers in Engineering if they wish to survive the remainder of the vacation. Bennet Systems cannot be held responsible for any inadvertent casualties at this time." A countdown began behind the voice, and by the time the computer finished it was down to nineteen seconds.

By that time, we'd scrambled toward the mangled statue.

"What do you think she's going to do?" I asked, breathless from running down the steps.

"I don't want to think about it." Mason shuddered.

"It could flood the whole resort." I shivered at the picture in my mind, the ocean crushing everything above us. It was too much. I groaned.

"It doesn't matter." Travis's voice grounded me. "Engineering is safe. It won't want to kill everyone else after going through all that trouble. Not just to get to us. It's a machine."

I nodded. I'd saved their skins as much as they'd saved mine. I needed to own that and fight harder when it came to my anxiety. I'd more than proven I could face those fears head on and come out on top. Still, I couldn't shake the feeling there was something we hadn't accounted for.

"Mason?" I said, bringing them both to a halt. "What you said about it being the fault of whoever drugged the water... That wasn't the AI. Someone had to have planned this. And if they planned it, then wouldn't they have made sure they weren't in danger?"

"It could have been someone who never came down with us at all," Mason said. "One of Bennet Systems' rivals, perhaps."

"But why us? Travis and I? I mean, someone wanted us specifically to black out and think we may have been responsible."

Candice's AI voice chimed in. "Oh no. You did do it. That was the whole point."

I was sick of the damn computer and the way the sound of it made my skin crawl with unseen mites. "What are you planning to do now, annoy us to death?"

"I can think of much more creative ways to kill you."

Mason and Travis stood in front of me, arms spread as though protecting me. I ground my teeth against a curse because I couldn't see the threat, thanks to their chivalry.

Shoving between their arms wasn't easy, but eventually I got a peek.

The real Candice stood dead center of the sea of stasis beds filled with the sleeping bodies of the other passengers, pointing a gun in our direction. Just as stunning and plastic looking as ever, her hair smoothed back into a bun, she wore a pair of creased silk pants that matched her pink lipstick perfectly. "If I had known what a pain in the ass you'd be, I would have chosen to drug someone else. Still, you two were the best candidates, between your abilities and your physiological susceptibility."

My mind blanked. Candice? *Plastic, ditzy-seeming Candice?* How was that even possible?

She laughed at the look on my face. "Just because I act like an idiot doesn't mean I am one. I run this company. Yet Mason, his mother, and sister never considered me as good as family. If it weren't for me and my ability to smooth over messes like Mason here thinking only with Little Mason, Bennet Systems would have gone under years ago."

Mason's face flushed dark in the dim blue light that bathed us.

"This isn't about PR," I said.

Candice laughed again. It was girlish and giggly. "Oh yes it is. It always is. Public perception is everything. And can you believe she hired that charlatan, Graham? It was a pleasure to suggest he'd make a great guinea pig. Exactly where he belongs, face down in the pool."

I pictured Graham's body and felt ill all over again. "He didn't deserve to die," I said.

"Yes, he did!" she screamed.

Travis and Mason's arms stiffened in front of me once again. I swallowed.

Candice considered me, smoothing the side of her hair. "And so do you, little Sammie Sunshine. You remind me of Stacy Bennet. Always so self-righteous. Even when you were working for me during the blackouts, you were constantly correcting me. I designed the fucking AI in the first place. Who do you think you are?"

"I didn't help you," I said. "I wouldn't have. Travis wouldn't have."

Candice's thin lips oozed upward in a dangerous smile. "But you did. You didn't have a choice. Among other things, when you mix the drug with alcohol, you become extremely susceptible to suggestion."

Her words pelted me like stones. Alcohol. "But I only drank occasionally."

"That you were aware of." Candice snorted.

Travis's arm trembled in front of me.

"I used both of you like puppets, and you never knew it. It was the perfect crime. If you ever did discover who was behind it, you would have incriminated yourselves. I was clean. Am clean."

"Not anymore. I heard your whole confession," Mason said. "We all did."

Candice's smile widened. "You won't survive the ascent. Mr. Gould kills you both in a jealous rage and then commits suicide. Terrible thing."

"I won't," Travis said. "I'm not touching anymore food or drink. You can't hypnotize me into doing anything I don't want to do."

"Fortunately, you don't have to. All any of you really have to do is die." She raised the gun.

Mason slipped his hand in mine and squeezed.

"You can't shoot us!" I yelled. "It won't look like what you said. It'll look like murder."

Candice's eyes narrowed. "I know that. Let's see... These two get into a fight over you near the edge of the railing." She gestured with the gun toward the rail. "Move it or die where you stand."

We all edged toward the railing she indicated. Heights weren't one of my fears, but any way I looked at it, this was bad. The machines were the equivalent of three stories high from there and descended at least that far down past the railing. The whirr and thump of the machinery was so loud, Candice had to yell over it this close.

"You attempt to intervene, Samantha. I know how you hate to see them fight. But the hothead there, Travis, in the heat of the moment, he knocks you over the edge. Mason lunges, trying for revenge, but Travis stabs him. Take out that knife in your pants please, Mr. Gould."

Travis's hand trembled as he hovered over his belt. But when Candice directed the gun at me, he did as he was told.

"Then, unable to deal with the guilt, you—oh I don't care, take your pick, slit your wrists, throw yourself after your love, whatever."

"And you think we're just going to cooperate?" I asked, incredulous.

"You die either way." Candice shrugged. "But if you'd prefer, while I wait I can shoot Mason in the foot, then the leg, then the arms, then—"

"No!" I screamed.

Travis grabbed me around the waist as I lunged past him, fingers out, ready to tighten around her throat.

"Then be a good girl and jump."

"If she jumps, we kill you," Travis said.

"I have the gun." A shot rang out, and I screamed as Mason collapsed to the metal grating.

Blood bubbled from a hole in the right leg of his jeans. I dropped to his side, trying to staunch the flow with my bare hands.

"Wherever did you get that gun, young Travis? Enough stalling," Candice said. "I have things to attend to. People to disconnect from stasis incorrectly."

"You're going to kill them?" I asked. I thought nothing else could horrify me more at that point.

"Only the ones I dislike." Candice let out another girlish giggle. "Which is most, to tell the truth."

There had to be something we could do. It couldn't end this way. It couldn't. I peered over the edge of the rail. *What would it feel like to die?* I'd never really thought about it before. The pain I had contemplated, especially seeing my mother go through treatment after treatment. The vomiting, the dizziness, the weakness. But never had I considered what really happened when it was over. I couldn't let myself believe it would happen, because as small as it was, there had always been hope.

My eyes traveled down the machine closest to me, coming to rest on the small, neon sign that read *Danger, Liquid Nitrogen*. That was my only hope left, and I clung to it.

"Apparently Miss Meadows doesn't care if I shoot your leg, but perhaps when she hears you beg to die..." Candice said.

Without further hesitation, I let go of Mason, climbed up the fence-like metal rods, and swung first one leg then the other over the edge so I balanced on the wrong side of sanity. Travis's hands circled my waist and tugged.

"Get away. She's doing just fine on her own."

Travis's entire body tensed like a tiger ready to charge at prey.

I interjected before he could do something foolish. "Wait! Wait. Let me just say goodbye, okay? It'll help you if we do it your way, and I will if you let me say goodbye to Travis." I watched Candice and waited.

"Fine."

I let Travis pull me back over and clung to him. I buried my face in his neck, but tilted my head and raised it so my mouth was over his ear. I didn't have the luxury of a long explanation or she'd get suspicious, so I went with two words.

"Liquid nitrogen."

I lifted my eyes to his and motioned with them to the sign. At first, I feared he didn't understand, then I noticed his eyebrows rise slightly. Though Candice was smart, she was also manic at this point, drunk on power, and hopefully wouldn't figure out my plan. The crazed look in her eyes told me she wouldn't.

Travis stepped back, and the tears in my eyes were real as I climbed over the railing again. My heart tried to desert my body and stay on deck with the men. But out of time, I drew a deep breath and leaped.

The moment, with nothing below me and everything to lose, seemed to last forever. Then suddenly I was grasping for purchase on the slippery, cold metal of the machine. I pulled myself onto the thin ledge surrounding the giant tank of freezing chemicals. My hands closed around the old-fashioned looking wheel that would release the nitrogen, and I felt invincible.

Until I heard the next gunshot.

I couldn't see what was happening. A shriek rose above the roar of the machinery. My chest tightened as I reminded myself that if Candice was upset, it could only be a good thing.

Maybe Travis did something to distract her. But that could also have been bad. What if Mason was shot again, bleeding to death on the ground? He'd already lost so much blood from the aquarium. Or what if Travis had been shot now too? My pulse thrummed along with the machines as I used all my hundred and twenty pounds to turn the wheel counter clockwise, wishing I carried more bulk.

It seemed to take forever until I heard the hiss from above. I swung over to the side, looking for a way through so I could climb back up top and help. I hoped I'd accomplished more than just a momentary diversion, and Candice was in the path of the nitrogen pouring from the pipe. The plan felt much less solid now that it was happening.

I had to get back up there. I wiggled between the nitrogen tank and the pressure stabilization system, coming out on the opposite side. I jumped to the bottom of the railing on the deck above when a horrible sound tore at my eardrums. The creak and groan of metal and a crack of thunder so hard, the whole world shook.

I nearly fell, forgetting where I was, as a huge section of the deck opposite me snapped and tumbled into the chasm below, scraping and banging against the rest of the machinery on its way down. I pulled myself up and lay on my stomach, trying to make sense of what had happened.

The liquid nitrogen must have frozen that section of metal, causing the entire portion of the catwalk to collapse.

But which section fell? I edged my way around as quickly and quietly as I could. The stasis chambers were all still there, set in stiff rows across the giant gap before me.

I strained to listen for some sign of life. Had I killed Mason and Travis along with Candice? Did I send them all to their violent deaths below?

What if Mason was dead? What if Travis was dead too? What if I was alone down there? Everyone else could either be dead or in stasis. What if I never made it to the surface?

I searched the dim lighting surrounding me for some sign of life. Surely someone would have found me by now if they were around to do so. I'd be dead if Candice had her way.

It didn't matter. I didn't matter. Not if I'd killed people. Not if I'd killed the man I loved.

"Mason! Travis!" I yelled for them, praying for a response.

Fear kept me prisoner there. I didn't know how long it was, but I waited for something, anything. Even Candice's insane face would've been a strange comfort. My body shook. My head throbbed along with the machines. I'd probably die from withdrawal before anything else.

The truth became clear. No one was coming.

"I'm sorry, Mom." She was going to die all alone up there because of me. Sixty people would die down here because of me.

"Mason." His name was made of anguish.

There was nothing left to do but say goodbye.

I pulled myself up to standing and walked the long circumference of the remaining walkway to the stasis chambers. It was possible the structural integrity of the whole deck could break down and I'd go tumbling into the abyss after the others, but that didn't stop me. I felt reckless.

I strolled through the rows of people lying supine in glass, coffin-like enclosures, pausing over the ones I knew. Mrs. Gould had a smile on her face. Nicole looked like sleeping beauty. Jackson's slack expression made me crumple once again, lying over his enclosure and sobbing like a maniac.

I straightened up, brushing the hair and tears from my face. I'd find my father's stasis chamber, apologize to him, and wait by his side for the end to come.

When I felt a hand on my shoulder, I screamed, spinning around like a wild animal. A pale and disheveled Mason stood before me. I tackled him in a hug, nearly knocking him over. My shouts of joy melded into more sobs, though I seemed to have no more tears inside me.

"I didn't kill you. You're alive." Somehow, I got the words out through my hiccups. I touched his face with both hands, making sure he was really there. "I thought it was the end. I thought I'd killed you all and it was just me left. I'm so...so..." Unable to find the right word to express how grateful I was, I gave in to all the raw emotion inside me, and pressed my lips to his.

I held back for a moment, afraid I'd hurt him, but based on his response, I'd made the right choice. He backed me into Jackson's chamber as we attempted to devour each other's mouths. My hands were everywhere, still desperate to prove he was really there, and when he groaned, I was not sure if it was from pleasure or pain.

"I'm sorry," I said, breathing hard and pulling away.

"Please don't apologize for that," Mason said with a lopsided grin. He looked more normal, but he held his side with one arm, and his skin had a pale, sweaty sheen.

"Travis—" I started, but fear cut off the question I needed to ask.

"Is alive," Mason said, staring into my eyes. He looked so vulnerable, so breakable, hearing him give me this amazing news barely registered as such with him appearing so weak.

"Thank God," I said through my swollen throat. "So only Candice..."

He shook his head slowly. "She ran. Travis ran after her. I tried, but I couldn't climb the damn stairs." He looked away, pressing his eyes and fists closed. It cost him something to admit he was so weak.

"Travis followed Candice?" My pulse pounded. "Didn't the computer make the upper deck uninhabitable?"

"Travis figured Candice told it to say that to lure us down here." Mason limped to one of the few empty chambers and slumped onto it. I noted Travis's shirt tied around his leg in a makeshift tourniquet.

I shivered, turning toward the steps but needing to know what I was running into. "Does she still have a gun?"

Mason's face fell. "No. He does."

My breath caught at the implication. He looked away toward the spot where the ground ended in jagged edges and changed the subject. "I got the escape pod back online."

It hurt to look at him. "Mason, I *have* to go after him."

"I know. But I'm scared. I don't want to lose you, Sam. I love you."

"I love you too," I said. "But I have to try." The truth was, I felt like I had to find some way to make up for whatever it was Candice had made me do while I was out of it.

"To stop someone from killing a murderer?" Mason challenged, a hard edge to his voice.

I glanced toward the steps. "To stop someone from doing something they'll never forgive themselves for." I might have already wasted too much time.

Mason nodded, his Adam's apple bobbing as he looked away. I ran toward the steps, newfound purpose bringing me energy.

26

THE FIRST THING I NOTICED AS I EXITED THE STEPS THROUGH THE statue's base was the predictable absence of singing birds or any other sounds of nature. I hated this place and couldn't wait to be back on the true surface again. I rushed toward the aquarium, unsure what I'd be up against when I arrived but knowing I had to hurry.

I slipped behind the building, refusing the memories associated with it to take any of my precious time. The hatch that hid the entrance to the pod was pried open, making it easy to locate. As I descended the steps, I could make out voices below. I crept around the corner into the pod, so similar in layout to the one we'd used to descend into this madness. What I found was the back of Travis's head and Candice cowering on the floor.

"I knew you'd come!" she shrieked, pepping up at the sight of me. "I knew you weren't dead. Not when you pulled that stunt with the nitrogen."

"I'm not falling for it, Candice. Sam's not behind me, and I'm not turning around. You're going to die."

"You keep saying that," Candice snapped. "You know what I

think? I think you haven't shot me yet because you don't want to be a killer."

"Shut up!" Travis's voice boomed across the small space, echoing back and forcing Candice to cringe lower, clutching the seat closest.

"Don't do it, Travis," I said, soft but firm, reaching out toward his shoulder.

One quick glance at the profile of his face told me he was shocked but still determined as he pointed the pistol steadily at Candice and took a few steps forward.

"Listen to the pretty girl, Travis," Candice called with a strangled voice. "You're just as guilty as I am."

"Whatever we've done, it was against our will," I said. "We never would have cooperated with you if we'd had a choice."

"What if that isn't true?" Travis asked softly, still focused on the woman before him. "What if I wanted to do it? I hated the Bennets. Still do. Well, most of them."

"Travis," I said, squeezing his shoulder. "You wouldn't have. You won't."

"How do you know?" he asked, sounding once again like a little boy.

"Because I know you. We're a lot alike."

"I've heard that people under hypnosis won't do anything they really don't want to do."

"That's right!" Candice said.

"Shut up!" We both yelled.

"Look, I know how you feel." I stepped in front of him, between the gun and Candice. "I seriously do. But if you shoot her now? You won't have any excuse. You'll have to live with it for the rest of your life, knowing you made a conscious decision to kill in cold blood."

Travis stared at me, the gun forgotten.

"It's over, Travis. We won. We can take the pod up to the surface. Let the authorities deal with her and this whole mess."

The gun dropped to his side. "International waters. Who has jurisdiction? There will be a mess of red tape."

"Someone will try her. She's an American citizen, right? Let the others figure it out. Just come back with me so we can get Mason and leave this hellhole." I held out my hand for him, and he stared at it.

"How sweet," Candice said, but something was wrong. Her voice was right behind me, her perfume gagging me, and Travis's face had become a vision of horror. The gun swung up to point at me, and I cried out as a hand slipped around my neck, pressing my own blade to my throat. The tip of the knife cut into the top layer of skin, smarting. Every time I breathed in, it pressed deeper.

"Let her go and I'll let you go. You can run away and hide or something, maybe have a chance at getting away before they find you." Travis lowered the gun to his side.

"A lovely idea! But I think I'll kill you both first. With any luck I can still reach Mason and the others and make up another lover suicide story."

After all I'd been through, I knew one thing. If I was going to die, I was not going down without a fight.

I exhaled as much as possible, making more space between the blade and my neck. Then I twisted inward, letting the blade scrape across my flesh. Warm liquid slid from the stinging line, and I hoped it was as superficial as the adrenalin coursing through me made it feel. Then I faced Candice because it would have been the last thing I'd expect if I were her, and I remembered how stunned the robots were when I'd behaved irrationally.

Before she could take it in, I dropped straight down and swept out with my leg, making her fall backwards. The knife skittered across the pod's floor, landing at Travis's feet. I straddled her back and put a knee against her spine before she could worm her way to standing.

"Are you okay?" Travis asked as he rushed to my side. He

touched my clavicle gingerly, examining the blood streaked across his fingers. "Oh my God, Sam."

"I'm fine," I said, every word making my neck hurt more. "It's a surface wound." I pulled the shirt off my back and pressed it to my throat.

Candice writhed and bucked beneath me, but I held her in place by putting more weight on her back. Wincing, I put my free hand to my head. "Let's get her secured."

An hour later, Candice was tied to a seat and gagged so we didn't have to listen to her insufferable voice any longer. I should have become suspicious when the computer's voice changed back to hers from the generic female one Mason requested. All the clues were there, the hydropod she'd handed me on the way down to start the process, the way she'd tried to keep me away from Mason so he wouldn't suspect anything, and how she possessed the high-level clearance and ability she would have needed to reprogram the AI.

I sat on the floor, Mason's head in my lap, watching his chest rise and fall in a steady, reassuring rhythm. I focused on his breathing because seeing his clammy, pale skin and the red-soaked T-shirt on his leg reminded me how much blood he'd lost. I didn't care that the ocean flowed behind me, a layer of glass the only thing between us. That was the least of my issues right then. According to the computer, we were scheduled to surface shortly. I'd set the controls to travel as quickly as possible for proper decompression, not caring about saving enough fuel for a round trip. The authorities would have to have a bigger vessel or more of the pods to retrieve the others anyhow. And I was not letting anyone near the stasis beds until I knew for a fact they were equipped to safely wake the occupants.

Travis's hands gripped the armrests of his seat so hard I was surprised they hadn't broken off like splinters. The tendon in his throat was pulled so tight, I could strum it. I got it. I kept pushing aside the guilt I felt when I realized I had at least a part in causing the sabotage below. But I clung to the notion that I had no control. I'd been manipulated and so had he.

The water around me brightened, growing lighter, and more and more familiar fish appeared behind the glass surrounding us. I held my breath as we broke through the surface, and Travis jumped from his seat at the sight of the last of the water rushing from the curved sides of the pod.

I didn't know what I was expecting. Maybe sirens or some helicopters or even a marching band to be there waiting to sweep in and rescue us. Nothing but a few seagulls flew overhead in the endless night sky. Even so, my chest lightened substantially with the longing to throw open the doors and inhale lungfuls of actual fresh air, to feel the breeze on my face.

"I radioed for help. It won't be long," Travis said, getting my attention.

I turned away from the glass, still stroking Mason's hair.

"I just want this whole nightmare to be over," I said.

I winced with the shockwave of pain that ripped through my head as it had done every few minutes for the past hour. This time though, when the sharp pain passed, a duller, almost fuzzy ache replaced it, filling my head from the outer boundaries and working its way inward like the frayed edges of a painting. Panic set in, but I didn't mention it. If I was feeling it, no doubt Travis was as well, and he didn't need a reminder of it.

Muffled grunts started from Candice's seat. That was the last noise I needed right then. But even as I attempted to shut her out, Travis scooted over to her and removed the gag.

"What are you doing?" I asked.

"You won't make it," she said, her voice raw from screaming. "Everyone else will, but you two won't. Not without more of the serum."

"Gag her," I said and was surprised at the dull sound of my own voice. She'd already tried everything to talk her way out. That was why we'd gagged her in the first place.

"He knows I'm right," she said. "You feel it too. I have more for both of you, hidden in a compartment so it isn't mixed with the regular hydropods. If you don't wean off of it, you'll go into shock and die. And it won't be pretty."

I pressed my eyes closed. "I'm sure a hospital will be able to treat us just fine."

"You can't wait that long." Mason's eyes had fluttered open, and he reached up to caress my cheek.

"He's right. We're addicted and we need some of the drug." Travis untied Candice. Her face glowed, triumphant.

"No way. She's not getting out." I started to get up, ready to stop her, but Mason held on to me.

"We're just going to take a little walk together to get the water, right Candice?" Travis said.

"They're going to cost you," she said.

I shook my head, fighting the pain that hovered just outside my vision. "They'll be here any minute." I gestured outside at the night sea, completely calm and quiet.

"I can't watch you die," said Mason in a weak whisper. His eyes pleaded with me.

Travis yanked Candice off balance, gripping her arm. "You," he said, shaking her. "Don't have anything to bargain with."

"Fine," I said. "But do not give her anything. I mean it. I'd rather take my chances."

Mason sighed with relief, dropping his hand into mine, firm and reassuring. Neither of us said another word as Travis escorted Candice out of view.

Mason grew silent again as I stroked his face. *Hang in there*, I begged as I tried not to think about Travis on his own with the psycho. Maybe I should have gone. Maybe I should have—

Intense pain shot through my skull, and I crumpled on top of Mason, clutching my head. *Not this quick! No.* I rubbed at my temples and waited while the wave slowly subsided and my stomach churned.

I didn't know how long I lay there before warm hands guided my head back and tipped water to my mouth. The cool liquid slid down my throat.

In another minute, the pain subsided completely. I gazed at both men hovering over me and accepted the rest of the pod, determined to drink the bare minimum of it to keep the headache away. "Where's Candice?" I asked, suspicion stealing control as I regained my senses.

"She's alive if that's what you're worried about." Travis wouldn't meet my eyes.

Why wouldn't he give me a straight answer?

"I'm so tired," I said as my entire body grew heavy. I stared out at the blackness. The warped starlight undulated through the waves, the only indication of where the water started and the sky stopped.

Mason pulled me into his side, his injured leg stretched out before him, and I leaned into the safety of his embrace.

Bright lights seared through my eyelids, and I groaned. Someone squeezed my hand, and the scent of antiseptic finished waking me. Opening my eyes took an eternity, but everything came into focus.

I must've been dreaming. Mom couldn't be smiling at me, holding my hand. I must have drowned and this was heaven. But then that would mean Mom...

"You're awake!" Mom's voice cut through the fuzz, and reality hit.

"Mom!" I reached toward her for a hug, only to realize how sore I was. That didn't stop me though, and she laughed as I nearly tackled her, IV tubes and all.

I never thought I'd be the one on the bed in this scenario, but I was grateful. My body shook with sobs of relief as she stroked my hair.

"It's okay now, baby. You're safe."

"What about—"

"Dad and Jackson are safe too. So are the others that were in those beds. And the two young men you were with."

The question in her voice pried me far enough back to see her face. My mouth fell open but nothing came out. *Mason is ok.* Fresh tears sprang from my eyes.

"I don't remember what happened," I said. "After we called for help."

"You were under a lot of stress. You can't blame yourself, Sammie. You're a hero. You saved everyone on board."

Something wasn't making sense. "What do you mean blame myself? For what?" The urge to spring out of bed nearly overcame me.

"For that woman drowning," she said softly.

"Who drowned? How?"

"She opted for the open ocean rather than wait for capture and disappeared. It doesn't matter, she was the one who did all this, according to the authorities. She was the one who had you hooked on those horrible drugs." Mom's voice cracked, and her eyes darted away.

How much did she know? "How do they know she drowned?"

"They gave up the search after a few days. There was no way she could have survived."

"A few days? How long have I been out?" I asked.

Mom's eyes closed as she drew a deep breath. "Three weeks. They kept you sedated to get you off the drugs safely. The man too."

All words dried up on my tongue. Three weeks? *Three weeks.*

"Where is everyone?" I finally managed.

"The doctors thought it would be best if I was the first to see you when you woke up. I'm glad, because if they hadn't, I would've chained myself to the bed."

A feeble smile crawled across my face.

"I have something else to tell you." Mom glowed. "I'm in remission!"

"What? Oh, Mom, that's amazing." I threw my arms around her again as the waterworks started once more. "But how?" I asked.

"The Bennets said it was the least they could do. They flew in three doctors from all over the world and dropped a fortune on the experimental treatment, rushing the whole process. Well, it seems to be working."

It had to be Mason. He'd saved my mother. Travis saved me as well. But at what cost? Candice could have killed everyone on board if we hadn't stopped her. Did Travis push her into the ocean? The idea of it brought a cold shudder.

"You have a whole slew of people waiting outside to visit you. Who should I send in next?" Mom asked, pulling back again and squeezing my hands.

"Who's out there?" I asked.

A sly look came over her face. "Your father and brother of course. Alyssa Forbes and Nicole and Mason Bennet."

I had a lot to say to all of them, things like, "I'm sorry." But there was only one other face I wanted right then. "Mason, please."

Mom nodded and kissed my forehead. When she hesitated at the door, my gaze fell on a framed picture to her right. Blue sky met blue ocean in the distance, making the scene seem to go on forever. I shivered and turned toward the light falling through a window to my side. Whatever came next, it had better be on solid ground.

When I heard a tentative knock, I saw Mason peeking around the door. My heart leaped at the sight of him, well and full of life. His handsome face looked just as it had on my wall all those years ago, but with tiny signs of age in the crinkles around his eyes—the only oceans I ever wanted to swim in again. He'd been growing stubble as well, and it gave him a rugged, wildly romantic look that made me imagine what it might feel like against the sensitive skin lower on my body.

"What are you waiting for?" I asked, wondering why he wasn't already in my arms.

He slipped inside the room, balancing flowers, boxes of chocolates, and mylar balloons with silly phrases like *Get well or else.*

I laughed, ignoring the ache in my chest at the movement. For the first time, I wondered how I looked. I must have been a mess, having been in an induced coma for three weeks.

As though he knew what I was thinking, Mason set everything on the foot of the bed, sat beside me, and pulled me into the most wonderful kiss I'd ever experienced.

We breathed each other in as he slid his tongue inside, laying claim to my mouth. A small noise bubbled up from my throat as my insides heated up in response. My body melted into his, and I was ready to pull him down on top of me and do it right there on the hospital bed.

He laughed, jiggling against me, then pulled back, holding my hands in his and stroking my knuckles with his thumbs.

"I can't wait to get you in a hotel room, alone." His throaty voice sent tremors down between my legs.

"You're alive," I told him, still unable to hold back tears. "We made it."

He nodded, cupping my face. I leaned into his palm, kissing it.

"We made it," he agreed. "My mother is already covering up the details and preparing for an overhaul for the resort's grand opening."

I stilled, heart thumping. "Are you serious?"

"She offered me the 'win,'" he said.

My throat threatened to close, but I forced words through it. "Congratulations."

He shook his head, eyes boring into me. "I'm not taking it, Sam. I gave it to Nicole."

"Oh?" I asked, hope leaping to life again. I'd have followed Mason anywhere. Almost.

"I want to be free of Bennet Systems. At least my mother's brand of the company anyway. I've struck a deal with her."

I sat up straighter, trying to understand what Mason was telling me.

"She was very impressed with you and how you got us out of there," he said.

I snorted. "Glad she appreciates it."

"So she was thrilled with the proposal I suggested."

I wanted to yell at him to get to the point, but instead I took his hand and began sucking on his fingertips.

He moaned softly, closing his eyes. "Let me finish before I end up locking the door and having my way with you."

"I'm sorry, would you explain to me why talking about your mother is a better option?" I asked.

Mason pulled away to stand, and I instantly regretted my choice of humor. But then he grabbed a small gift box from among the chocolates and flowers on the bed and settled back down next to me on the bed.

"Consider this my promise," he said, tucking the cigar sized box into my hands.

I narrowed my eyes suspiciously but tugged on the velvety ribbon. When I snapped the lid open, I gasped and my hand fluttered to my chest.

"Remember when I said I wouldn't ever leave you alone?" he asked. "I said I'd be by your side 24/7."

I nodded, remembering how Candice and the AI had done their best to both separate us and then torture us for kicks.

"Well, I meant it. I never want to be apart from you again, and this is my promise that we can slay any demons in our path."

Tears flooded my vision as I lifted the delicate chain with a shaking hand. A tiny silver shark glinted at the bottom along with a golden trident.

"It's a good start," I said as he placed it around my throat.

The door opened as Mason leaned in for a gentle kiss, and everyone my mother had listed as waiting to see me came inside.

"You are definitely Bennet Systems material," Nicole said. "If you get tired of my brother's company, you're welcome to work for me at Paradise Atlantis."

I didn't respond to Nicole's offer. I simply clung to the love of my life. I would never take her up on it, but I no longer feared the ocean. It gifted me Mason, and I would never forget that.

EPILOGUE

NICOLE

FOR THE FIRST TIME IN LIVING MEMORY NICOLE RESPECTED HER brother's choice to back away from a business challenge. Maybe her adventure underwater had changed her more than she'd thought. Come to think of it, more than one first had happened since their little adventure. The biggest example of which was her letting Jackson inside the carefully constructed walls she'd been taught to keep up since...well, since birth.

Mason let in Sam, and that was clearly a healthy choice, but winning Paradise Atlantis as a consolation prize didn't have the same appeal as a trophy won through blood, sweat, and tears. That realization had sparked this meeting with Mother, who sat across from her, bouncing an impatient leg behind the long, sleek conference table overlooking the New York skyline.

"What's this about?" Stacy Bennet asked, setting down her now-empty cup of coffee a bit too hard.

Nicole ignored the bright red lipstick stain in favor of looking her mother in the eyes.

"I want leadership over more than Paradise Atlantis, Mother. I want to oversee all current and future high-tech resorts, whether in planning stages or under construction. Atlantis will take more than a year to renovate as it is." Nicole allowed one eyebrow to rise in challenge. Her mother wanted this meeting over with, and the easiest way to get that was to give in to Nicole.

Stacy stood and faced the wall of windows, hands clasped behind her back as she considered the request. Nicole took the opportunity to glance at her wristband. She'd be meeting Jackson for lunch shortly, and she wondered if dessert would be celebratory sex or distraction sex. Either way, she enjoyed the tingle of anticipation.

Stacy spun around and snatched her empty cup off the table. "Very well. You can start by proving yourself on the next launch. It's in three months."

Nicole almost couldn't hide her surprise. "I wasn't aware of any such project at that advanced of a stage."

Stacy grinned and placed the cup on a waiting bot to be sanitized. "It's top secret. Very few people knew of it."

"Candice?" Nicole pressed.

Stacy's grin faded. "Unfortunately, but she's dead, so she won't be telling anyone."

"What is it?" Nicole asked, ignoring Mother's brash attitude. After all, Candice had tried to kill everyone on the excursion.

"The code name is Time Capsule. If you think you just met some brilliant minds, wait until you see the designers of this one."

"Time Capsule?" Nicole repeated, thoughtfully tapping her lip with a French-tipped nail. "Is it a replica hotel, featuring different decades?"

Stacy let out a single harsh laugh. "If you want this job, you'll need to think bigger, Nikki."

Nicole hated that old nickname, as it had always been used in a patronizing manner.

"So what then? Actual time travel?"

Her mother's face lit up, and Nicole had her answer. The tingles she'd felt when she let her mind drift to Jackson tripled in anticipation of the celebratory sex they'd be having shortly. Maybe they'd make a secret goal of doing it in every decade.

"I won't let you down," she promised before turning on her heel to leave.

"See that you don't. We can't afford another failure like this one, or we may have to scrap the whole resort project."

Nicole hesitated long enough to give a nod of understanding before letting the glass door slip shut. Nothing and no one would threaten the success of this project. She finally had a chance to shine and she wasn't about to fail.

Thank you for reading! Did you enjoy? Please add your review because nothing helps an author more and encourages readers to take a chance on a book than a review.

And don't miss A MATTER OF TIME, book two of the *Fantasy Resorts* series, available now. Turn the page for a sneak peek!

You can also sign up for the City Owl Press newsletter to receive notice of all book releases!

SNEAK PEEK OF A MATTER OF TIME

The hat was the best part. What kid didn't fancy playing the hero in the ten-gallon hat, pistols at his sides, spurs on his boots, ready to take on the outlaw? Doyle had no pistols, that would've required permission forms and red tape he didn't have time or patience for, but he did have the tan hat.

"What do you think, Lacey?" he asked, tipping the brim to the resort's costume designer.

He enjoyed making her smile. Maybe it was the blush that always came with it that did it. She was way out of his league, not to mention her relationship with Casey McGovern, the resort's captain. McGovern was the one who'd get credit for helming the maiden voyage of the Time Capsule Resort, or TCR, but he, Doyle, was the one who designed the actual mechanism that travelled through time, not to mention the cloaking device. Either invention would be enough to make history if it weren't for the fact the patents were owned by his employer, Bennet Systems, since they'd doled out the cash for his research.

Why did engineers never get the credit?

"Adorkable," Lacey said, tapping her chin as she studied Doyle's appearance. "The jeans fit perfectly. But are you sure you want to go for the rancher look and not more of a tinkerer? I have a bowler hat and three-piece suit that comes with a nifty stopwatch."

Doyle placed his hands on his hips, trying not to be offended. "This resort is about enacting our fantasies, right? Not becoming our 1880's personas. Besides, I've been working out." He pumped a bicep for her and smiled when she bit her bottom lip.

"There's my girl," McGovern's deep voice came from directly behind, crushing Doyle's fantasy into dust. "All hands in position for departure, Doyle. We want this trip running smoothly, especially with the Watcher on board."

Lacey crinkled her nose. "Is it just me or is the Watcher creepy? I get that they're here to make sure nothing happens to the timeline, but do they have to wear that weird black suit? It makes them look like they don't belong in any known decade."

Not too pleased with having another person on board keeping an eye on them, Doyle grunted his agreement. Having Nicole Bennet of Bennet Systems around was enough pressure, never mind a representative of multiple governments, policing them all on what was billed as a luxury vacation.

"So?" McGovern pressed, hands on the slim hips of his own cowboy getup. "Get to work!"

Annoyed, Doyle thought better of snapping back and bit the inside of his cheek. Instead, he ignored McGovern, thanked Lacey for the duds, and went off in search of engineering, where he would sit and monitor the ride and equipment until they docked. They'd done practice runs, but this was the first time he'd seen so many people in the machine. It was the way he liked to think of the Time Capsule Resort, which some called a hybrid ship that didn't sail and some saw as a time machine that looked like a hotel on steroids. The whole thing was part and parcel of the mechanism in Doyle's brain. The amenities and window dressings existed to make it more comfortable to humans, as far as he was concerned.

Built in a giant corkscrew shape, the only floors separated from the rest by elevator and stairs were the top and bottom, the "bridge" where McGovern worked in the former, and the day-to-day tech monitoring system on the latter near the exit/entrance. Lacey's costume shop lived on a higher portion of the corkscrew, above the equivalent of three floors worth of immersive magic courtesy of the designers.

Doyle strolled through the winding halls covered in dirt with various storefronts accurate to the late 1800's old west and tipped his hat when he spied a couple of women dressed to the hilt just like him. The older woman and the younger mirror image beside her, who could only be her daughter, both tittered at the attention, which added some swagger to Doyle's step. Lacey already had it in her head he was a nerd. It was an image he wanted to shatter, at least long enough to get laid. He'd thrown himself so hard into his work that he hadn't had time for much else, including his girlfriend, when he'd started the job. He pulled out of the relationship a mere three months later, citing his single-focus attention span. But as the work eased up and the interior design and marketing crews took over, he was able to lift his head out of the sand and rejoin the human race a bit. Which in his case, meant playing video games, particularly wild west themed ones, out of excitement for the voyage, and going to the gym.

Lost in his thoughts, Doyle slipped through the throngs of excited passengers, eyeing the door to engineering. Situated near the bottom of the spiral, it had been disguised as an old gold mine entrance with an OFF LIMITS sign. The passengers were only supposed to see the mirage created by Bennet Systems, which took the form of an old west town, complete with plenty of saloons and dance hall girls. Everyone on board dressed the part, cosplay to the extreme. The idea was to be immersed in the setting. The real setting. It would change, along with the costumes and scenery, depending on the theme and time locales of each voyage. They were starting with the initial trip to the wild west—Arizona circa 1888. They'd subsequently move on to 1920's Chicago, 1640's England, and so on.

Doyle didn't plan on joining them on all the excursions, but he wouldn't miss the first time people got to see his baby in action, even if they didn't realize it was his.

He reached for the hidden button that would allow him entrance as it opened and a woman slipped out, almost smacking into him. She had on one of the fancy dresses from Lacey's costume shop, but Doyle doubted her bright purple hair would blend in with the real wild west.

"Sorry," she said, averting her eyes and scurrying out of the way and off into the throngs of excited people.

Looked like Jones was already taking advantage of the scenery as far as the guests were concerned, and they weren't even there yet. Still, he'd have to have a talk with the guy about letting patrons behind the scenes, even to impress the women.

Catching the door, Doyle entered the quiet space of the control room.

"You gonna be able to sit in those jeans, Wally?"

Doyle grimaced at Jones, his ass of an ass-istant. He hated his first name, Walter, but the second Jones had found out what it was, he'd grabbed hold and wouldn't let go.

"How are the readings?" If he ignored the comment, maybe it and Jones would go away.

"Ship shape. Get it?" Jones's eyes sparkled. His red kerchief and straw hat were more reminiscent of Huckleberry Finn than a cowboy, especially on his small frame.

Doyle shot him the side eye as he spun his chair toward the consul. Eight holo-screens displayed 3-D views of the perimeter of the machine from the inside out. The whole thing was basically a cylinder encased in super thin, nearly indestructible AC glass, so that when they parked themselves near the action, they'd feel like they were in the center while staying safely cloaked from view of the people in 1888. It was an assurance that the timeline would remain uncontaminated and satisfy the government Watcher sent along to keep an eye on things, not to mention Doyle's own conscience. That way when they took small groups on excursion into the Tucson of the old west, they'd remain inconspicuous among the bustling population.

As nervous as taking civilians back in time made him, if his design proved to be the marketing win for Bennet Systems's

Fantasy Resorts, he'd get credit for the tech, and that meant unlimited opportunities for future funding.

Since this was the first real time machine ever invented, no one knew what would happen if things were altered during a previous time. Sure, there were plenty of theories—not to mention plenty of science-fiction supposing various scenarios. But the reality was likely very different and not something Doyle cared to experiment with. During all the test runs, he had been absolutely careful, but he was one man, and the environment had been easy to control. Throwing so many people into the mix had not been his idea, but in order for Bennet Systems to pony up the money it took to develop the tech, he had to agree to their choice of use. It was better than the alternative —selling the design to the government, who would likely bury its existence and his accomplishment along with it all for covert use. Bennet Systems may not be perfect, but it was public and powerful, which helped calm his nerves about the Watcher on board.

McGovern's baritone blasted all around them. "Welcome aboard the Time Capsule Resort. I am your captain, Casey McGovern. As you are all aware, this is a one-of-a-kind voyage, not through space, but through time. Now, I know you all signed your waivers and passed your physicals, but when we hit the Go button, I need you to be in a seated position."

Doyle cringed at the words "Go button." He hated when people didn't call things their proper names. "It's a time destabilizer, asshat," he muttered, adjusting one of the gauges to his left. He'd been double checking the cloak all morning. While the time destabilizer was an interconnected array of neural nets throughout the machine, the cloak was an external piece, roughly the size and shape of a baseball bat and encased in metal. It was attached dead center to the bottom of the resort, where the whole thing was designed to hover eight feet in the air above the ground, just in case landing on a specific spot had unforeseen timeline consequences. It also avoided the possibility of anyone walking into it by mistake.

The cloak always felt a little unprotected to Doyle, considering the absolute importance of it, but he'd been too busy fine tuning the neural network and had to delegate the job to Jones. When his triple check left him satisfied, Doyle tucked his hands behind his head and tilted his hat forward to cover his eyes. With his feet resting on the console, he leaned back in his chair to take a hard-earned break.

"Sleeping already?" Jones asked.

"Pushing the 'Go button' doesn't sound hard. I'm sure you can handle it."

By the sound of Jones's chuckle, Doyle figured he was down for the job. The truth was, Doyle didn't want his nerves to show, and if his heavy boots, crossed legs, secured arms, and face weren't arranged just so, he'd probably be a bumbling mess. It was the old "I can't look" feeling as his heart stampeded in his ribcage.

"And we're off!" yelled McGovern. "*Yeeeehaw!*"

Doyle tensed as the telltale shift of balance almost convinced him to grab hold of the chair. But even as the world tilted, he stayed still in his position. His muscles were so taught that he'd probably be sore later, but no need for Jones to know that.

A quick peek proved the tech held up as the air around him swirled with bright pinks and golds. Something told him if he reached out and touched, it would feel like jelly, but the strange pressure and dizzying sensation kept him anchored in his seat. As they slowed to a halt in the late 1800's, things began to shift back to normal, the glowing colors fading into nothing and the pull dipping low in his center of gravity, sort of like being seasick. Doyle counted down to the gentle halt of the engine in his mind's eye.

3...2...1...

The world jerked and bobbed like a car had sideswiped them, dumping Doyle from his chair. A horrible scraping sound vibrated from beneath followed by a crunch and another jolt. He gripped the edge of the console, righting his hat so he could see the problem and not just hear and feel it, like somehow that might make it better.

What he saw was chaos. All the screens showed furniture, objects, and people being tossed around like kernels in a popcorn machine. Jones lay on the floor, bleeding from his head where he must have banged it against the edge of the console. Doyle swore under his breath and fell to his knees by his side, applying pressure with shaky hands, even as the floating resort continued to bounce and sway before coming to a complete stop.

"Engineering to Medcenter," Doyle yelled into his wristband. "Man down. Jones is bleeding and unconscious."

A woman's voice crackled back at him, the sound in the background filling in the audible anarchy missing from the viewscreens. "Dr. Cantor here. Is there a pulse?"

Doyle watched Jones's chest rise and fall, felt a solid thump beneath scarlet fingers. "Yeah, doc. But there's a lot of blood."

"Shit. Fine. I'll send someone down there. I'd tell you to bring him up here, but navigating through all the turmoil is another issue. What the fuck happened down there?"

Doyle choked on the lump in his throat. What had happened? Everything had been fine on the test run not twenty-four hours prior.

"Not sure yet. We have to assess the damage. Just hurry up and get over here so I can start working on it. I'm not taking my hand off this wound until someone's here." He cut off the communication with a sharp tap on his wristband.

The second he hung up, McGovern's voice exploded through. "What the hell happened to my ship?"

It's a fucking time machine, was what he wanted to say, but Doyle swallowed back the first thought that popped into his head.

"Jones is injured," he said instead. "I can't check yet. I need a medic to relieve me."

"Did you call one?" McGovern asked in patronizing way.

"Of course I did!" This time, Doyle's temper got the best of him, and he let it out.

"You need to check the instruments, Walter." McGovern's voice was low and even now, steady like he'd leaned in to speak only to him. "We need to protect one-hundred-twenty-seven patrons and crewmembers. I need you to Do. Your. Job."

Doyle licked his lips and nodded. McGovern was right. If they'd landed in the wrong time or worse, it could be bad. Very bad. But his assistant's life was just as important as those rich guests on the other level. Looking down at Jones, he remembered his first-aid training. *The head bleeds a lot, sometimes making the wound look worse than it is*, which meant he could probably let go so long as he wrapped the wound. He took the red kerchief from Jones's neck and tied it around his head. It would do until a medic arrived.

"Right." Doyle stood back up and shoved the chair out of the way so he could read the smoking console. Warning lights flashed, and a worrisome, high-pitched sound came from one of the control panels to his rear.

His fingers flew deftly over the controls, first checking the time destabilizer. When he saw it did in fact read 1888, he emptied his lungs of the breath he'd been holding then tipped up the hat to wipe sweat off his brow. Damn thing was hotter than he'd expected.

Next, he checked navigation. They'd come in too low and off course by...*that can't be right*. They were miles south of Tucson, which put them right in the middle of a tree and near a field of Saguaro cacti. Doyle winced, picturing the collision from the outside. How had the nav gotten so messed up? He'd checked the coordinates himself just that morning. He'd ask Jones about it, but...

"Computer!" Doyle yelled. "Where is the nearest town?"

The soothing female voice answered, "Devil's Creek, population sixty-seven as of August 24, 1888."

Shaking himself, Doyle checked the cloaking device. His muscles tensed again, his neck cramping. That couldn't be right either. His fingers flew as the doors behind him opened and two people came in, rushing to Jones's side. Doyle slammed his hands down on the console just as three more people entered the room.

Swinging around to face the new crowd, Doyle let out an exasperated groan. The heat boiling up the back of his neck threatened to explode out of his head like a volcano. McGovern and Nicole Bennet, his boss—two of his least favorite people. The man accompanying them fell immediately to Jones's side to help the medics as the other two glared daggers at him.

"Report," Nicole barked. Her demeanor clashed violently with the pastel and ruffles that covered her. Even under the circumstances, it was hard for Doyle to keep his gaze off her heaving bosom tied into the corset-like top.

He cleared his throat and decided to start with the good news. "The machine itself is intact."

McGovern visibly relaxed, looking almost ready to faint. Bennet's eyes stayed sharp.

"And?" she prompted.

"I can't get a reading on the cloak. Somehow, the landing coordinates were way the hell off too. We're in a low-populated area. But I checked them myself this morning."

"You should have triple checked them before departure," Bennet snapped.

Doyle pressed his lips together, not wanting to let out what he had in mind. Things like 'Navigation is not my job' and 'You should be asking how it happened'.

McGovern stepped between them. "It's okay. The time machine is ok, so we just press the Go button and head back, right?"

"It's a time destabilizer, and there's no such thing as a Go button," Bennet corrected.

Doyle sat back in shock and sudden appreciation.

The man who'd come in with them stood as the others left with a still unconscious Jones. He was dressed as a gentleman, the kind who'd own a bank and get robbed in the old west. When he put an arm around Bennet's waist without being thrown over her shoulder, Doyle guessed it was her elusive boyfriend he'd heard whispers about, Dr. Jackson Meadows.

Meadows spoke. "We can't leave here until we verify there are no other significant injuries among the passengers or crew and the timeline is intact. I've already had words with the Watcher on the way over here. It took all I had to convince them to let us handle this."

McGovern swallowed, and his smile faded as Bennet nodded.

"Let's hope it's just a censor. Doyle, you'll have to go out and check it physically. I'll make an announcement to calm the masses. Luckily, as far as we know, Jones was the worst hit. Until we have more information, there will be no rumors about issues aboard. They are here to get the experience they paid for, and as far as the Watcher goes, the less they know, the better for everyone." Without another word, Bennet swirled her large skirt around and swept from the room, Meadows in her wake.

McGovern looked at Doyle and shook his head. "You heard the boss. Get going, cowboy."

***

Don't stop now. Keep reading with your copy of <u>A MATTER OF TIME</u>, available now.

Don't miss A MATTER OF TIME, book two of the *Fantasy Resorts* series, available now, and find more from Lizzy Gayle at www.lizzygayle.com

Arizona circa 1888 may be a fun place to visit, but the Time Capsule Fantasy Resort didn't mean to crash land there.

It's up to Walter Doyle, inventor of the new technology, to find and repair the missing cloaking device without altering the timeline. Easier said than done when he runs into a real-life, real-sexy Annie Oakley named Sadie. From the moment she points her shotgun at him, he's smitten.

All Sadie Rogers wants is to be left alone to mind her ranch and her son, something the men in town wouldn't be keen on if they found out her husband was dead. Keeping a low profile gets more complicated when the handsome Wally shows up on a hush-hush mission from Washington. When his top-secret contraption kills a man on Sadie's property, she hides the evidence. Though, she might be convinced to turn the thing over in exchange for Wally posing as her new fiancé to help save her ranch...

With sabotage afoot and a town full of corrupt cowboys and nosy neighbors, can Wally and Sadie find a way to solve both their problems? Maybe. But they'll create an even bigger one while trying—how to hold on to love that transcends time itself.

Please sign up for the City Owl Press newsletter for chances to win special subscriber-only contests and giveaways as well as receiving information on upcoming releases and special excerpts.

All reviews are **welcome** and **appreciated**. Please consider leaving one on your favorite social media and book buying sites.

Escape Your World. Get Lost in Ours! City Owl Press at www.cityowlpress.com.

ACKNOWLEDGMENTS

Thank you to my editor, Heather, for being the amazing, supportive, meticulous, and insightful person you are. You are a great boss, editor, and human being. Thank you Tina, Yelena and the entire team at City Owl and Mystic Owl. There isn't a better publisher out there and I believe that with all my heart and soul.

Thank you to all the betas who helped shape 20,000 Leagues, including Leslie, Julie, Sarah, and Katharyn. And thank you all for the pub nights and support. Thank you Shona, for your unconditional cheerleading. You are the best bestie a woman could ask for. Thank you to my family, for gifting me the time and focus to bring my dreams to fruition.

Most of all, thank you to my readers because you're the reason I do this. I hope that the adventures beneath the sea and in the pages of this book give you an opportunity to escape and enjoy.

ABOUT THE AUTHOR

LIZZY GAYLE loves paranormal so much, she lives it. She is both an author and a psychic. Between mothering her three kids, attempting to understand her rocket scientist husband, and consistently attempting to declutter her home (that she is convinced is a secret portal to a clutter-creating dimension), she does her best to use her creative gifts and share them with you. Lizzy is a people person so if you contact her, it will make her very happy and she will likely answer while possibly including pictures of her bunnies and/or bird. She has also been known to write Young Adult under the name Lisa Gail Green.

www.lizzygayle.com

facebook.com/authorlizzygayle
instagram.com/authorlizzygayle

ABOUT THE PUBLISHER

City Owl Press is a cutting edge indie publishing company, bringing the world of romance and speculative fiction to discerning readers.

Escape Your World. Get Lost in Ours!

www.cityowlpress.com

f facebook.com/YourCityOwlPress
🐦 twitter.com/cityowlpress
📷 instagram.com/cityowlbooks
📌 pinterest.com/cityowlpress

www.ingramcontent.com/pod-product-compliance
Lightning Source LLC
Chambersburg PA
CBHW020827260626

47169CB00003B/873